SENTINELS: WOLF HUNT

BY
DORANNA DURGIN

MILLS & BOON

All the characters in this book have no existence outside the imagination of
the author, and have no relation whatsoever to anyone bearing the same name
or names. They are not even distantly inspired by any individual known or
unknown to the author, and all the incidents are pure invention.

First published in Great Britain 2010
Harlequin Mills & Boon Limited,
Eton House, 18-24 Paradise Road, Richmond, Surrey TW9 1SR

© Doranna Durgin 2010

ISBN: 978 0 263 88227 8

46-0510

Harlequin Mills & Boon policy is to use papers that are natural, renewable
and recyclable products and made from wood grown in sustainable forests.
The logging and manufacturing processes conform to the legal environmental
regulations of the country of origin.

Printed and bound in Spain
by Litografia Rosés S.A., Barcelona

Doranna Durgin spent her childhood filling notebooks, first with stories and art and then with novels. After obtaining a degree in wildlife illustration and environmental education, she spent a number of years deep in the Appalachian Mountains. When she emerged, it was as a writer who found herself irrevocably tied to the natural world and its creatures – and with a new touchstone to the rugged spirit that helped settle the area and which she instils in her characters.

Doranna's first fantasy novel received the 1995 Compton Crook/Stephen Tall Award for best first book in the fantasy, science fiction and horror genres; she now has fifteen novels of eclectic genres on the shelves. Most recently she's leaped gleefully into the world of paranormal romance. When she's not writing, Doranna builds web pages, wanders around outside with a camera and works with horses and dogs. There's a Lipizzan in her backyard, a mountain looming outside her office window, a pack of agility dogs romping in the house and a laptop sitting on her desk – and that's just the way she likes it. You can find a complete list of her titles at www. doranna.net, along with scoops about new projects, lots of silly photos and a link to her SFF Net newsgroup.

This is for my friend Lorraine Bartlett/Lorna Barrett,
for all the stuff behind the scenes,
and for Writers Plot!

With my thanks to the Magna Owners of Texas,
who helped me find just the right motorcycle for Jet.

Mythos

Long ago and far away, in Roman/Gaulish days, one woman had a tumultuous life—she fell in love with a druid, by whom she had a son; the man was killed by Romans, and she was subsequently taken into the household of a Roman, who also fathered a son on her. The druid's son turned out to be a man of many talents, including the occasional ability to shapeshift, albeit at great cost. (His alter-shape was a wild boar.) The woman's younger son, who considered himself superior in all ways, had none of these earthly powers, and went hunting other ways to be impressive, acquire power. He justified his various activities by claiming he needed to protect the area from his brother, who had too much power to go unchecked...but in the end, it was his brother's family who grew into the Vigilia, now known as the Sentinels, while the younger son founded what turned into the vile Atrum Core.

Glossary

Sentinels: An organization of power-linked individuals whose driving purpose is to protect and nurture the earth—as befitting their druid origins—while also keeping watch on the activities of the Atrum Core

Vigilia: The original Latin name for the Sentinels, discarded in recent centuries under Western influence

Brevis Regional: HQ for each of the Sentinel regions

Consul: The leader of each Sentinel brevis region

Adjutant: The Sentinel Consul's executive officer

Aeternus contego: The strongest possible Sentinel ward, tied to the life force of the one who sets it and broken only at that person's death. Meghan Lawrence has placed one of these on Fabron Gausto, reflecting any workings he performs back on himself

Vigilia adveho: A Sentinel mental long-distance call for help

Monitio: A Sentinel warning call

Nexus: The Sentinel who acts as a central point of power control—such as for communications, wards, or power manipulation

Atrum Core: An ethnic group founded by and sired by the Roman's son, their basic goal is to acquire power in as many forms as possible, none of which is natively their own; they claiming to monitor and control the "nefarious" activities of the Sentinels

Amulets: The process through which the Core inflicts its workings of power on others; having gathered and stored (and sometimes stolen) the power from other sources

Drozhar: The Atrum Core regional prince

Septs Prince: the Atrum Core prince of princes

Septs Posse: A Core drozhar's favored sycophants; can be relied on to do the dirty work

Sceleratus vis: Ancient forbidden workings based on power drawn from blood, once used by the Atrum Core

Workings: Core workings of power, assembled and triggered via amulets

Prologue

Marlee Cerrosa, stuck in a boring internal security meeting where everyone else had more seniority than she, pretended her cell phone wasn't ringing.

Is he insane, calling me here?

She smiled apology at the others, wishing that the *Mission Impossible* ring tone didn't come through quite so clearly. Their understanding amusement came through just as clearly, along with a hint of condescension—although she didn't imagine they knew it showed. She was the youngest on this Brevis Southwest team, and the most human of those working internal tech support—barely enough Sentinel blood to be here at all. And so she still worked out of a corner cubicle, batting cleanup and grunge work. They knew she could do more; it was nothing personal. A matter of putting in her time, earning her way up.

Just how much more she could do, she didn't think they knew.

And she was *sure* they didn't know who'd just called. Or that although she scribed notes during the meeting, looking as concerned as anyone about the recent system aberrations, she knew exactly how those aberrations had occurred. She didn't blame the Sentinel field agents for their concern about security, but she knew better. There was no actual breach.

Just…a little sharing.

They needed a reality check.

When the meeting finally ended and they all gathered up for their predatorial meat-heavy lunches, Marlee grabbed up her Tecra computer tablet and her chilled Scooby-Doo lunch box with fruit and salad and went up to the roof for some fresh air and some privacy, not to mention the best cell phone reception in the building.

A place she could use her phone scrambler without question.

"I can't believe you called me here," she said, as soon as he picked up the phone. "I can't believe you called me in the *middle of a security meeting.*"

"Oh, come. Don't tell me it didn't give you a thrill. A deep, secret little thrill." His tone was beguiling… personal.

She hated that.

"I'm not doing this for thrills."

"Ah, there, now." He backed off; he always did. It was how she knew he needed her.

But dammit, he always *tried*—getting personal, making insinuations—and she was tired of it.

"Nick Carter will be out in the field," he said.

She didn't question it, as unlikely as it seemed—for the brevis adjutant rarely went into the field, and when he did, he didn't go alone. After all, Nick Carter, Sentinel shapeshifter extraordinaire, was the primary assistant to the Brevis Southwest Consul. Brevis Southwest, Brevis Northwest, Brevis Central…north into the Canadian regions and south into Latin America. All huge swaths of land overseen by men of too much power and tied by allegiance to their Brevis Nationals—although men at Nick Carter's level usually wielded that power from behind closed doors.

But he wouldn't have said it unless he knew. Not this man. "I need you to interfere with his incoming communications. Phone, e-mail…whatever."

She laughed out loud, as ill-advised as it was. "You must be kidding."

His brief silence served as a response. "I want a virus on his personal computer system—turn it into mush. I want them locked out."

Now she let her own silence speak. She leaned against the giant EVAC housing structure on the roof—there, where she'd set up her lawn chair and shadescreen, habitually hiding from the sun even on this relatively pleasant early November day. Up on an old town roof in Tucson…the sun always seemed warm to her.

He said sharply, "You can do these things."

It wasn't a question.

She said, "I don't work for you. I take suggestions when it comes to keeping the balance. If I didn't truly believe—if I hadn't *seen*—" She didn't finish the thought. They both knew why she did what she did. Because the field Sentinels, the shapeshifters…

They were far too powerful. They called themselves protectors of the earth, but they'd gotten above themselves…beyond themselves. And while Marlee didn't think the Atrum Core family branch had taken the right path when choosing to work against their druidic brothers those thousands of years ago in a Roman dominated Britain, she could understand why they felt the need to do it at all.

For not only could the Sentinels shift to another shape—each to his own, and invariably something powerful, something predatory—they often took on enhanced abilities even in human form. Keen of vision, keen of hearing, of scent…swift on foot, strong in hand. And most of them had their own individual talents. Wards, healing, shields…there was the field agent in northern Arizona who rode power, and who had been in not one but two scandals. How brevis had cleared him a second time, Marlee couldn't imagine.

It was for men like him that she did what she did, driven by a childhood of watching subtle injustices and power plays. Made her small changes, her small interferences. Helped to keep the balance between the Sentinels and the Atrum Core, without actually benefiting the Core.

She watched a raven swooping down between the redbrick buildings, knowing that it, too, might well be a Sentinel, and happy it came no closer. "What you're asking will expose me."

"Ah, no," he said. "Not my Marlee. You're too important to us all. We'll make sure you're covered. And while this level of interference might seem extreme, it's only temporary. A few days at most."

Cover her? She'd assumed she wasn't the only

Sentinel in her position—mostly human, but come of long-established bloodlines. Not quite special enough to fit into this world, but with eyes open far too wide to merge happily into the world that knew nothing of Sentinels or Atrum Core or the ancient battle between them.

But she hadn't truly considered how many others might be right here at brevis with her.

"I would not ask, my Marlee…" He let the words trail away, the implication clear enough. *If I had a choice. If it weren't important.*

She hated the way those words made her feel. She loved the way those words made her feel.

As if he possessed some part of her…as if she'd forever given up something of herself to this man who was so used to taking what he wanted. And yet…as if she was making a difference, here among people who assumed she couldn't. As if she was the only one who *could*.

"I'll see what I can do," she told him.

Chapter 1

He saw her in stages.

Pure feral grace...

Surrounded by the chaos of the Pima County Fairgrounds with a complex breed ring and performance dog show cluster in full swing around him, Nick Carter caught only a glimpse of dark, lithe movement as the woman ducked wind chimes at a sheltered display and disappeared around the end of the vendor row. And though his vision was full of pop-up shade shelters and colorful wares, people lingering in the wide aisle with a variety of dogs ranging idly along beside, the desert's seasonal wind gusting and lifting swirls of fine desert grit until it was all one big dance of color and motion—

In truth, in that moment, he saw only one lean woman: swift, bordering on rangy, dressed in black beneath an early winter desert sun. Black fitted vest with no shirt beneath, black crop pants, black leather shoes, tight to her feet. Black hair, short and artfully mussed. Pure bed head. Pure feral grace in her movement, taking her so quickly out of his sight.

He saw it all in that instant—a stranger, on his turf. A shifter, so obvious and yet unknown.

Forget about the troubles within brevis regional, forget about the increasingly problematical stealth amulets being employed by the local Core. Hell, forget about the very concerns that had brought him out here, signs that Fabron Gausto had returned to run amok once again.

Pure feral grace...

Not here. Not without his permission.

He followed her. Around the end of the vendor row, past the main building with its reserved grooming stations, show superintendent's table, and show committee setup. Past the tall wire exercise pens teeming with packs of small breed dogs, all of whom invariably crouched or cowered or rolled over as Nick passed by— and now all of who still lingered that way from the woman's recent passage.

At least he knew he was on the right trail.

Another glimpse of her, nothing more than a black-shod heel, a toned calf—but still his shoulders and nape tightened. It was her, all right.

It wasn't a trespass he could allow to stand. Not with the entire Southwest regional office compromised from within, the aging consul a man who hadn't taken his javelina boar in years, Nick's own handpicked Sentinel echelon team wounded and recovering, and dammit, every sign that they were all still defenseless against the recently employed stealth amulets.

And as incongruous as it seemed, not with the recent incidents at dog shows in the area—dogs stolen, dogs missing. While the local law had chalked up such problems to animal rights activists, Nick had the feeling it was more ominous than that; it smacked of the Core's endless experiments to harvest power that didn't belong to them. With the Core, ominous was never simple, never moral.

And someone always died.

She's only a woman, he tried to tell himself, as a twinge of the absurd touched him—chasing after that lean form here on the busy dog show grounds when he should have been interviewing the breeders he'd come to see. Except...

Not "only a woman" at all. He could recognize the wolf in another as easily as he could see it in a mirror, in his own hoarfrost hair and pale green eyes—but mostly in his manner, as though at any moment the civilization might simply fall away, leaving gleaming teeth and laughing eyes and blood-spattered fur.

And he knew it because of how very often he'd been counseled against it. *Blend in,* he'd been told in training. *We will always know you, but no one else should.* And so he'd cultivated the expensive haircuts and the expensive suits and the other trappings of civilization that somehow never seemed to fool anyone.

This woman wouldn't fool anyone, either. She wasn't quite tame—no matter how she might try, whoever she was. And that was the most important point. *Whoever she was.* Because here in Brevis Southwest, Nick should know her. Field Sentinels—those who could take another form—were not thick on the ground in any region, and if Nick hadn't actually worked with each of the Sentinels in his region, he nonetheless knew their dossiers.

Not this woman's.

Nor had anyone reported anything unusual from other regions—Sentinels gone missing, Sentinels gone traveling, Sentinels following a trail across borders. She was a complete unknown, an anomaly during restless and uneasy times when Nick could not afford anomalies.

So through the outdoor show rings he followed her, giving wide berth to the obedience rings and the utility dogs who performed exacting feats of scent discrimination and directed retrieving. Farther yet, where the agility dogs barked excitement through their courses, the teeter slamming to the ground and handlers shouting top-speed course corrections with the panicked note that meant *oops, too late*.

Here, Nick was at home—the very reason he'd come here today, hunting interviews with handlers and owners. Of the brevis Sentinels, he was the one with a pack of retired show dogs. He was the one with co-owned dogs on the circuit, a common arrangement in the world of showing and breeding.

He was the one to whom the affected handlers would speak freely.

To judge by the startled expressions the woman left in her wake, the number of people doing double takes over their shoulders…she not only didn't fit into this world, she hadn't ever learned to glide through it, either.

Just past the agility grounds, he stopped—with nothing beyond but groomed, remote fields bordered by a man-made tangle of trees and brush. Past that, a midland desert choked thickly with its own native growth—creosote and brittlebush and wild, gorgeous bird-of-paradise, all scattered about with a variety of cactus. But right up close, a field of nothing but informally parked cars, people going to and fro…but none of them startled, all of them chatting happily as they juggled gear and tugged along rolling carrier wheels, their conversation lost in the flapping of the shade canopy setups behind him.

An elusive scent played hide-and-seek on the gusty breeze; Nick whirled.

There she was.

Waiting for him.

Everything that first glimpse had promised—rangy athletic grace even in stillness, only a few feet away and tucked up against the back side of the agility scorekeeper's tent. Her features came as no surprise at all, they so suited the rest of her—short, mussed hair a glossy black, wide-set eyes a deep whiskey gold and tipped up at the corners over the world's most amazing cheekbones, and a wide, serious mouth that wouldn't have to say a word if she only ever let those eyes speak for her.

Only a foot away now, and an unexpectedly swift step brought her closer. She found his gaze, direct and unflinching. "You're following me."

"You meant me to." He said it without thinking, while his mind caught on her voice—lower than he'd expected, smoothly musical, the edges of the words softened by the slightest of unfamiliar burrs, the faintest softening of consonants.

"Did I?" She cocked her head slightly as she examined his words, his demeanor—everything about him.

"You don't belong here," he said, but he kept accusation from his voice. *For now.* "Were you looking for me?" And on second thought, more warily, "You didn't come here about the missing dogs."

At that she smiled again. Slowly. She shook her head. "No," she said. "Not about the missing dogs." She glanced over to the agility rings, where an overwrought Border Collie flung itself around its own made-up course as the judge signaled fault after fault and the handler laughed helplessly. "They are but infants."

It startled him, as much as he hid it. So a wolf would think, indeed—for compared to a wolf pack's complex social structure and interaction, the domesticated dog led a simplified and limited life. He thought of his own rowdy, cheerful pack of little hounds. "They have their charm."

But her response had been too honest, too true. *She's not involved—but she's not one of mine....*

Before he could take that train of thought any further, she said, "You knew me," and she said it with some satisfaction.

He found himself smiling—all wolf. "How," he said, "could I not?" And then, narrow-eyed, "Is that why you're here? To see if I would know you? To see if I would follow you?"

"To see if you *could*," she said.

She's not involved, she's not one of mine....

"There's protocol," he said, the reality of it pressing in. Too many things happening, here in Southwest. "You need to check in with brevis if you're—"

"Run with me," she said, turning her head to a sudden

gust of wind, glossy black hair buffeted, eyes flashing gold in the sun. Wild invitation from a wild child grown.

He stopped short. In those eyes—in the lift of her head and the lines of strong, straight shoulders, in rangy legs promising long, ground-eating strides—he suddenly remembered something of what he was.

"Run with me," she said again, looking out over the remaining fields of the fairgrounds to the thick tangle of irrigated wooded borders between the tended green land and the natural desert grit and caliche and sand, filled with thorns and things that bit and stung and knew how to survive their harsh land.

Nick looked out at that land, and he looked at the woman flinging *wild* in his face, and without even realizing it, he grinned again, dark and just as feral as she. *All wolf.*

She hadn't expected him to respond to her—not personally, not in any way. She'd expected to fail.

She hadn't expected to respond to *him.*

She'd seen pictures—flat and uninteresting, without scent or texture. They hadn't told her what she truly needed to know. They hadn't revealed the deeper truth of him.

They hadn't told her he was alpha.

Not alpha as reckoned in the world of cities and people, as among the Sentinels or the Atrum Core. Meaningless, those appellations. But alpha in the truest sense of the word.

So now she'd found him, and now she'd drawn him in, and now she knew she would not fail.

But now, she wanted to.

Not an option.

This open area in which they spoke held little shelter for changing—nothing more than ugly plastic portable bathrooms tucked beside the scorekeeper's tent. Jet wrinkled her nose at them and targeted the informal parking lot beyond—full of oversized vans, small RVs, and big SUVs.

A moment earlier, he'd been amused. But she'd left him with his civilized human thoughts too long, and now he held out a beckoning hand. A commanding hand, as if he had every right to demand her response.

She supposed he did, when it came to that. But she tipped her head just so, and she dropped her jaw in light wolfish amusement…and she backed away. Just a step, then two…hesitating in invitation.

"Later," he said, his voice grown hard in a way that didn't quite match the yearning in his pale green eyes. Humans might have trouble reading the truth of those eyes, but she had no such hindrance. He held firm nonetheless. "You've got questions to answer."

"After. If we run," she told him, jogging a few easy strides away from the hustle-bustle *barkbarkbark* before hesitating again—knowing *just* the pattern of tease and entice, though he'd likely not recognize it until too late. For all his wolf, he was far too human to see the subtleness of what she could wield.

"No," he said, though his glance at the spit of woods as it reached through this field showed him to be just a tad more perceptive than she'd thought. A little faster.

And so she moved again, body fluid and beguiling, expression clear. *Romp with me.*

He shook his head. "I'm not bargaining. I want you out of the field until you're formally cleared."

She couldn't help a laugh. "That is for no man to say. I am my own person." Not strictly true at the moment...but true for so much of her life that it clung to her, curled up inside her and aching to be set free again.

"You," he said, and those light green eyes darkened as he lowered his head slightly, "are in Brevis Southwest. Without permission or notification." Not a good sign, that challenging look, or the set of his shoulders. If he wanted to take her, he could.

Then never let him get close enough. She slipped farther away, a few light-hearted steps toward the beckoning woods. "After," she repeated. She closed her eyes, flung her head back, let flared nostrils scoop in the scents of this man-made wild spot that had outpaced any attempts to keep it tamed. A hundred yards away, the scattered cars defined the edge of the parking area, more sparse than the clustered vehicles around the entrance to the performance grounds they'd just left. The noises and odors of that place had grown more distant, and the woods, the desert beyond...they called all the more loudly.

And besides, she was close enough now.

This human form could run, too.

Run she did, straight for the woods, all smooth easy speed and loping strength, taking advantage of his momentary surprise to gain ground. And once there, she didn't hesitate. She spun to face him even as she toed off her shoes; she tugged impatiently at the buttons of the vest. So confining, these clothes! She skimmed free, rolling them into a quick, practiced ball and standing to face him, wearing only Gausto's necklaces on this lean, naked human form, skin tightening against the shadowed breeze.

He stopped short at the sight of her, eyes gone dark, jaw gone hard. He took a step toward her—

She smiled, showing teeth, and crouched into a tight ball of flesh, reaching within to free the wolf. It swelled from inside her, a rising wave of relief and power, swirling blues and grays that expanded to obscure her from the world and the world from her. But that veil quickly shrank back, showing her the world now through her wolf's eyes. And still she showed her teeth, a laughing curl of lip—a challenge. *Come run with me if you dare.*

He took it as such—but he took off none of his clothes. All the specially made Sentinel clothes with their warded pockets and natural materials—useless to one whose changes had been instilled by the Core, triggered over and over and over until she learned to do it herself, then trained with powerful aversives to remain human while they taught her more.

His gaze latched on to her even as the glorious flicker of blue lightning gathered—her first sight of a Sentinel's natural change, flashing and strobing until he finally closed his eyes and lifted his head just so—and then the light obscured his form, twining and crawling around him until she had to look away—if only for an instant, and then she drank in the sight of him, well-pleased.

They stood together for an instant—close enough for him to have snagged her, had he truly wanted to. Black, rangy wolf-bitch with long legs and a gleam in her eye. Hoarfrost gray wolf, a big male with substance and power and size. Two wolves in the midst of humanity—strangers, but, as wolves were wont, confident in their quick assessment of one another, their equally quick camaraderie. Nick Carter as wolf relaxed more easily than as human, relying on an instinct that told him she was only just what she was. Wolf-bitch, comely and strong and wanting a good run.

In unexpected choreographed unison, they each gave a good shake—an ear-flapping, tail-popping shake, dismissing the residual energy of the change. After that, his tongue lolled out, ever so briefly. And then he seemed to remember why he'd followed her this far, and his ears canted back and his muzzle tightened over his teeth.

Time to run, oh, yes. At first full-bore, slipping through the trees like darkness and shadow, irreverence on the run from authority. But soon enough it became obvious to her…he could have caught her at any time. Caught her and shoulder-checked her off her feet; caught her and grabbed her up by the scruff. Instead he merely flanked her, waiting…giving her, ultimately, the chance she'd asked for before he demanded his answers—and she finally broke free of their subtle sparring and blew out of the woods and into the desert.

She'd been waiting here for days, lurking at the edges of the fairgrounds at night and coming in during the day to hunt for him as she'd been told. So she already knew the trail, and already knew the best paths in the desert— the way to the nearest wash, the cholla thicket where the jackrabbits thought they could hide, the barrel cactus damaged by an illegal off-roader, now a temporary source of juicy pulp and water.

She led him there, and they trotted along the wash, bumping shoulders. She made a quick, flirty dive at his foreleg; he snarled horribly and pretended to go down; they tooth-fenced there under the bland midday winter sun, the wind gusting at their fur, a cactus wren shrilling a warning above them just in case their fierce mock growls had gone unheard by any potential prey within reach.

She ended it by leaping to her feet and loping back toward the woods, pushing speed and surprised that he could keep up with her, too used to the larger males who couldn't match her lithe movement. But they reached the woods together, found the shade and the cool dirt together, pressed themselves down behind the cover of leaves to watch the distant fuss and bother of humanity.

A nudge of her long muzzle and refined nose brought his head down; she commenced to cleaning his face—his eyes, his strong cheeks, his ears. The only submission an alpha would give, to a wolf-bitch of his choosing.

Of his choosing. That's what this was. That was what it had turned into, beyond her intent and surely beyond his, but inescapable and irrevocable. And so he gave her such trust, this man who had tried to stay so distant and yet had let the wolf in her beguile the wolf in him, half-closing his eyes to tilt his head into her caresses.

Maybe that's what made it so hard to trigger the amulet, the one Fabron Gausto had given her—the one that was meant to immobilize him, to fetter him. Maybe that's why his widened eyes, pale and green, held such stunned betrayal as the power of the thing surged up and wrapped itself around him, catching him even as he bolted upward, a snarl on his lips. Maybe that's why, as his body stiffened and trembled and then went limp, she thought she heard a cry of denial invade her own private thoughts.

Or maybe that had just come from within, after all.

Chapter 2

*"**B**ring him in, Jet."*

Fabron Gausto had said those words with confidence. No doubt he'd fully expected Jet to obey.

He had every reason to.

Confused by the changes in her life, by the changes in her body, Jet had accepted the things done to her at Gausto's hand…so that she might survive them, as so many had not done. And when he held the rest of her pack hostage to her good behavior and sent her out to take down the enemy—one, he'd said, who would see her coming and yet never truly see her at all—she'd had every intention of doing just that.

But he'd been wrong. Nick Carter had truly seen her. He'd recognized the wild in her; he'd seen her nature.

He'd seen her heart.

And she'd seen his.

The feelings were strange to her—they came differently than they had before Gausto had forever altered her. Sweet and hard and twisting, more complex…conflicting desires, conflicting needs. She didn't know how to reconcile them…what to do with them.

She knew only that she needed time to understand them.

And so instead of bundling the stricken wolf into an unwieldy package on the back of her sleek, growly Triumph Tiger motorcycle, alone, she'd ridden the thirty-one miles north to Oro Valley much more quickly than she should—speeding and ducking and dodging through traffic, nipping at the heels of larger vehicles and sprinting on by, close enough to catch the hint of unease in the other drivers' expressions.

Also against directions, that aggressive riding—but if Gausto had expected anything else, it only proved that he'd learned less about her world than she had about his.

This route, she'd practiced extensively, though she knew few others. She peeled off I10 and onto Route 77 without second thought, skimming west of the Santa Catalinas and through Oro Valley, up to the foothills of the Tortolinas. She left bike, helmet and leather biking jacket in the sprawling driveway of the desert estate, parked in the shadows of stately, groomed saguaro that looked no happier, leashed by civilization, than she. Past the unobtrusive guards with a lift of her lip they pretended not to see; past the entry landscaping cameras that showed of her approach.

Gausto knew, then, that she came alone.

He waited for her.

Past the public entrance to the house, the big double front doors of rustic wood enclosed by decorative steel privacy screening, and around the side to the entrance. Unlike the front half of the house, this hallway was narrow and dim, unexposed to exterior light; it led to rooms with no windows and no escape.

Jet had reason to know.

It led, too, to the far workroom, a deep place of murky memories and illness and brethren trapped and dead.

But today Jet went to none of those places. She went instead to the tiny vestibule of a room that was hers alone—flat off-white walls with token but classic southwest texture, a plain overhead fixture with a dim bulb, a tiny rectangular window near the ceiling. To her furniture, her cot, a small trunk of clothes and the chair where Gausto would be sitting.

He was.

Never taken unaware, that was Gausto.

He sat with his legs crossed and his hands quiet in his lap, but Jet was not complacent of him. Not this man, with his precisely tailored suit, his silver flashing jewelry, black hair drawn back in a tight tail at his neck. And dark eyes—cold, flat eyes. He didn't wear amulets as so many did here; Jet had heard enough to understand that somehow, he was protected. Fully, completely protected from any workings anyone might try on him.

She was human enough to feel bitter envy at this fact, and wolf enough not to show it.

"Jet," he said, using her name with flat authority. Well he might; he'd given it to her.

And she did as she'd learned; she showed him submission. The form was her own—down to one knee, hands quietly on the other, body twisted ever so slightly aside in token exposure, head tipped just as subtly to show her throat. Always a careful balance, there—she'd seen those flat eyes of his go alive at the sight of her tender flesh, and she thought that even in his fully human existence, he felt the flicker of impulse to go for her throat.

Especially when he was angered.

Slowly, she went down to one knee. Slowly, she gave him her vulnerability. Her very caution seemed to please him.

"You failed," Gausto said. "I'm surprised. Perhaps I didn't explain the stakes carefully enough? Another demonstration—" He stopped as Jet stiffened, and smirked slightly in the satisfaction of it.

She wanted to tear his throat out.

And she could have done it, could have shifted and been on him before he so much as moved from the chair. His blood would have splashed across these walls, his mysterious ward of protection of no use against her teeth and speed.

But she didn't. Not with the scent wrapped around this house, ever reminding her...her pack, trapped beneath, some already dead at Gausto's hand, the rest awaiting salvation only Jet could provide.

It should have been enough. It *would* have been enough. But Gausto had also promised her something else again.

Freedom.

For Jet, freedom had turned complicated and elusive—much more complicated than the simple return of a pack to the distant mountains from which it had come. For among them, Jet was no longer fully wolf…nor completely human. She was Gausto's prize tool, his *thing*. That he would even contemplate releasing her…

He must want Nick Carter very much.

But Jet, in spite of her own best efforts, was not as biddable as she was meant to be.

Now she tipped her head just a little more, looking up for permission to speak. He made her wait for it— of course he made her wait—and then gestured assent, pleased with his own benevolence. She said, "I found him." She used the words carefully; he had made it clear he found her natural way of speaking displeasing.

Nick Carter, she thought, had not minded at all.

"But you did not bring him back." Gausto flicked invisible lint from his knee. "Finding him is no great accomplishment, little Jet. Did I not provide you with the details of where he would be, and train you in the exact route, the correct clandestine approach? *Finding* him was nothing. But I also gave you amulets to use on him. My dear wolf-child, all you had to do was take him aside and trigger the amulet as you've been trained." He regarded her with disdain at the corners of his mouth. "You will try again tomorrow. And the next day, if necessary. But Jet—mark this well. For each day you fail, one of your pack members will pay the price."

After an instant's spike of alarm, she schooled herself. As long as he still wanted Carter, her packmates would not die. Because if she truly failed—if she died in the attempt or she died at Gausto's impatient hands— he would need them to start again. And her pack was not such a very large pack that he could afford to discard any one of them.

Not until he'd given up on Carter.

And still, she couldn't stop herself from saying, too quickly, "I have him."

Gausto snorted, most genteelly. He must be in a mood. He was far from genteel when it suited him. "My dear, don't insult me. The cameras would have shown him to me when you arrived." His eyes narrowed. "But you're smarter than that. Explain yourself."

She straightened, watching to make sure it didn't displease him—but he'd forgotten about such subtleties. He often did. It only proved to Jet that he was far less civilized than he pretended to be—but the same could be said about any of the humans she'd met here. "I found him. I used the amulet."

Gausto's expression swapped out triumph with a frown. "Then why have you not brought him to me?"

"I had questions," Jet told him, and thought it reasonable.

"Questions?" Gausto repeated, his tone instantly telling her he thought no such thing. "It is not your place to have *questions*, Jet. It is not your place to *think*. You do *as* you're told, *when* you're told, *how* you're told."

"But if I understand, I do it better." She tipped her head, looked at him in cublike question...she'd learned early that he interpreted this as an eagerness to please. "Yes?"

It did indeed settle him, if only infinitesimally. She took the moment. "I don't understand your world," she told him. "He is alpha, your Nick Carter. Is this how it is done, the challenge? From behind?"

Gausto sucked in a sudden breath; Jet knew she'd misspoken badly, but had no idea how—sometimes it seemed to her that the truth was not *his* truth. His lips thinned. He reached for her, and she forced herself to be still, not to react—not to cringe or lift her lip or retreat, all hard-learned lessons—as he grasped the short, romp-fluffed hair at the back of her head, digging his fingers in to pull hard. "Nick Carter," he said, "has committed crimes against my people. He is alpha to nothing of mine, do you understand that?"

Jet understood that Nick Carter knew alpha where Gausto knew bullying. She understood on a level so deep it needed no words. She understood that where Gausto held sway over her through dint of his cruelty and advantages in this human world, through his ability and willingness to manipulate her and change the very essence of what she was, Nick Carter had connected to her with heart, with the things he had chosen not to do as well as those things he had done. He had run with her; they had forged an afternoon together with the instinctive, spirit-deep communication of creatures who could not lie about their souls.

He had not bullied her. He had not snarled her into submission. He had not gone beyond fairness to coercion.

Maybe that's why, somehow, she had left a piece of herself behind with him, felled by that amulet right along with him.

If Gausto noticed her distraction, he didn't indicate it. "Nick Carter is a criminal and he must be stopped. And unless you don't care anything about protecting your own people, that's all you need to know."

But Jet already knew much, much more.

He'd almost made it. Had almost bolted up out of reach, out of range.

He'd thought she might be so many different

things…from undeclared field agent to outright rogue—until there at the end, when her shift had gone so differently, he began to realize she might be something else altogether.

But he'd never thought she could be Core.

And he hadn't realized it would shred something deep within him to have it so. He didn't know her; he hadn't done anything more than let his guard down for an uncharacteristic lupine romp. Or so he'd thought.

He knew better now.

Too late for that.

Barely conscious enough for the thought, gasping under the weight of the triggered amulet and the poison of it in his system, he nonetheless found it hard to reconcile the betrayal with her subsequent flight, leaving him tucked away here in the wild strip of growth protecting the outlying fairground fields from the desert.

Hard to think at all.

The amulet, triggered, hung around his neck with a stench he couldn't avoid—corruption and coppery astringency and sharp acrid wisps of power—sickening him. His human form could have grasped the amulet and wrapped his hands around it and if he suffered for it, he could still break it. Unique, this skill in action. A mere handful of field Sentinels had seen it in use; fewer yet within Brevis Regional. She couldn't have known. *Coincidence. Luck.* But it left him no less trapped. No less sickened.

And getting sicker.

He hadn't realized it at first. Gone down hard and fast, the proverbial ton of bricks, darkness not only closing in on him but clenching down tight. He'd woken already panting, tongue lolling onto the scant, gritty leaf cover, to find her crouching over him—back to her human, clothed, and the pure wolfish scent of her cutting cleanly through the amulet stench. "I don't want this," she'd said, resting her hand in his thick ruff, black hair painted heavily with silver. And she'd opened her mouth to say something else, but after a hesitation, rose silently to angle out of the trees.

Moments later, a powerful motorcycle engine roared to life, settling to a growl…moving away at uncertain low speed on the off-road terrain and then abruptly smoothing out, shifting up in pitch, and winding up for asphalt…fading quickly into the distance.

The silence sat most heavily on him in that moment—the realization. Only Fabron Gausto would break the rules of the uneasy Sentinel-Core detente so completely—and only Fabron Gausto had little to lose, and everything to gain.

Gausto had already deeply embarrassed his Core Septs Prince, using forbidden blood workings on Meghan Lawrence and Dolan Treviño this past spring. But he'd been released for Core justice, for even the brevis regional adjutant—the consul's executive officer—didn't take the fate of a Core drozhar into his hands. Not with relations between the Core and the Sentinels already teetering.

Not with Brevis Regional Southwest so vulnerable, with field ops gone subtly wrong and bad luck plaguing them, and confidence in the ageing consul wavering.

Nick didn't think Dane Berger—consul, Sentinel, and javelina boar—was in on the deeply buried conspiracy, but his willful blindness had allowed things to get this far. Far enough that his original adjutant had been killed and Nick, after only a year in his place, could see the growing danger.

But not well enough.

Gausto, in trying to redeem himself, had then sent a Core team to the San Francisco Peaks in northern Arizona, Joe Ryan's high desert turf. And if Nick had initially targeted Ryan as the cause of the area's problems and sent Lyn Maines to investigate…well, maybe it was the best thing he could have done after all. Now the Peaks were secure, and Gausto…

Gausto must be desperate. Enough for an all-or-nothing bid. Nick could all but hear that flat, arrogant voice in his head, inveigling the septs prince. *Leave me my life, and I'll give you Nick Carter.* And then, because neither he nor the Core could be tied to any such operation, he'd found someone else to do it.

Someone wolf.

Pure feral grace.

Something wrenched inside him. He thought at first it came from the amulet, but a sudden flash of whiskey gold eyes, of laughing invitation—of the perfect flirtatiousness every wolf knew with her partner, pure and unfettered—and the twist of pain sent him thrashing in the underbrush.

Not just the amulet. The amulet's working, reacting to the energies within him. That deeply, she'd reached him.

Sonuvadamnedbitch.

He took the battle inward, eyes unfocused and halfclosed, the heat of the day reaching him even in this protected shade but the panting gone beyond mere heat. It ate at him, this amulet. Wormed around deep inside his body and chewed away at the foundation of him. Worse than maybe she'd thought—or Gausto, for that matter. Because Nick was pretty sure Gausto wanted him alive.

For Gausto liked to play.

He cleared the murk from his mind, shoving away whiskey gold and edgy movement, a flash of black…he focused on his inner voice, gathering it, channeling it— pulling together a wordless *adveho,* sent straight to Annorah at brevis—their communications star still intensely determined to prove herself with perfection after her misjudgment during the Peaks incident. Not coincidentally, the single brevis-based operative currently in his small circle of trust.

But the *adveho,* the call for help that no Sentinel would ignore, went nowhere.

His focus faded; his awareness of the details around him faded, too. The scents, the sounds, the active fairgrounds so very close and yet way too far away to do him any good…

Didn't mean he wouldn't try. One inch at a time, rolled on his chest, head too heavy to lift. Paws, pushing against dirt and weeds…slipping, losing strength…hind legs splayed out behind like a puppy on ice. Barely budging the weight of him. But still…budging.

Try again.

And again.

Gausto wouldn't get him without a fight. And if it meant fighting those whiskey gold eyes and pure feral grace…

So be it.

Try. Again.

Chapter 3

Jet washed her face in the tiny bathroom down the hall from her own room. It calmed her. She liked the sensation, and the soap, and the lotions—even the very basic scentless hand lotion provided in this bathroom. She liked shampoo and conditioner and flinging her head back from the faucet to send water droplets flying from her hair.

It didn't make sense, that. She was wolf, and wolf needed none of those things. But she liked them nonetheless.

She had this time because Gausto was fielding a phone call—one he thought she couldn't overhear. He'd never bothered to test her hearing; Jet thought he had guessed it was more acute than any born human's but simply didn't think it mattered to know how much.

His mistake. For Jet was a made thing, might be a

temporarily controlled thing…but she wasn't truly bound to him, not by blood nor pack nor heart.

And she knew what it was to be wild. More, she wanted it back.

Gausto had that tone in his voice, now. The deference. Only one man brought that out in him—his Septs Prince.

Gausto's was a pack of many localized packs, Jet had decided. Gausto ruled one of the local packs…but just barely. He'd made too many mistakes, shown too many weaknesses, and now the alpha of all the packs combined was displeased with him.

And no wonder. Gausto still considered his mistakes to be bold strikes against Core prey, worth the risk and worth the failure. But Jet knew the difference—and she could see it in the eyes of his men. The occasional flares of doubt, the fears that Gausto would lead them to disaster.

Wolf packs were not so very different. They were simply less forgiving.

And so she not only heard his phone call, she understood the byplay of it. Leaning over the sink to peer at her face in the small mirror and search for any sign of the wolf, she quite absently absorbed Gausto's words.

"He's as good as contained." Gausto's trouser legs brushed against one another with the faintest susurrus of cloth against cloth; his footsteps sounded slightly gritty against the thin floor covering as he paced. "That amulet was developed specifically for him." A pause. "I still don't know how he's evaded so many of our more subtle amulet attacks over the past year. But once I get him here, I'll find out."

The eyes, Jet decided. Still wolf there. But not the face—features too refined, jaw a little too sharp. The nose was good—a strong nose, even a hint of a bump at the bridge. And the mouth…it was not wolf at all, but she liked it. She touched her lower lip with hesitant fingers, prodding the fullness of it, feeling the pliability.

Unaccountably, thinking of Nick Carter. Of how well she knew him, through those moments with his wolf. Of how the thrill of it still lingered with her…and how the cold hard dread of what she'd done still sank deep.

"Later this afternoon," Gausto said, his voice still carrying that oily note, the one that came through when he thought he was smarter than everyone else but didn't dare say so to the Septs Prince. "No, not at all—we're completely covered. If anything, given my agent, they're going to think it was one of their own."

Nick Carter, Jet thought, had the wolf in him—right there on the surface, visible for all to see even if they didn't recognize it. His hair, for one thing. True hoarfrost, dark hair brushed with gray…not just black and white hairs intermingled, as she'd seen in some of the Core guards and the one woman who'd tended her through the early transition.

And his eyes—not just the pale green color, but the nature of his gaze itself—steady, self-knowing. Alpha eyes. But more than all that, the way he moved, all that strength and smooth power, the impression that he always knew where he was and where everyone else was, always knew just where and how to place himself to keep the advantage. She wondered if she, too, showed the wolf in her movement.

They *had* to see it, she decided. The other human-born. They just didn't know what it was.

"Security has scrubbed this place clean," Gausto was

reassuring his prince. "I've got a table waiting for Carter. He's going to talk like he's never talked before." Jet looked away from the mirror, startled, toward the sound of Gausto's voice. Toward the meanness that had come into it. "Before this day is over, he's going to understand just how much I owe him."

Jet froze there, the towel still in her hand, the dread drilling deeper. She didn't understand all the implications of those words, but she didn't have to—she understood his intent.

She understood for the first time that to get what he wanted, Gausto used not only threats and punishment, he used untruths. That Gausto intended not to force postponed negotiations as he'd told Jet, but that he intended to acquire information. That he intended to do it with pain...and that he looked forward to inflicting that pain.

More than that. He yearned to do it.

And he was using her to make it happen.

Marlee pondered her options. Log sheet up on her monitor screen, an Apache phrase book open on her desk—idle background reading—and the phone headset hooked over one ear. "No, seriously," she told the field Sentinel calling in from the home. "Check to see if it's plugged in." And then she waited past the annoyance, the denial, the sudden silence—all the while thinking about delivery options for the virus Gausto had ordered her to insert into Nick Carter's computer—*if only they knew*—and just about convinced she'd need a hand delivery. Finally she heard the sheepish acknowledgment that the Sentinel's monitor plug had indeed wiggled loose.

"You're welcome," she said, keeping her voice to strict customer service cheer. *She* knew she was better than this. Underutilized, underappreciated. But if she was going to stay here—if she was going to stay above suspicion—then she had to use the team spirit that ran through this office like a braid of loyalty.

Loyalty to Nick Carter, of course.

The virus. Yes, it would take a hand delivery. And she'd do it today, while Carter was out at the fairgrounds pretending he was still a field Sentinel after all.

She pulled off the headset and picked up the thumbnail drive beside her keyboard, turning it thoughtfully in her hand. No big deal to create a work order for a nonexistent problem, head for Carter's office, and infect his machine while she was "assessing" it.

"Did you really just ask me if I had the *right day?*" The voice was pleasant alto and just barely familiar, and at the moment it had a touch of tooth. It also wasn't far from Marlee's cube, there in the entry aisle of the IT section.

Something about the responding voice made Marlee want to lean into the sound of it, soaking up…something. Power. Security. Grounding. She closed her eyes against the impulse and shuddered. *Sentinels.* They had a sway over people that no one else could imagine. Just like Carter, trying to cover up the truth of what he was with *GQ* haircuts and *GQ* suits and still managing to suck the air out of Marlee's lungs anytime he walked into a room.

Now this one said, with just the right surprise, "Me, imply that you had our appointment mixed up? I don't think so. Don't think I'd do that."

"Nick was supposed to be here," the woman said.

"Today. Now. It's time to get this Vegas thing sorted out. You were set up and it's time everyone knew it."

He snorted. "That's not what you said not so long ago."

She didn't back down an inch. "Just be glad I'm on your side now."

"That's the truth." His reply was somewhat fervent, and they'd said enough, then—Marlee knew exactly who they were.

She cleared her throat and leaned back in her chair. "Hello? Can I help you?"

Not that she wanted to deal with Lyn Maines, Carter's tracker friend, or Joe Ryan—the very Sentinel who'd very nearly destroyed the balance of the San Francisco Peaks. And Lyn—when she'd first gotten here, when she was helping Carter find the *Liber Nex* manuscript out on Encontrados Ranch where Dolan Treviño had gotten tangled up with coyote's daughter Meghan Lawrence…

Then, she'd had her head on straight. Then, she'd been dedicated to keeping the Sentinels honest. But Joe Ryan had turned her somehow, and now she was no better than all the rest. Using illicit power to take advantage of those who didn't have it.

"This place overwhelms me," Lyn murmured now. "All the trace…" She and Ryan came around the doorway, a few matter-of-fact steps while Marlee dredged up a smile of greeting and kept it there—until Lyn stopped short, startled.

Ryan reacted with the wary responsiveness that told Marlee he knew the meaning of the expression on Lyn's face, and she struggled to maintain her own composure, realizing instantly that the pictures she'd seen of

Ryan conveyed nothing of the man himself. Mountain lion shifter, he was easily a foot taller than Lyn, maybe more. Where neat, petite Lyn barely showed her ocelot—just a certain smudgy look at the outer edges of large eyes that the average person would take for makeup—Ryan pretty much oozed his cougar. Tawny hair gone short and dark at the nape and temples, a solid, muscular presence, fresh scars still healing—a powerful man used to wielding power.

Marlee kept her smile where it was. "If you're looking for Nick, he's not here. I think he's out in the field today."

"This morning, maybe," Lyn said, sounding distracted. Overwhelmed by trace, she'd said. "He'd have called if he was delayed."

Ryan's hand lingered at her waist. "Things aren't always like that in the field."

"That's what I've heard," Marlee agreed, adding a little laugh. She thought it convinced them, and relaxed a little. They didn't, after all, have any idea she'd been sitting here thinking about planting a virus in Carter's private system.

Her computer dinged at her, a cheerful little instant message notification. Like Pavlov's dog, she glanced at it—and froze. Just for an instant, seeing the screen name there. *FG347*. Acprince. So subtle. And lately, not nearly enough care. Too pushy, too cavalier with her security, too assured of her compliance. She was no puppet, doing his bidding unquestioned. She was no traitor.

She only wanted to make sure the Sentinels didn't grow *too* cocky.

Done? Gausto asked her in his IM.

She hit the space bar with a casual thumb and then the return, barely glancing at the keyboard. An empty reply—a message of her own. *Back off. I'll let you know.*

Maybe it was time to see if she could work with someone else as contact. Fabron Gausto made her feel…

Dirty.

"You're busy," Lyn said. "Sorry about that. We just thought we'd look around rather than disturb the whole building by having Annorah page him."

Right. Annorah. Carter's pet communications Sentinel. Another whom Carter seemed determined to keep on active duty regardless of her behavior in the field. Marlee wondered that Lyn could even say the woman's name so calmly, given Ryan's injuries at the time. True, she hadn't meant for the consequences to be as grim as they'd turned out…

But that was the problem, wasn't it? Sentinels interfering, and thinking *oops* was reaction enough when things went wrong.

"No problem," Marlee said. "His system's been a little hinky lately, so it's possible he tried to mail you an update and it just didn't reach you." *Ooh, nice one.* Lay the groundwork there for when the virus took Carter's communications down.

"So, listen, if you see him…" Lyn said, and let the words trail off. Ryan had gone silent, contemplating Marlee in a way that made her itchy. *Sentinels.* They were all like that.

"No problem," Marlee said. "You'll be here for the afternoon?"

"A while," Lyn agreed. She nudged Ryan with her hip. "Let's check with his admin. Nick might have set him to digging up information on the clerk who—" she glanced at Marlee and didn't finish the sentence. "Anyway, it's worth a try."

"You done here?" he asked.

"Everything I need," she told him, which made little sense. Marlee waited for them to turn around, and then frowned fiercely at their backs.

They'd hardly gone when her computer dinged at her again.

When?

Admit it. More than just annoying and pushy. These days, Gausto downright scared her.

Jet pushed the Triumph into the tree line, just enough to obscure it—here, on the desert side of the buffer zone, where she'd done as directed and cut the barbed range fencing to approach from this angle. She toed the kickstand down and gave the sleek leather seat an absent pat of appreciation.

Gausto had bought this bike expressly for her, and try as she might to treat it with the same disdain she applied to everything human he forced upon her, she couldn't help that since her awakening to nonborn human, this one thing had restored to her the fleeting taste of running wild. Powerful on the road, quick with speed, sleekly responsive to the lean of her body…it floundered a little in this brief foray off-road, but she loved it no less for that.

So she patted it and she left it, jogging silently through the man-made belt of wooded overgrowth to where she'd left Carter—unharmed but incapacitated, and no doubt cursing her.

But Nick Carter was gone.

Instant panic assailed her. *He can't be gone.* For she'd seen the results of this amulet—Gausto had shown her, using one of his own men, so she'd know what to expect. So she'd trust him.

Never that.

But she trusted the consistency of the amulet, and Nick Carter should be here. The same as tranked and bound. Gausto would blame her if he had escaped. And worse—as she stood there, staring at the place he'd been, the flattened foliage and scuffed sandy soil—*worse*—

She wouldn't see him again.

That made her stop. Made her frown. For it wasn't part of her world, that bereft feeling. *He* wasn't part of her world.

Or he hadn't been.

But now...

Now he was.

She gave a little shake—a stress-release shake, flowing through her neck and shoulders—and she put herself back in her wolf-thoughts. Letting her primal self take over, even in this form.

Her primal self saw clearly past the emotions and found the trail. Bent twigs, disturbed soil, crushed leaves in this place where so much was spiny and waxy and hard to damage at all. Her nose scented it; her eyes saw it.

And more. There was sickness here...a certain raw flavor of effort and distress.

It was a trail she could follow. But she did it with care, not assuming anything in this strange place with its many people, so close. One slow step at a time, confirming the sights, the sounds—checking out of this shadowed buffer zone and into the bright sunshine full of dogs and huge white tent canopies and people and noise, a loudspeaker announcing in the background about *Sporting Group* and *Ring Five*.

Busy people. No one looked at her, or noted her slow movement among the trees. And so she tracked.

Not that it took long.

He hadn't gone far.

He shouldn't have been able to move at all, but…

He wasn't moving anymore.

Too late, too stupid.

He'd figured it out, all right. The amulet strung around his neck held a containment working, but…so much more.

The more Nick tried to break it, to fight it, the more it drove back at him, insinuating itself into his energies—replacing good with bad.

Poisoning him.

Realizing it—realizing how far it had already gone—he did the only thing left to him. He poured everything he had into one final effort. All his intent, all his focus—clawing his way across the ground, one excruciating inch after another, hind legs splayed out behind him. He had no thought for what he'd do if he was spotted or if he broke free, only that narrow little goal. *Move.* Break the working. Leave the amulet smoking.

Find the woman who'd left him here. The Core agent in wolf's clothing. That, too.

Move.

But it occurred to him, finally, that he no longer made progress. That what felt like heart-bursting effort from within resulted in nothing without—only his head sinking toward the ground, lolling off slightly to the side with his mouth barely open to pant. Air puffed past his flews. Heavy sickness spread through his body, weighing it down.

The next panting breath brought an influx of scent, both ambrosia and anathema.

She was back.

He growled, a ridiculous and weak token—but an unforgiving noise. A statement.

She'd come in her human form, all black-clothed and lithe. She made a noise of dismay; she went to one knee beside him. With all the effort he had in him, he raised his growl to something distinctly audible.

It gave her not an instant's hesitation. Her hand landed on his ruff, fingers kneading in. For a long moment, she said nothing—for that long moment, his growl hung between them. Unmistakable.

Until he had to break it off and resume panting, more heavily now, eyes slitting closed.

"I don't understand," she said, and frustration laced through her words. Frustration and more. *Grief.*

Nick didn't think it was for him.

"He said you wouldn't be hurt." Her accent, whatever it was, came thick. Or no accent at all, perhaps—a difficulty in forming the words. A slight speech impediment, almost Castillian in nature. "He said he wanted only to talk." Her fingers kneaded his fur, then smoothed it. "When he said you took the wolf, he made it sound…*wrong.* Stealing. Faking." Nick growled at her again…but it came weaker. Barely there at all. "Yes," she told him. "He was wrong about that. And this…I can see how it harms you." She found the thong around his neck—the amulet strap she'd placed there herself—and her hand hesitated.

Nick tried to growl again. Somehow it came out as a faint whine.

"He said he wouldn't hurt my pack." She covered her face with her free hand—an unusual gesture, putting the back of her wrist against her nose, her hand loosely curled and oddly graceful. As if the hand itself wasn't as familiar as the paw. "He said if I did this…"

Nick panted. The amulet worked on him, tugging at all the corners of his being. Fever washed over him.

She repeated, slowly, "He said if I brought you to him…"

Breathing suddenly seemed like too much effort. His lungs burned; he realized he'd let them lie fallow for long moments and dragged in a gulp of air.

Quite suddenly she bent over, laying her face against his—nuzzling him ever so slightly. Just as suddenly, she straightened again. "I think he lies," she said. "He will do to my pack what suits him, no matter what I bring him." A gentle lift of his head and a flick of her hand, and she removed the amulet thong. "No more do I heed him. You, I help. And my pack…I save on my own."

Instantly, breathing seemed natural again. And if his body shuddered with waves of flame and ice, he nonetheless had his growl back.

She gave a little laugh, laying her head against his for a long, long moment. "Good," she said. "That suits you. Now be the human again, and take yourself away from here. Gausto will not wait long before he comes for us."

Chapter 4

Gausto.

Nick had known it, of course. Or guessed it, the moment that amulet went over his head. But to hear her say it…

A wave of dizziness swamped his thoughts.

She stood up and back, and made as if to fling away the amulet—stopping herself at the last moment. "No," she said out loud, a lurking anger behind her words. "Someone else could find it."

It shouldn't matter. It had been triggered; it had connected with Nick. Separated from him, it was worthless.

Or should be. With Gausto, you never knew. The man seldom cared about consequences when he drove for power.

So yeah. Best not to take chances. As she tucked the

amulet away in a tight front pocket, he lifted his head—
wobbly at that, but still a significant improvement. Not
for long—it thunked back to earth, a jarring thud.

In an instant, she was there beside him. "You have
to take the human," she said, cradling his head in her
hands, lifting it to face him nose-to-nose. No fear, not
even with his crazed eye and the snarl on his lips. She
stroked his face from the muzzle back, awakening all
the myriad nerves there, flattening his whiskers. Past his
cheeks and the massive carnassials that could have
sheared off her arm, firmly down his ears…tugging ever
so slightly and waking those nerves, too. Bringing him
back, even if his head still lolled in her hands. "Nick
Carter," she said, "I heard him talking. He wants you.
He will hurt you. Do you understand this?"

He snarled for her.

"Be the human," she told him, one more time,
whiskey-gold gaze latched onto his with ferocity. "I
must leave this place, too."

Too many things gone unspoken there—too many
pieces unknown.

But he heard her urgency. He believed it. *Be the human.*

Easier said than done. Took every fuzzied bit of concentration he had. He thought she'd back away, giving
him space—but when humanity settled around him,
there she was, still holding his head—turning it, gently,
so he wouldn't end up face-first in the goats' head burrs
and stiff ground cover—and then releasing him.

She did it like someone who'd been there.

He coughed, clearing his throat of weakness—or
trying to. "What?" he rasped, and made it clear enough
with an unyielding gaze that he referred to her. *"Who?"*

She shook her head. "I have to go." Right. To help her people. Whatever that meant. "You have to go, too. He won't wait long." She shook her head again. "He almost sent men with me, but his prince spoke loudly of not being caught. I think, though, that they are not far behind. So go, now."

"Not without you," Nick said. He made it to his hands and knees, limbs shaking visibly, a feverish hot and cold chasing itself through his bones—but he didn't take his gaze from her. Didn't release her. *"Who…"* Too much going on in brevis these days to ignore that fact. "It matters…"

"It matters to *me,*" she told him. "But it is not yours to have." She rose, a fluid motion, and strode away down the buffer zone. No looking back…but there, at the edge of the trees, the slightest of hesitations.

But then she moved on.

And Nick's shaking arms gave way, and he plowed down into the dirt without grace. He spat an unequivocal curse and rolled over to his back, wiping dirt from beneath his lip with the careless and uncoordinated swipe of his wrist.

All right. Fine. He hadn't intimidated her into sticking around. It had been a long shot. He tried Annorah again, got nowhere—his focus was too scrambled, his energies likewise. So he needed to get up on his feet and find his way across the fairground to his car. Or at the least, onto the agility grounds where someone would have a phone.

Because he had no doubt his mystery betrayer-and-savior was right. If Gausto was behind this, if he'd had any doubts of the outcome…he wasn't far off. Or his people weren't far. No matter how the Septs Prince had instructed him.

Get up. Walk. Stagger. Crawl, if he had to. To the phone, in the car. Across the show grounds. Gausto would seed these grounds with his people if he realized that Nick was here, loose and vulnerable. And unlike the Sentinels, the Core agents carried guns. Guns and amulets and no compunction about damaging their prey.

His fingers twitched; fever cold chased him. And he realized, some moments later, that he hadn't moved at all.

Son of a bitch.

...no, still hadn't moved at all.

He didn't hear her coming.

There she was, standing over him, and in his mind he rolled up and sprang to his feet and he caught her— claiming every bit of the intimacy she'd established with her invitation to run in the desert, every bit of the conflicted tangle between them, driven into place with her four-footed romp and lighthearted play.

But no, he still hadn't moved at all.

"You," she said, glaring down at him. "*Have. To. Go.* Are these the wrong words?" She made a frustrated noise deep in her throat, something that probably hadn't started out human. "He said it would *not hurt you.*"

Nick coughed out a laugh. He hunted words, found only another wry truly amused laugh, even if it turned into a groan of effort as he did, finally, roll back over to his elbows. "Honey, he *lies.*"

"*Jet.*" She leaned over to grasp his upper arm, hauling him halfway to his feet with one smooth effort. He staggered into her, but she took advantage of the movement, hauling him forward.

"Jet?" he asked, the word a gasp as she slipped under his arm, wiry strength in that lean frame. "Where—?"

"Can you drive to leave this place? No. Then you come with me."

"Wait!" Still a gasp, but more emphatic—and when she hesitated, there on the edge of the desert, he managed to keep his own feet. "Compromise." Because he'd gathered this much—she was on the run, as of now. Breaking away from Gausto, and lucky she'd be to survive more than a few hours of that defiance. "You have no place to go. I have no way to get there. Come with me. "

She stared at him, the lowering sun slanting down to light whiskey-gold eyes into a glow. More of a glower, really—a demand. "Did that make sense?"

Nick waved off such details. "In fact," he said, "it didn't. But I think you understand me. Because I'm pretty sure I understand you."

She snorted. "You understand nothing," she told him. "But I will take you to your place, and then if it pleases me, I will consider staying." She adjusted her grip on his arm as it draped over her shoulder, and turned back to the motorcycle propped up against the tree line, a blazing red Triumph Tiger for which he couldn't help but make a sound of appreciation. Pride flashed across her face. "Even if they are near, they will not catch us," she said—and then cast him a dare of a look. "As long as you don't fall off."

He didn't fall off.

It was a tall bike, but she handled it ably on the desert caliche and once on the road, shifted smooth and fast up to speed. Good thing, that smoothness—the back suspension wasn't adjusted for his weight, and it wallowed.

They managed the turn onto Houghton; he clamped his hands at her hips and lurched into her back. He sent her across the bridge to the access road and south, staying off the highway. They cruised down along the Pantano wash, and then onto the little side roads toward Pisto Hill and towering Rincon Peak. The developments fell away and turned into worn, distant homes, baked dry in the sun over the years. A country store and post office, a small farm supplies store, a mom-'n'-pop grocery…

Nick didn't truly see any of them, sidetracked by the tremendous effort of staying upright on the motorcycle, of hanging on. And his dimmed and fuzzy senses were otherwise full.

Of her. *Jet.* The scent of her, swirling around them with the billowing dust, settling into his pores. More wolf than anything he knew, the scent of fresh clean *wild* and honest effort and some edgy unknown element that came through as pure Jet.

Then again, that was the problem, wasn't it? *More wolf than anything he knew.* Because far too much about her didn't mesh with Sentinel blood. Not the scent, not the way she'd changed, not the way she spoke.

Not the way she worked with Gausto.

And here I am, bringing her home. Lurching and slumping against her until the strong, athletic lines of her body became familiar—until his hands took for granted what they would find when he adjusted his grip, and yet still that shape—the flex and stretch of steady muscle as she handled the tall bike, the neat curve of her ribs and the quiet tuck of her waist, the swell of her hips and the push of a gorgeously rounded ass against his thighs—made him greedy for more.

Dumb bastard. She'd poisoned him. She'd left him helpless for Gausto.

And then she pulled me out of there. Saved his wolf hide.

Dammit, I can't think. He leaned his forehead against her shoulder, let it settle there.

Eventually, he realized they'd stopped again—that she needed direction. "Little," he told her. "Adobe… Beagles."

She turned her head; her voice came muffled by her helmet, full-face sport helmet in stark red and white against black. "I don't understand."

But Nick wasn't going to be much help. The best he could do, as he slid down against her back and tipped off the bike, was not take her with him.

Jet stared at him, oddly bereft without the sensation of lean, hard muscle pressing up against her, the warmth of his hands at her waist. He sprawled in the dirt at the side of the road—gritty pale sand scattered over caliche, full of rock and dryness and surrounded by all things spiny. An ocotillo soared above him, its thin, spindly arms offering no shade; a cactus wren churred nearby and flittered away.

Her hand slipped the clutch; the bike stalled out. Silence settled around her, until the sound of her own breathing within the helmet magnified, filling her mind with a surreal susurrus of white noise.

She'd never been out on her own before in the human world. Entirely on her own. Not on an assignment with carefully learned routes, not accompanied in the Tortolita foothills while learning to ride the bike. Not accompanied by Gausto out on training runs on the street. No one looking, literally, over her shoulder.

It was simultaneously exhilarating and terrifying.

And what of Nick Carter? Did it even matter?

Oh, yes. That answer came swiftly and inexplicably. It didn't particularly make sense, not with so much inner drive to simply start this bike and step it swiftly through to sixth gear, heading out to some wild place where she could change to *wolf* and gather herself to save her pack.

But, oh, it mattered. Sitting here in the silence at the side of an ill-defined desert road…she was just as fettered as ever, this time by the sight of Nick Carter, sprawled ungainly in the dirt. A scant breeze stirred his hair, ruffled by wind and dampened by sweat here in this dry climate where the air sucked away perspiration before it ever had a chance to soak anything.

Sick. Damaged by the amulet, in spite of Gausto's assurances. Not likely to survive out here in the open.

Run. Oh, run. Do it now. The instinct spoke strong in her—spoke smart.

Jet lifted her head, gazing around the foothills— the fingerlike extensions of raised earth, extending every which way—some low and long, some sharp and high. Here, in this spot, she saw no houses, no buildings. No humans at all. A power line in the distance; a windmill pulling a slow turn in another direction, a barely visible stock tank beneath it. *Run, Jet. Do it now.*

Jet started the bike, and her hands on the clutch and throttle felt like someone else's—so fundamentally wrong, neat fingers and trimmed nails folding gracefully around the clutch lever on one side, the throttle and brake lever on the other.

And, as though they were someone else's, they throttled the bike up and forward, feathered the clutch to a release point, and sent her off down the road.

Chapter 5

Marlee knew better than to carry the viral thumbnail drive around with her. Even flush from success, with Nick Carter's machine simmering in viral malfunction and his phone redirected to the prepaid cell currently in her pocket, she wouldn't be an overconfident fool. She jammed a screwdriver through the thing and dumped it down the incinerator shaft, and then she got an iced tea from the vending machine on her way back to her own floor and her own cubicle. In her mind she practiced just the right disdainful tone to use with Gausto when she let him know it was done.

Of course, she'd wipe the virus and reverse the phone forwarding after today—it was all the time she would have given Gausto even if he'd wanted more, and he hadn't. Just one afternoon…a distraction. Big deal.

Phoenix APS could cause them more trouble than that with a slow response to a service outage.

Besides, it very much suited her. After everyone else failed, Marlee Cerrosa would be the one to restore Carter's computer. The hero. And if all went according to plan, no one would even catch on to what she'd done with the phone.

In fact, as she jogged down the stairs to her floor, her cell phone trilled the special ring she'd assigned to the forwarded calls—bypassing Carter's admin, who could still call out but might well go hours before even wondering why there hadn't been incoming calls, especially with Carter out of the building.

She tucked herself off to the side, turning toward the wall to keep her voice from echoing up the stairwell—even if it was carpeted to keep echoing noise from hammering against sensitive Sentinel ears. "Nick Carter's office."

Just that easy. Marlee breezily told the caller that her boss was out of the office, and then she took a message.

She was grinning when she exited out into the stairwell. So she wasn't as strong as these Sentinels, and she didn't have the special skills and senses they shared. She was still strong enough. Skilled enough. *Human* enough.

The grin faded right off her face when she rounded the corner and found a whole little pack of them in the hallway. Lyn Maines and Joe Ryan, from earlier in the day, nodding a greeting without breaking off their conversation. And oh, crap, was that *Treviño?* The last Sentinel she wanted to see, this hard man who took the jaguar. He hadn't softened a bit since Meghan Lawrence had snared him—she who had been raised without Sentinel training and had her own very human ways of dealing with things.

There'd been talk, of course. And Marlee made no apologies for listening. She'd known, long before she hit true Sentinel training, that these thickly blooded shapeshifters needed to be watched.

She just hadn't realized she didn't have to be alone in it.

So she knew of Dolan's history, his grudge against the Sentinels, his barely tolerated independence in the southern-most Southwest territory. He'd also not been to brevis for years…until recently. Marlee had to stop herself from scowling at him. *Why now?*

Meghan stood beside him—pure lean cowgirl in worn, hard-worked jeans and boots and a rolled-sleeved flannel shirt over a snug tank top—her features a bit sharp and her eyes faintly tipped up at the outside, coyote eyes in shape if not in color. No one, Marlee thought, should be that comfortable standing next to Dolan Treviño.

And there was Annorah, come out of her communications shell. Annorah, Marlee could admire. Envy, even, for her vast skill, uncoupled with physical prowess as it was. But not trust. Not when she'd worked with the others so closely, even if she *was* still atoning for her misjudgment in her first and last field assignment.

The final member of their little group, she'd been watching. Maks, who took the tiger. He was big; he was quiet. He'd been badly hurt in Flagstaff, and he hadn't quite been released from care. Why he didn't bear a grudge against Joe Ryan, Marlee couldn't figure.

With Marlee hesitating on the edge of them, Meghan said, "It won't be long, Maks. You look so much better than the last time."

Treviño snorted. "You mean back when his eyes were still crossed?"

Maks muttered something Marlee couldn't hear, but it was short and sweet and emphatic, and it made Ryan snort in laughter.

"A happy ending is nice when you can get it," Lyn pointed out, not nearly as relaxed as the rest of them— as if she ever was. "Even Michael is recovering, and I honestly thought Shea was dead. But Nick—"

Meghan ran a hand over the wall beside her. Never just a simple gesture, with Meghan Lawrence—she was always reading the wards around her, soaking them in and sorting them out. "Do you really think…?"

Ryan shook his head. "He's been out of contact for a couple of hours, that's all."

Completely? That startled Marlee; she wondered what Gausto had done to Carter's cell phone. And why hadn't Annorah been able to reach him?

Ryan added, "But it's time to find him."

Treviño shifted, impatience on his face. "Dane doesn't need to get wind of this."

The consul. Not a man many people saw; not a man considered at the top of his game. Not anymore. Ryan agreed, apparently. He snorted, no amusement at all this time. "Not Dane, not his people."

"I think it's already beyond that," said Annorah, a plump woman who moved with strength and assurance. "I don't think you're getting it. I haven't been able to reach him at *all*. There's only two ways that happens— one is if he's been closed off somehow. The other is if he's…" She hesitated, looked uncomfortable, and said it anyway. "Dead."

Meghan frowned. "What if he's sleeping?"

"Then I still get a sense of him. He can shield me out, too—not many can, but he's got the way of it. But I can still *sense* him."

Marlee said, without really planning on it, "I bet he's just caught up in that dog show."

As one, they turned to her. Oh, crap. "I'm sorry," she said. "It's just…well, I need to get through, and I got caught up in your conversation."

"No problem," Ryan said, so laid back that she floundered a little. Had she been wrong—? Then again, he had that reputation: laid back, easy to take lightly… until it was too late. That new scar…a cogent reminder. Now he added, "You're not worried?"

She found a smile, offered it up. "The thought that Nick Carter can't take care of himself at a dog show…" She shrugged. "Nick is good at what he does. It's not convenient, having him out of touch like this, but he'll be back soon and we'll figure it out."

Meghan shared her smile. "It's hard to imagine things going wrong on quick check into disappearing dogs."

"He thought the disappearances might be tied to bigger things," Annorah said, a bit sharply—defensively. Had a crush on her boss, did she?

It was then that Marlee realized she was reveling in the moment. Tense at the prospect of being caught, yes. Anxious to make sure she walked the line she'd set for herself without crossing it, yes. But she also knew more than they did—if not the exact nature of Carter's disrupted communications, she at least knew who was behind them. She knew that there were parts of it they hadn't even discovered yet, and weren't likely to discover. And she knew it would be over when she removed the virus—half a day of disruption.

She knew all those things, and it made all the difference in the world. Didn't it?

"Back to work," she said. "But it'd be great if someone lets me know when you hear from him."

"You know," Meghan said, her words drawn out with the pondering of it, "I'm thinking that it's a good day for a dog show."

Marlee wondered at the relief she felt.

Maybe not so complacent after all.

Can't be good.

Dry, hot ground dusting close by his face, full of sharp desert scent. The sun beating on his chest, his legs…his shoulder grinding into hard, gritty caliche. *Can't be good.*

Could be hours before anyone found him here. Longer.

He tried to consider the amulet, to consider Jet, to understand how the one was tied to the other, and to pull together what little he knew. She'd been with Gausto. Now she was on the run. She had answers that he needed.

He couldn't trust her for a moment.

He had no idea what she really was.

And he wished like hell she would get her ass back here so he could find out.

But since she was running, and since no one would find him here, and since his Sentinels had to be warned that Gausto was making some sort of move…

This time, he really did roll over.

And found himself staring at a pair of black leather lace-ons, soft slipperlike shoes over sturdy, well-arched feet that would have been happier barefoot.

"I found it," Jet said. "Little adobe Beagles. Maybe."

He hadn't heard her bike. He looked for it, dull and thick and slow to think.

"I left it there," she told him. "You would fall. So we walk." She stepped back to look at him, hands on hips, head cocked...frowning. "Or I carry you."

And she did.

Jet rubbed her feet. These shoes hadn't been meant for walking alongside a desert road, and they definitely hadn't been meant for carrying a man over her shoulders across that same terrain.

Gausto's men had thought her freakishly strong, like the Sentinels they hated so much. She thought herself no more than what was necessary to survive.

And now she had no way to get inside that small adobe house, which was nothing like Gausto's ostentatious residence. More welcoming; more lived-in. A human den. She took Nick through the side yard gate instead, trailing a hand over the fence coyote rollers and taking note of the small tricolored and red-patched hounds who gave her instant berth, circling at a distance with their noses lifted to scent the air—hanging ears, bright eyes, tentatively wagging tails, brows wrinkled in worry...but seeing her. Knowing her. Not daring to bark at her.

She lowered him from her shoulder-carry into a patio lounger and stepped back to look around, finding the back door—steel security screening with a geometric design that couldn't hide its stout purpose. Locked.

No matter. He was in the shade. And there was water. Jet had already dumped her jacket and her helmet in the front drive; now, after a thoughtful glance at the dog water buckets, she stripped her shirt off, bundled it up, and dunked it.

She carried it back to Nick Carter, letting it drip all over his face…letting it trickle into his mouth. The flush on his face highlighted the hard line of his cheek and the echo of it in his jaw; even in the shade, the strong light of the desert day brought out the silver scattered on his eyebrows, made the silver hoarfrost of his hair shine bright.

She pulled his shirt up, became impatient with the inconvenience of buttons, and ripped it aside so she could sit on the edge of the lounger, spreading water over his chest. Goose bumps rose on his skin, tightening his nipples and raising the hair, more silver than black, that grew crisply across his chest.

She thought, then, of their desert romp. She closed her eyes and felt it—the connection they'd forged out among the cactus and creosote, the wolf in them driving past human concerns and human interference. Deep and pure and as strong as any instinct…stronger than any rational understanding. It had resonated in her then; it tingled in her now.

Jet shivered. She looked down at herself in surprise, at her own tight skin, and then out at the hot sunny yard. By no means was she cool enough to be chilled… and this feeling was far from it. No, this feeling was hot and vaguely uncomfortable and seeking—*wanting*. On its own, her wet hand drew down along her body, from collarbone past the thin material of her bra and across her stomach—hard and toned, and yet somehow softer than his.

With no more thought than that, she trailed fingers down his torso, feeling the smoothness, the hard strength beneath…the texture of the crisp hair and distinct flutter of his skin beneath her touch. She lingered at his collarbone, following the curve to his shoulder and arm—so different from her own.

She had examined her body often enough, those first days. Looking down at herself, or in the mirror Gausto provided. Never had it looked quite as it did now, simply for being in contrast with his. A sweeping curve of waist, a lean flare of hip; her muscles, while just as hard as his, ran sleeker beneath the skin. Her hair stayed fine and downy soft, nearly invisible in most places. Not at her crotch, which had surprised her at first. Not on her head.

She frowned at her breasts, now—even beneath the one-piece hosiery bra, they looked different to her. Fuller, tighter, nipples distinct beneath silky material. They *felt* different—hot and heavy and aching. She crossed her arms, cupping herself with protective uncertainty. Trying to ease herself. Being held…

Yes, she wanted that.

And she wanted…

She didn't know.

And, too, she did. She needed, she wanted, her body *demanded*. She felt hot in places she'd only considered with matter-of-fact practicality until this moment. She wanted to touch herself; she wanted to touch this man before her. She put a hand on his damp skin, above his waistband where his abdomen hollowed out as he breathed.

For that instant, his breath stopped.

She found him watching her.

"I—" she said, and nothing else, because while she had plenty to say, she had no words to say it. How did one talk about this feeling, a sudden raging howl within her? How it stammered through her chest and wrapped around her heart, or how looking at him, human body with wolf's soul, made her want to laugh and cry all at once?

He still struggled with himself, his skin twitching beneath her touch, his gaze ever so faintly confused.

"I—" she said, and ran out of words all over again, even if her hand still reached.

Nick's hand shot out to capture her wrist. "Jet," he said, from between gritted teeth.

But oh, she *wanted*. She searched his gaze, looking for understanding—looking for the clues to this world, to the way things should be. And she knew what she saw there. *Also wanting.* "You, too," she told him, in case he hadn't known it. She drew the back of her knuckles lightly across the hot skin of his cheek, ever watching his eye. "Still, you are not well."

He grasped her wrist again, more gently this time. He bit gently at the knuckles that had touched him, and then simply held her hand against his chest, trapped and still and as gentle as he might hold a living bird.

"Jet," he said, full of wonderment. "Who are you?"

How could she explain such a thing? How could she truly explain what she'd done for Gausto—done *to* Nick? She tried to tug away; that gentle grip turned insistent. She tipped her head ever so slightly, exposing her neck. "He said you would not be hurt," she told him, unable to hide the anger. "He told me he wanted to talk to you."

Nick snorted. "The talking is long, long over."

"I didn't know," she said, felt her ears flatten…or so they would have. "So many things. How he lied. How he planned."

"He'll go to those lengths for anything in his sights." He gave her a sharp look—or one that was meant to be sharp, and didn't quite make it. "He's not going to let you go that easily, either."

"I'm *not*," Jet said, although she hadn't realized it until that moment. "*Going*. He has taken too much. I want it back." Her people. Her life.

And Gausto's people didn't truly know what she was. They had seen her only when she'd been fresh and bewildered and frightened, and after she'd come to believe that she worked to gain her pack's release.

They had never seen her free to follow her own nature.

"I need to go back," she told him. Head north to Ojo Valley. Secure the bike and her clothes, and live as wolf while she watched and chose her time and whittled Gausto's men away. "They'll figure out it's me, eventually," she told him, forgetting he hadn't been in on her thoughts—it was something she did, something that drove Gausto to quick fury. Gausto could not abide the sense of being left out, left behind…left out of control. But Nick just looked at her with alarm as she added, "It will be too late for them."

He barely let her finish, half rising from the lounge with the emphatic nature of his words. "You *can't*. He'll *tear you apart*. He'll literally tear you apart." That he fell back to the lounge, breathing hard, seemed to surprise him.

"He talked about cutting you off from your people," she said, using the word *people* when her mouth and heart wanted to say *pack*. "You need help. Can you call them?"

He closed his eyes; it seemed to her that he gathered strength just to finish the conversation. "There's a wireless phone just inside the door. Spare keys are in the dog igloo."

"Dog igloo," she said blankly.

"Dog house." He didn't yet open his eyes. "Den. But watch out for Baroo."

She looked at him blankly. Perhaps he felt that puzzled regard. He tried again. "If he's in the igloo, he'll bite anyone but me."

So the dog igloo would be the pale, rounded little fake den with the white-blazed nose peeping out of the shadows to regard her with concern. "I can get the keys."

"Bites," he muttered, somewhat nonsensically.

"Not me," she said, already halfway to the little den in the shade. Incongruous to see those soft-faced Beagle lips lift in a snarl; doubly so when the snarl was all she could see, the rest of his face hidden in the shadow of the den's overhanging entrance. He didn't even lift his head—at least, not at first. Not until it became evident that the snarl wasn't working.

She walked up to the dog igloo—right up to the entrance of it. "This is my place now," she told him. And stood there, crowding his space. Owning it. The snarling crescendoed from within the dog igloo—a structure large enough for half this pack, and probably at some point they filled it to overflowing, snuggling against the cold nights this desert had to offer. Horrible sounds, those snarls…and all for show. She waited until they faded in intensity, and finally died away, and then she stepped slightly to the side. Not giving up ownership, but leaving him retreat.

He took the opportunity to scoot to freedom, shooting out into the middle of the yard with the milling dogs there. "As a child," she murmured, and groped within the dog igloo to find the keys—shoving aside the floor pad, feeling beneath it. As her fingers closed on cold metal, an even colder nose touched the back of her arm. "Ah," she said, twisting around to see. "Yes?"

The muzzle looked familiar, except that it wasn't snarling. Big worried eyes, ears hanging long, wrinkles of concern on the forehead, body seated at absolute attention.

"Baroo," she said.

He shifted from one front foot to the other, and looked at the dog igloo. Looked hard.

"Come to me," she told him, "and you may have it back."

For she knew dogs. Gausto had kept her with dogs, after that first change.

She didn't like to think of it, that first time. Or the second. Or any, until she had made the process her own. But those days—thick and hazy physical misery, language being crammed into her head with Core workings, a deep confusion between the two states of existence—were indelibly stamped into her memory. And they included time with dogs, simply because Gausto continued his experiments with them.

The dogs died, mainly. But now she knew them. She knew from this one's reaction that it understood her basic imperative, if not the promise she was making. "Come to me," she told him again, "and you may have it back."

Simple, these dogs, but they gave their trust in a way she never had...and she never would. This Baroo of Nick's gave a tentative wag and came to her. She touched his head and indicated the dog igloo, and his sturdy brush of a tail beat faster, his thoughts completely transparent. *Mine again,* he told himself.

Jet felt the pleasure of her own small smile—if only for the briefest of moments. It fell away again as she stood, keys in hand, and went for the back door.

The screen opened easily and silently, well-oiled. The main door lock turned over with a solid *snick,* the feel of it somehow reassuring in her hand. Artificially cool air washed over her, and the house greeted her with pleasant visual warmth—desert tones throughout, rusts and turquoise in the accent pieces with tile corner pieces near the ceiling and set in adobe walls; obscure wall art made her feel like closing her eyes and lifting her wolfish nose to the wind. Skylights flooded this back entry with light, an open area from which the rest of the house spread away. The kitchen, this way. A larger public area, over there. Across from the kitchen, an open room with huge windows facing north, filled with a neat row of dog crates, a table piled with food bowls, various jars and bottles and things medicinal, and a pile of crate pads. Leashes hung from the walls, as well as a few framed pictures featuring posed dogs and people and ribbons.

She almost let herself be drawn in there. If she was to get any additional sense of this man—this Sentinel so hated by Gausto and his kind—then this room held what she needed to know. How he treated his dogs.

But beyond the room of crates was another. Even with her human nose, she could perceive the scent of him there. This was *his* place...his bedroom. His private den.

She took a step in that direction, without even realizing it. One step, and another...

A dog barked outside. A single bark, taking note of something. Jet stiffened. But none of the other dogs rose to it, and she slowly relaxed—but she didn't lose herself again. She turned around, found the phone, and left the cool air behind to return to so many different kinds of heat she couldn't name them all.

Chapter 6

Marlee eavesdropped. Unabashedly, and all too easily. No one had yet realized that Nick Carter's incoming calls…*weren't*. But his admin had twigged to his wonky computer, and that meant Marlee to the rescue.

Theoretically.

In reality, she made herself look busy, she planned out her announcement of the virus and the need to isolate the machine and the need to research at her cubicle…and she listened. No one else paid attention, all closed away in their cubicles, focused on their small little worlds—but Marlee always paid attention.

"His car is there." Distress colored Meghan's tone. "It's locked and hasn't been touched—ward view is clear. I found someone who saw him early this morning, but no one since."

"And then there's that strip of woods." Treviño's

voice came grim, and the startled silence afterward told Marlee that Meghan was taken unaware.

"Out past the far fields, you mean?" Lyn said. She sat with the rest of them, out in the admin's office—the poor man had fled, ostensibly meeting a detective to deflect questions about an ongoing op, and looking markedly relieved to be facing such an inquisition rather than sitting in the middle of the rising tension and concern in his own office. "I know that area. I can't think what Nick would have been doing there."

"Well, he was." An aside, obviously to Meghan. "I found trace, while you were talking to people."

"Ah," she said, understanding.

"You booted Dolan away while you were asking questions at the grounds," Lyn said, amusement behind a neutral tone.

"Damned right. He scares them. He scares their dogs. Dolan, what *was* it?"

"I have no fu—" Right. Treviño and his mouth. But Lyn must have given him a *look*—Meghan didn't seem to care—and the words, cut off, continued more blandly if with a darkness in them. "I don't know. Untangling that is Lyn's turf—but I'm not sure it's even possible. All dark holes and hellish intensity...pain and nothingness."

"You should have—" Meghan started.

He cut her off. "No way in hell. There weren't any wards to deal with. You didn't need to feel that."

"Or know about it, apparently," she muttered.

"You know now." Perfect example, Treviño taking his own way no matter what anyone else thought. Marlee made a disdainful little face, there in the inner sanctum of the missing brevis adjutant—and felt it turn to a startled little open mouth when Treviño added, something entirely new in his voice, "I couldn't, Meghan. Not to you."

Lyn cleared her throat. "He's no longer just absent, then. He's missing. *Taken.*"

"I think so," Treviño said, startling Marlee all over again. *Taken.* What the hell was going on? Who *took* the brevis adjutant? Who *could?*

No. That's not what this was about. She wouldn't believe. That's *not—*

Their sudden silence brought her back to what she was doing—or what she was supposed to be doing. It made her realize she hadn't keyed anything into the computer for a while, as she ought to have been had she truly been struggling with a recalcitrant system.

Maybe they wouldn't notice. They certainly had other things to think about.

And so did she.

He'd fallen asleep. Or passed out.

Either way, Nick woke to find the phone tucked on one side of his body and Jet tucked up against the other, and the shadows growing long in the yard. Her shirt still sat on his chest, nearly dry now; she wore nothing more on her upper body than a stretchy one-piece bra, cradling those beautiful breasts. See-through.

Heat and lingering fever warred within him, bringing out a shiver. It didn't help that although she had one hand curled up under her chin, the other rested low on his belly. A proprietary hand.

That romp in the desert had meant something to her after all, it seemed.

As it had to him. So much more than he'd thought it would.

But where she'd come from...why her change to wolf had felt so different...

Jet dozed, her hand twitching, her lip quirking. A dream, Nick thought. But heat spread from his low belly from the movement of her hand and he sucked in a slow breath, reminding himself of so many things. All those questions unanswered. Gausto. The reason he was in this condition in the first place.

Not to mention the need to get some brevis help out here—a Sentinel healer, for starters, to flush these lingering poisons from his system. And someone to go after that amulet...figure out a ward against it.

And then, maybe, just maybe, it would be time to go after Gausto. If the Septs Prince wouldn't rid himself of this problematic drozhar, then it was time for the Sentinels to handle it.

For *Nick* to handle it. This was his brevis region, now, far more than Dane Berger's—although Dane's official status suited Nick just fine; it left him more freedom. It gave him the room to circle in on the brevis leak that he'd at first only suspected, but now...

Too many things had gone wrong at just the right time for Gausto. Too many messages gone astray, too many field agents left vulnerable, too many operations inexplicably failed.

Jet sighed deeply and opened her eyes. Amazing whiskey gold with dark brown rims and black lashes. She had the goth look down cold, except...it wasn't a *look* at all. It was simply Jet. She flexed her fingers and slipped her hand over his skin, splayed fingers taking possession of the slight hollow in front of his hip and the gap it left in his waistband. She had to stretch only a little to nuzzle his neck, and Nick stiffened with startled pleasure as she nipped and then licked tender skin. "Jet—" he said, strangled sounding at that. Conflict reverberated through his body—the need to distance himself back into brevis adjutant versus the instant response to her, above and beyond all other instinct.

Maybe he was lucky, then, that the vast blue sky pulled a sudden dip and whirl overhead.

She sensed the change in him. "Amulet," she growled—an alto growl, so perfectly suited to her. "Gausto. Lying son-of-a-*human*."

He grinned at that, if through clenched teeth. "Exactly so."

She nudged him—her cheek against the spot she'd just left tingling with teeth and tongue. "Call your people."

He lifted the phone, thumbed the autodial. The familiar number tones of Sentinel brevis played out, and then…nothing. Frowning, he hit the flash button, hunting a dial tone.

Nothing. With a single, precisely uttered curse, he set the phone aside.

Jet sat, retrieving her shirt and pulling it over her head. "No?"

"Line's dead," he told her. "Probably this entire switchbox. Well-planned." Not even Gausto would dare to intrude into Nick's private home. Such forbidden action would open a veritable floodgate of retribution upon the Core, and the Core wasn't ready for that. "Give me a moment. I'll try for Annorah."

Expression dark at the thought of Gausto, she pushed

off the lounge to pace the yard, the dogs swarming around her with tails waving—cheerful, utterly clueless about things Core. Probably thinking about dinner. So might Jet be, for all of that. So. He'd feed her.

But not until he reached for Annorah. It hadn't worked with the amulet in place, but if he was lucky…if removing it was enough to let him through…

Mental feedback static blasted back at him, jerking through his body and very nearly emptying his stomach. He swallowed hard; he breathed shallowly, eyes closed, as the moment passed.

"No?" she asked again, and somehow she was right there, crouching beside him.

"We should be all right." He spoke through gritted teeth. "Gausto isn't going to bring this fight here."

"Why not?" Jet asked. "A challenge should be done to face."

He found wild intensity glimmering in her eyes. Not hard to imagine that she was thinking of doing just that.

But any Sentinel knew exactly why Gausto would stay away from Nick's home—that the two organizations maintained a cold war pretense of distance and strained civility, a detente with certain unbreakable rules—and that the very foundation on which they both operated demanded a low profile. It had kept the Core in check all these years, even if it on occasion proved an impediment to Sentinel operations as well.

And any born Sentinel would know it. Sentinels trained from infancy, with age-appropriate immersion into the hidden life of talent and shifters. Any Sentinel child would have known why Gausto didn't dare come after Nick here at home or anywhere near it.

Any born Sentinel.

If she was Sentinel and she didn't know, she was an even greater risk to them all than he'd ever thought. And if she wasn't Sentinel at all...

No such creature. Not and shift so beautifully from woman to rangy black wolf and back again.

But if she wasn't...

"Why not?" His voice went hard as he repeated her question. "Any of us would know *why not.* But not you. Who are you, Jet? *What* are you?"

She froze; she knew alpha. And she resisted, eyes narrowing and head tilted in such a way as to invoke an inner vision of wolf with slant-back ears and defiant posture, giving nothing and ready to spring away from his reach. Had he reached for her, she would have snarled. That same warning sounded in her voice as she said, "Not of yours."

He rolled off the lounge, so focused on her that he barely felt one knee almost give way. She scrambled backward; the dogs wuffed with alarm. Another step or two and she was up against the house and now she *was* snarling—eyes narrowed, a little curl of her lip, a low alto sound in her throat. He grabbed her upper arms; his fingers tightened heedlessly. "Jet," he said. "*Whose* are you? *What are you?*"

She shifted, then—right there in his hands, the energy coursing through him like a sudden shock, his hands on skin and then fur, his eyes blinded by the release of energy, so close. *Clean pure essence of Jet and pure wild and moonlight over snow, the spurt of blood at night, the crush of bone and the exhilaration of the run*—seared into him, seared through him, and howling in his throat. Her pants fell away; her shirt fell askew and off. Black fur so crisp and clean it shone even in shadow brushed the skin of his arms even as she clawed at him with her hind legs.

He gave her no time to orient—he shifted his grip upward, holding her on either side of her ruff, her hind legs still off the ground and her eyes furious and her jaws snarling. But he knew his grip—he knew better than anyone just exactly which grip to take. Just beneath her ears, up tight and close, thumbs bracing her jaws.

She couldn't bite him; she could only flail at him with her paws—the claws of which would deal considerable damage, and so he threw himself forward, pressing in close.

"No," he ground out at her. Golden-eyed ire glared back at him, those jaws so close to his face, the snarl unending—each breath in, each breath out. "This is *my* turf, Jet. And dammit, *you owe me.*"

The snarl eased to stressed panting; she never released her glare. Tough bitch. Alone in this city, on the run, and yet still fighting for retribution. Facing down a wolf so alpha he ran an entire region of shapeshifters.

Adrenaline ebbed; he braced his knees. He tipped his head beside those gleaming white, exposed teeth, murmuring in her ear, "Jet. You *need* me."

In an instant, she went limp. And then, in an abrupt change that almost triggered his own shift, sending his breath hissing through his teeth as it invaded him so deeply—familiar this time, achingly and hauntingly so—she shifted back. He pressed up against her, holding her against the rough adobe exterior of the house... reeling from the glory of her.

And then he was glad for the rough nature of the adobe, for there went his knees. She ducked around to shove her shoulder beneath his, and drag-walked him back to the lounge, where she scooped up her pants and underwear, but made no attempt to put them on. "*You* need *me*."

"Because of what you did to me." Calm words. Controlled. As if he wasn't still reeling from the touch of her. He handed over her shirt. She pulled it on, where it only served to accentuate what it was meant to cover. "And you know nothing of Sentinels. You know how to ride a bike. You know how to slip through a crowd, but not how to be part of it." He shook his head. "You know something of Gausto, but not enough to anticipate his lies. So now you tell me—"

She interrupted him. "He taught me only the necessary things."

He went very still. Something important hung in the moment, in the nature of her expression. A defiant sorrow. A look that said he would never understand, but that she wanted more than anything to find someone who could.

"Necessary," he said, reining in his intensity with such effort he had little left over to spare, "for what?"

She gave him surprise. "To move between his residence and the place I found you. To other places he thought I might find you, until he was sure of that one. To use the amulet he gave me. To use the cell phone."

Nick frowned. It made his vision go vaguely fuzzy; he rubbed his eyes in a weary gesture. "He didn't just pluck you off the street. We keep better account of Sentinels than that...but you damned sure know the wolf."

She looked down at him, those steady golden eyes. For an instant, she looked surprised, as if she'd thought he already knew. And then she said, "I *am* the wolf."

Chapter 7

Surely if *anyone* could see her, truly see her, it would be this man. The one who knew the wolf from the inside out, but from the human perspective.

Not the perspective of a gangly adolescent bitch who, along with her pack, had been plucked out of the wilds of the rugged mountains far north of here and brought here with Gausto's other prisoners. His *experiments*.

"We didn't all survive," she told him, watching his face for acceptance—searching for that understanding. Instead she saw only the struggle to fathom what she'd said.

Gausto had said Nick would shove her aside and stalk away. Gausto had said that Nick and his Sentinels would laugh in her face and then lock her up because she'd broken their rules simply by existing. But she'd always thought there was a contradiction in that assertion.

"He tried dogs first." She stepped into her under-wear matter-of-factly. "He wanted to have his workings refined before he wasted any wolves. We're harder to get, he said."

"Much harder," he said, deadpan. Still flushed and sick, but so clearly improving she could feel only relief when she looked at him.

"He tried dogs off the street, but they weren't healthy and strong. So he started taking the breeds. Then he tried it with us, and…it didn't work very well." She looked away from him, realized she was still holding her pants, and stepped into those as well. "Until me. The others… maybe they were too old." She didn't think about those moments—the first turning for her alpha bitch, and what had come from it. Human screams and lupine screams and a twisted mishmash of body parts.

No, she didn't think about it.

"He went back to the dogs," Nick said, understanding crossing his face. "He already had what he needed…you. And he could afford to take time to return to the research."

"He thought they might be easier to train." She lifted her chin, her shoulders tall in a direct stare—and then felt her mouth go vulnerable, thinking of those early days and how Gausto had tried to break her.

But Nick…

Nick looked stunned. He looked at her with sudden, true understanding—and then he quite suddenly unfolded from the lounger, rising to stand toe-to-toe, face-to-face—and if Jet had grown accustomed to matching the height of Gausto's men, she realized anew that she had to tilt her head to meet Nick's gaze. She held her ground as he cupped her face in his hands.

"My God," he said. "You—" He shook his head. He ran his hands over her shoulders, a hair's breadth away from her skin—a reverent gesture—stepping closer while again somehow not quite touching her, a dance both erotic and respectful. He bent over her neck, scenting of her, his hands finally landing not at the small of her back but lower, where his touch tightened the skin all the way down her buttocks and the backs of her legs.

Jet let herself go in it. She tipped her head back and opened her neck to him; she bent back into his hold, arms relaxed and open—supplication, exhilaration. She gave to him that which he'd truly won out on the desert with their romp, when the instinctive connection between them had gone so deep.

A fine tremble ran across his shoulders and down his arms; his breath caught. But then something in him stilled. He stepped back, gaining just enough distance to look down at her face again, his hand touching her cheek, her lip…her brow. He shook his head. "I'm sorry," he murmured.

She frowned, ferocity in this as in everything. "Be sorry because you back away, not because you came close."

He laughed shortly, a sound with bite to it. "I'm sorry for what was done to you. I'm sorry that I want so much to compound it."

"Gausto promised me the pure wolf again…but I don't believe it." She scowled at him. "Not for a moment do I stop living, waiting for it to happen."

"The Sentinel healers—"

"No!" Jet said, and now she did step away from him. She stabbed a finger at Nick, and then at herself. "I am

free of Gausto, and I will not then walk into the hands
of your Sentinels."

"Heart," Nick said, "I *am* Sentinel."

"You are *wolf*," she said, certain of that. "I am wolf.
Just that."

He laughed—short and bitter. "There's never been a
time I wasn't Sentinel," he assured her. "I'm adjutant of
a region whose consul hasn't taken his javelina boar in
years…do you understand that?"

Gausto had told her that Sentinels were a corrupt and
powerful people. He'd said that Nick was driven to
destroy Gausto's people, and that Gausto needed the
chance to talk past their misunderstandings—that he
needed Nick separate from his Sentinels, simply so Nick
would stop trying to kill him long enough to listen. To talk.

Then again, he'd told her the amulet wouldn't be
harmful.

So she didn't answer Nick at all; she only looked
back at him. He watched her wariness a moment, and
scrubbed a hand over his face. "God," he muttered.
"Where am I even going to start?"

"Feed me," Jet suggested.

He looked startled. "Hell, yes," he said—and then
looked around to the Beagles, all of whom had arranged
themselves around the lounge with an attitude of atten-
tive patience, except for the two who, with wild ferocity,
wrestled over possession of an old plastic milk bottle.
"And them, too." He reached for the phone, seemed to
remember it wasn't working, and let his hand drop.
"I've got to reach Darla, or she's going to show up here
in the middle of this."

Jet felt an instant flash of jealousy; she didn't try to

hide it. Nick had accepted her attentions in the desert; he'd taken that which she offered—if not all of what she offered—here in his yard. He was *hers*.

He grinned ever so slightly in response—it looked predatory, that grin—and said, "The woman who comes over to feed the dogs if she can't reach me around this time every afternoon. Never mind. She'll see your motorcycle."

"Cell phone," Jet said. "I have one of those. But it only calls Gausto."

Nick looked briefly nonplused—and then his mouth set in a grimmer line. "I'm sure that's what he told you. I'm also damned sure that if he gave you a cell, he's got the means to locate it."

Quick anger surged through Jet, raising hackles that didn't exist and coming out as a small growl deep in her throat.

"Yes," he said, fulling disengaging from her—putting real space between them. "Destroy it."

It was the work of moments to return to her bike, flip up the saddlebag flap, and pull out the phone. Another moment to find a significant rock and grind the phone to pieces beneath it. Jet tossed the rock aside, and returned to Nick's backyard.

He wasn't there.

The dogs greeted her with their steady wagging tails; the lounge still held the indentation of his body…his scent. She closed her eyes, breathed it in…wondered if she had done right to come here with him, to stay here at all. He had his own history with Gausto, and his own plans. He seemed willing to interfere with hers.

She'd keep it in mind.

A muffled sound from within the house caught her

ear. With some hesitation, she opened the door and slipped into that back entryway—keeping her glance oblique, her head tilted slightly down. Acknowledgment of his turf. She followed the sound away from the private denning space and toward a bigger, brighter area. High ceilings, tile accents, another skylight…the kitchen. Nick stood by the sink, kitchen machinery in front of him as he poured something goopy and thickly scented from a tall container into a mug. "It's not food," he told her, so matter-of-factly that she lifted her head, accepting her welcome. "But it's a start. Protein. I made enough for you, if you—" He stopped at the sight of her cell. "Thorough."

She moved closer; he handed her the glass. She brought it to her nose, took in the thick, spongy odor of it, and returned it.

He grinned. "I don't blame you. Steak, then? Raw to rare?"

Gausto had tried to feed her raw steak. Jet had never convinced him that this human side of her preferred something with a crusty singe on the outside and lingering pink on the inside. "Burnt," she told him, waiting for the resistance. He only opened the refrigerator door and pulled out two steaks, so, she added, "Not all the way burnt."

"We'll get it right," he said easily.

"You feel better," she observed, circling around the kitchen to touch the counters, the cabinet handles. With Nick as the center of her movement, she explored, tasting with her fingers and eyes. Pale wood cabinets, natural tile countertops, pale stone floor.

"I found a quick-acting Excedrin," he said, somewhat ruefully. "Food will help."

"Food always helps," Jet said, which is how she found herself embroiled in the very practical chore of helping Nick Carter fix dinner. From the salad with spring greens and walnuts she couldn't stop nibbling; corn on the cob, so satisfying to her teeth, and steak, so satisfying all around. With Gausto after them both and her pack needing rescue and Nick still recovering, they sat in a sun-washed alcove and ate what he told her was a perfectly normal meal.

She liked it. As restless as she was, her backside in this chair when her four feet wanted to be running free in her home territory, she let herself wallow in the small moments—his murmured directions where to find the dinnerware, the spatter of the cooking steaks in the broiler, the scent of it filling the kitchen. Her very own steak, burnt around the edges and still pink inside, because for the first time someone had listened to her.

She liked the crunch, and then the tenderness.

She also learned about corn on the cob. Treacherous stuff, spurting juices and dripping butter and setting her off into rusty giggles. And then, in the middle of the most wondrous ice cream, her questions bubbled up again. "So one woman had two different men? And that started it all?"

He looked at her in surprise. The food had revived him considerably; aside from a feverish gleam in his eye, he looked much the man who had found her that morning. Jet looked at that gleam and thought his energy would not last, but it made her think of the day to follow…the things that needed to be done.

He returned her regard and said, "Something like that. Is that what Gausto told you?"

"He said that it was many years ago. Generations."

"A couple thousand years, if that means anything to you."

"No." She tended the ice cream. "It's too big."

"And nowhere near here. Overseas—"

"Also too big," Jet said, for she had seen maps.

Her feet on the ground, that made sense; her toes digging into the soil on the run…that made sense, too. Following scent over the earth, defining territory by that scent as much as sight or touch…

But not looking at a flat piece of paper and calling it a map and pretending it represented her world. Not supposing that so much of it was deep water. *Salty* water. She thought Gausto had been lying about that.

"It doesn't matter." Nick slouched back in his chair. Along the way of making dinner, he'd also fed the dogs, and now here they were. No phones available to reach Nick's people, no computer Internet connection. Nor could he reach the woman named Annorah with his thoughts, which didn't surprise Jet in the least. Who could do that, anyway? "What else did he tell you?"

"This woman had two sons by two fathers. One son was sired by a druid. He could make himself a boar, and he killed people's dogs so they couldn't hunt for food, and then he killed people, too." She gave him a darkly sardonic smile. "Fewer people might work out well for my kind."

"This was back when there weren't so many of us," Nick said, and though his jaw had hardened with annoyance, she knew it wasn't at her. "And that's not exactly how it was."

"The other father was sired by a Ro-man—"

"Roman," Nick said, coming out of his annoyance at

Gausto. "It's all one word. It's not a type of man—it means where he came from and who was his pack leader."

She liked that. How matter-of-factly he made it clear to her. How he didn't give her that superior little look that slid onto Gausto's face so easily. "The Roman was a warrior, and he taught his son to protect the people. He tried to stop the boar, and he is still trying to stop the boar."

Nick snorted. He stood and picked up their plates, waving her back when she would have stood with him. "Do you believe him?"

"I don't know what happened *then*," Jet said, sinking into the seat cushion of the iron-backed chair. "In *now*, Gausto stole my pack from their land and put them into locked rooms and cages so far away from home we can't even smell our territory on the breezes. He killed some of us, and he changed me. He lied to me. Now I wait to see what to believe."

"His basics are right," he said, sliding the dishes into a slide-out rack that already held dirty items. He refilled his glass, dropping ice cubes into the water with a careless splash. Jet followed suit...just a little bit of water and a whole lot of ice.

Gausto had laughed when she'd tackled her first glass of ice water by fishing out the cubes to crunch them down. He hadn't laughed when she'd fastened those same strong teeth on his arm as he reached to take her ice water away.

She'd paid for that moment. But she still thought of it fondly...a day when she was still naive enough to do what came naturally. What he *deserved*.

Nick ran the glass over his forehead—it was flushed again, as if the amulet's poison came in waves. He leaned a hip against the counter in a casual slouch—a deceptive slouch. Gausto had spoken of Nick as though he spent his days indoors, sitting and passive. Jet looked at this man and saw through the slouch to the wolf running in freedom and power.

She looked at him and she wanted to be next to him, touching him. With him.

If he saw any of that, he didn't let it show. Cool pale green eyes, crisp-cut silver-skimmed hair askew, hanging over his right eyebrow. He said, "The druid's son realized his great skills, and began to use them for the good of the people—which in those days, meant using them to defend Gauls from Romans. The Roman's son was determined to prove himself in his father's eyes, and to his mother. He began to gather power—but he did that by taking it, because he had none of his own." The run of words had the sound of rote to them; they did not sound like Nick's own. "So the druid and his family—for by then they each had family—protected the earth from what the Roman was taking. And the families grew, and the Roman side claimed they acted only to keep the Druids in check, and the Druids had their hands full cleaning up after the Romans."

Jet made a face, full of disdain. "They needed the right pack leader over both of them."

Nick laughed—short, bereft of humor. "Maybe they did at that. And now the battle waxes and wanes—and the rest of the world has no idea any of us exist." He gave her a sharp look, setting aside his glass. "The same needs to apply to you, Jet."

"He said so." Jet fished out a small ice cube and slid it into her mouth, reveling in the cold smoothness of the ice cube before she crunched it down. "You, I thought safe. You have your own wolf."

Nick laughed. He outright laughed. "Safe," he repeated. "No one's ever said that before."

"No one's ever been wolf before," Jet told him, giving him a hard and sudden look from beneath lowered brow.

It froze him there, leaning against the counter. Just for a moment. And then he took a deep, long, and obvious breath, and he shook his head—but he never looked away from her. He never broke the connection she'd forged. "No," he said, his voice rusty. "There's never been anyone like you."

Out in the hallway, Lyn Maines sneezed again, interrupting the muttered conversation there. Marlee rolled her eyes at the sound—alone in the IT area, she was safe enough to express her frustration. She'd about had enough, between Gausto's Instant Messages and the various field Sentinels—still hoping for Nick's return, starting to get pushy and nosy and acting as if they ran things…which might be the case in the field but most definitely wasn't the situation here.

Remember that, she told herself, over and over. *This is your space. And they were definitely not the boss of her.*

Then again…where *was* Nick Carter? They were right, all of them. He should have been back by now. And his empty car at the dog show, but no sign of him? No one who'd seen him since early morning, with the crowds growing thin and Best in Show underway? Nasty trace scattered around the edges of the grounds?

But alone in the room, she didn't even flinch when Gausto IM'd her again. *Acprince.* Of course.

Stand fast, he told her, another command to leave the communication blockages in place.

Too long already, she typed back, fingers flying. He'd asked for an afternoon; she'd given it to him. But with Carter still gone, the situation had gone beyond inconvenience. Brevis needed clear communications.

Stand fast, he repeated.

And because she was IM'ing, and because sometimes her fingers thought faster than her brain, she tapped out a quick, blunt, What have you DONE?

Stand fast, he said, and then more ominous words, *or you'll be the one to take the blame for it all.*

Marlee froze at the keyboard. She tapped a reflexive letter, then pulled her hands away from the keyboard— putting them deliberately, stiffly in her lap, where they clenched into tight fists in spite of her best efforts.

What has he done?

And then Lyn Maines sneezed, and it was closer yet, and Marlee quickly shut down the IM window and pulled up the diagnostics she was running on a server. Only to freeze again, almost immediately, astonished to hear the voice then joining the unintelligible conversation. A male voice, rough as a file with age and impatience.

Holy crap-pile. Was it really—?

Silently, she pushed her chair back; silently, she moved to the arched doorway—reminding herself to act as any of the IT drones would, startled and curious and even a little bit awed.

The brevis consul didn't often come to this floor. He didn't often leave his office, if he came into the building at all. More often, he commanded from home, telecommuting and working through his personal assistant.

And there, in the small group of people she found gathered outside the elevator, that very same altogether too-smug assistant lifted his head from a dutiful nod at Berger's words and glanced down the hall—and at the sight of Marlee in the doorway, nodded.

One more time, Marlee froze, her stomach clenching cold and her skin hot. That had been more than a nod of greeting. That had been *acknowledgment*.

She wasn't the only one here doing Gausto's bidding.

She forced a breath. She tried to think. She didn't even consider moving out of the doorway as the group came down the hall—not when they were obviously heading for the IT room. All of the pushiest field Sentinels—all of those who had been here earlier. Ryan and Lyn Maines, Treviño and Meghan Lawrence, Maks the quiet tiger and even Shea the coyote, who from the looks of him should still be in the crisp, superbly equipped underground medical and healing section.

Ryan said something she couldn't completely hear, but she got the important part "—It's got to be a virus—" and she realized with a sudden flush of relief that they were coming for help.

"That's not good enough," Berger said, making no attempt to lower his voice. He wasn't as tall as most of them, not as predatorial. A beefy man of thick muscle and thick waist, he moved with purpose but no grace; strength but no speed. His hair was a bristly gray—the same gray it had always been, to judge by the photos in the brevis common area—and his square jaw jutted ever so slightly in an underbite. All handsome enough, with hard, neat features to go along with it, even if his eyes were a little small and it wasn't hard to imagine the tusks that would appear with his shifting. "Why the hell didn't you either call me earlier or wait until you had something more definite? Now it's too late to act swiftly, and too early to know what's going on."

Marlee could hear Treviño's snort from where he stood apart from the others at the back of the group, Meghan looking worried beside him—no doubt concerned that he might say enough to get himself thrown into a Sentinel Justice hearing. And Ryan, too—all too familiar with Sentinel Justice.

Oddly, the thought had Marlee relaxing. These field agents might be shifters; they might be strong and capable. But in this office, they were known as trouble-makers and Marlee was known as the one everyone could count on.

But Lyn was the one who put words to Treviño's rude noise. She looked the assistant squarely in the eye and told Berger, "We were informed that you were unavailable."

"Eh?" Berger said, and made a strange little throat-clearing noise—a gestural tic of sorts, and it wasn't hard to imagine it coming from the boar he was rumored not to have taken for several years now. He glanced at his assistant.

"A misunderstanding, I'm sure," the man said—slender and aesthetic, dishwater blond hair, eyes of some color or another and hidden behind glasses. Marlee had never liked him—had found him too happy with little displays of pointless power. The thought that he might consider them to be working together...

Her stomach tightened up all over again. Her stomach, her nerves...and the small little voice in her head wondering what she'd gotten herself into. If it wasn't all just a little more significant than she'd ever thought, these *favors* she'd been doing for Gausto.

His last message had been on the computer, but she quite suddenly could hear his voice in her head.

…take the blame for it all.

Somehow she thought he meant more than the virus.

After that intense, silent moment in the kitchen, everything changed. Nick went out to the backyard—locking up the gate, speaking to the dogs…settling them in for the night.

He returned pulled into himself, but Jet saw something else there—a sadness, layered over the poison-fever and the flush and fatigue. She wanted to ask him—she opened her mouth to ask him—but he must have seen it coming, for he spoke first. "There's nothing else to be done tonight," he said. "The phones are out, the cable's down—we can't reach my people. We can't save yours. Tomorrow, we'll get through."

"Will Gausto try to keep us here?" Jet felt herself bristle at the thought.

Nick shrugged. "He might try. But you can bet my teams already know there's something wrong, so it won't happen."

She pushed the ice cream away. "He is *up to* taking you. Hurting you. It's the reason I *am*."

"Then he failed," Nick said simply. "We're safe tonight. Tomorrow, he'll learn what *failure* means."

"But—"

"Tomorrow," Nick said, his voice bottoming out.

She saw it, then. The way he stood with one hand casually on the arch of the entry. The way his feet were spread, his legs slightly braced. Whatever Gausto's amulet had done to him, he'd made a remarkable recovery—but he'd run out of that spurt of energy some time ago.

And still, because she was who she was, she said steadily, "And if you reach your people, will they help mine? Or will they want me for their own, because I am what I am? Because I have been Gausto's?"

His reaction was what might have come from a man too tired to be startled. "That's not—" But he shook his head. "Yes," he said. "Probably. But—"

"I won't let that happen." She caught his gaze in a direct stare, her shoulders back and her head lifted. "You know that."

He met that gaze, but his words came reluctant. "It's complicated."

"Do I leave now? The desert is safe for me. Are you?" No matter what stood between them, strong and deep and wanting more. No matter what two wolves had forged together in the Pima Valley sands.

His fingers tightened on the archway. "Jet," he grated.

"Are you?" she asked him again. *Safe for me?*

He released a long breath; a struggle. And if she felt for him, she could nonetheless not let it go. He said, "I don't know about safe, come tomorrow. But I can be honest, always. Please. *Stay.*"

Tonight, then. She nodded.

He scrubbed a hand over his face—dark stubble against pale skin, relief in his eyes. He held himself tightly upright as he led her to the sleeping side of the house, where he showed her a bathroom and an unused room where the air hadn't been stirred for a while but the bedding was unused.

And then he went to the back corner of the house, where his scent came strongly to Jet's nose. Water ran, briefly—Jet had not brought herself to move as it shut off. Nick reappeared, minus the shirt she'd ruined. "Okay?" he asked her briefly.

"I—" She stopped, sensitive ears catching the low noise from outside. It grew to a mellow *woo-ooo* of a howl, a solo singer. A second dog yipped and a third joined in, and then the chorus swelled, filling the desert night with melodious song. Jet's throat tightened with the ache of longing—of wanting to sing not with these dogs, but with her own pack. She found Nick looking at her—looking *through* her, understanding her as Gausto could never hope to try—and she said brokenly, "But…why? They are already home. Already together."

Nick shrugged, the merest lift of one bare shoulder. "Sometimes they hear something, but sometimes…I think it's just in their hearts." A flicker of pain crossed his features, jaw gone tight.

And that, she saw, was a pain not of Gausto's doing. It was the pain of a wolf looking for his own pack.

Chapter 8

Jet lay awake. Down the hall, Nick had fallen immediately into sleep—deep and uneasy and sometimes still sounding pained, that last expression of his lingering between them in this darkness.

It didn't take Jet long to slide from the bed, the sheets smooth against bare skin, and pad down the hallway. She slipped inside his room, standing just inside the doorway where she'd be the hardest to see. He didn't wake, and that told her something.

That told her a lot.

She'd put him in this position. She'd done what Gausto had told her; she'd believed what Gausto had told her.

This morning suddenly seemed like such a long time ago. Years of experience and maturity, packed into one day. Until now, she had not liked Gausto. She had resented his training, his hold on her. She had wanted freedom from him. She had thought him vain and indulgent. But she had, in fact, believed him.

No more of that.

Now she had run with Nick Carter as wolf. She had, with her invitation, created something unexpected and deep and *forever* between them.

Now she knew what it was to touch a man—to be touched. Now this man who had once been her prey was teaching her how to be both wolf and human, simply by being who he was himself. Showing her what her body could feel; showing her what her heart could feel. Showing her that humans, too, had loyalty to drive them.

Gausto had made her. He had trained her, coercion and punishment and intimidation. He had set her on Nick Carter...

And now he would reap the results.

Unexpected energies twitched Nick awake. A moment of disorientation—sheets twisted around him, moonlight from the unclosed blinds casting unfamiliar shadows in his blue-tinged Sentinel's night vision. The scent of something equally unfamiliar bathing his senses—tang of sage, a hint of fur and desert dust.

He oriented. Found the door, the closet, the dark lumps of his furniture. The pool of black at the bottom of his bed.

The pool of black at the bottom of his bed.

Jet. Jet as wolf, blacker than the shadows, staking her claim. She opened her eyes, a golden gleam in the darkness.

He found his mouth tugging on the hint of a smile.

"Yes," he murmured, not even sure what *yes* entailed. But it was good enough; the whiskey-gold eyes shuttered again, and Nick fell back into sleep with that smile still tugging at his mouth.

Marlee Cerosa gasped herself awake.

Another nightmare.

Because while she'd removed the virus from Carter's computer and unblocked his phones—staying late to do what no one else could get done, and walking out of brevis with overly strong claps of appreciation still stinging her back and shoulders—she couldn't stop thinking about...

Everything.

Whether they'd figure out she'd been behind the problems in the first place.

Whether they'd figure out that she'd been behind any number of problems in the past.

Whether Berger's admin, growing bold, would give them both away.

And just how much Gausto had been using her all along.

For it was clear that she'd bought into his pretty song of paranoia and keeping balance and *no one gets hurt.* It was clear Nick Carter was in trouble. Gone from the fairgrounds, leaving a wash of anguished trace. Not answering his home phone. Not answering his cell. Not answering Annorah or his e-mail.

Marlee had grown up bullied and intimidated; she'd learned things with her early forays into computer hacking that no one ever knew. She knew in her heart, in her soul, that the Sentinels needed to be kept in line.

But she wouldn't work with Gausto any longer. She'd find her own ways. She'd work for herself.

For today she had let Gausto push her past what gut instinct said was right…and now Nick Carter was missing.

Marlee Cerosa stared at the ceiling, and sleep would not come.

Chapter 9

Jet whimpered in her sleep, paws twitching, spirit quailing before memory and nightmare…a helicopter on the hunt, the *phut! phut!* of tranquilizers taking down her packmates…the sting of a dart in her flank. How quickly her feet had grown heavy and slow…

The weapon stabbed deeply into her flesh, as much quarrel as simple dart, spiking hot pain in strobing slashes. She yipped and jerked and—

Woke up.

Here, curled up on Nick's bed in the wolf, rolling wildly until she fell off and over and landed hard, human and naked and sprawling.

With caution, she peered back up over the bed.

He slept.

He slept hard.

He had his own dreams, she thought.

But the pain hadn't faded with her sleep; she caught her breath on it, pressing down on the spot beside her spine, above her hip—there, where in wolf, the dart had struck her.

If she'd known what it had meant, she'd have fought harder. Or she liked to believe she would have.

He still didn't move.

So much better than he'd been when she'd brought him home...and yet he'd looked ragged when he'd left her in the guest room, as if he'd been standing there on the memory of strength.

I didn't know. I'm sorry.

My fault. Mine to fix.

She'd call his pack. She'd shift back to the wolf and run the desert road until she found the nearest phone. The gas station out by the throughway exit, if that's what it took.

The spot she'd been darted twitched in pain, shooting from her back to her belly; she bit her lip on a whimper, folding over it. Never had it done this before, not during all the time she'd spent with Gausto.

"Bring me this man," he'd told her, *"and you may go home. Bring me this man, and your pack may go with you."*

"I'm sorry," she whispered. "I'll make it right."

Except as she crept from the room, dismay sitting cold and hard in her stomach, she couldn't be sure it was safe to call help for him.

Gausto had people there. In Brevis Southwest.

He'd bragged about it to her once; he'd gloated. He had people there who made his work easier. People who would make her job easier, too.

But she didn't know who they were. How could she tell any of brevis, not knowing who was safe?

She hesitated in the hallway…wanted nothing more than to crawl into that bed with him, curling up with every part of her body touching his. She touched it, this body—ran light fingers across one collarbone and down her torso, trailing off over the crest of her hip.

No. More than body. Her hand returned to her chest, flattening over her heart. She had known longing as a wolf; she had known randy flirtatious first heat. But she had never known loyalty and longing and sweet deep embers, all the gift of one man who had been willing to reveal to her his innermost wolf, romping through the desert.

She could not repay him by doing the wrong thing.

She could find his phone, and find the phone numbers of his brevis regional connections. Any of his people would surely leap to help him.

Except for the ones Gausto had bought.

I cannot repay him by doing the wrong thing.

Not when doing the wrong thing had gotten him into this position in the first place.

But she couldn't chance that he might grow weaker. Or that Gausto might come here after all.

Indecision tore at her. The house closed in around her. It stifled her, sturdy walls and muffled sounds and strange scents all enfolding her and separating her from what was real.

Jet left her clothes behind. She headed down the hall, not as cautious as she should have been. She hesitated long enough to snatch up his useless phone from the kitchen table, thumbing through the contacts there, soaking them in. Memorizing them so quickly, in the way that had so annoyed Gausto.

She didn't know who at brevis was safe, and who was Gausto's.

So she'd just have to call them all.

Then she left the phone and she left the house, striding right through the sleepy dogs; they lifted their heads and thumped their tails. Baroo poked his head out of the dog igloo and went *wa-woo* at her in soft inquiry. She merely looked at him, quiet and steady, her body full of alpha and clear enough even for a dog-child to read; he sighed and lay down with only his nose visible in the doorway.

Through the gate, a few steps into the driveway, gravel biting at her bare feet and the cool desert night biting at her skin...she reached for the wolf, stretching out into a run on the way. Energy coalesced around her, scattered her...brought her back as black-furred and swift and loping into the darkened desert range.

The miles to the gas station fell away beneath her feet. She ignored the scent of prey around her—the startled mice darting off to the side, the owl swooping low overhead. Miles gone...soothing, steady rhythm. *Wolf.* She eased down to a trot at the sight of the station lights, and came around the back corner into the parking lot.

In the darkness and at the edge of the lot, the man carrying his giant drink and his strange fake-meat burger didn't pay any attention to her until she was on him— blocking his way back to the station and convenience store, close enough so he'd never reach his car before she brought him down. She lifted her lip in a snarl, the one that had such an effect on Gausto's men. The one with plenty of lip-curling, all her teeth showing. The one that a wolf would know to read as pure warning, but which these humans seemed to see as the fiercest of threats.

The man froze. Past his prime, out of shape…he instantly smelled of fear-sweat. It made the top of his bald heady shiny. Jet took another step. She eyed the heavy sag of his front pocket and took another yet, panting through the snarl—plenty hot, plenty thirsty.

"Be a good dog," the man said. "Maybe you need water?" Without looking away from her, he pried the soda lid off with his thumb, and carefully—so very carefully—set the soda on the ground. "Maybe you need a burger? It's just a cheap road burger. I left it in the microwave too long." Nervousness infused his voice; he fumbled the wrapper and put the burger on the asphalt, too.

Jet stepped forward, owning the asphalt. She lapped at the soda—yellow and strong, it made her nose wrinkle of its own accord. She sniffed around the burger, trying to decide if it was truly food and truly worth eating. By then the man thought himself safe, and started to back away.

She lifted her head, transfixing him with her stare…snarling. And as his eyes widened, she leaped for his pants.

Jet gulped the burger down in a few measured bites; she took a few more laps of the soda. Coins from a torn pocket rolled and danced down old asphalt.

No one had paid any attention to the man's cries. Nor to his dash to the car, not taking any notice that she hadn't followed—she had what she wanted—or to his wheel-screeching departure from the rough edge of the parking lot.

Not a lot of people here at this time of night.

Jet detoured around the backside of a battered delivery truck perma-parked nearby, taking back her human form. The human form had a speaking voice; the human form had fingers. She commenced to gather the scattered coins, and then—walking around broken glass and bottle caps— she went to the phone booth at the side of the building.

Marlee didn't dare close her eyes. Not again—not on the nightmares that had strained through her sleep this night. And she hardly dared to keep them open, with her imagination turning darkness into shapes and monsters. Her blood was too weak to confer upon her the easy night vision the Sentinels took for granted. She didn't have their ability to heal from wounds that could easily have been fatal; she didn't have their extra strength, resources they could draw on even in human form.

She had only her determination, her quick wit, and her unrelenting sense of fairness.

And for now, her determination wavered. Her wit might well have failed her. And her fairness seemed to have left her open to the worst kind of influence.

The worst of it all was, she just wasn't sure.

So, finally, she got out of bed. If nothing else, to turn on the aquarium light and watch the stop-and-start swimming of her Rasboras, listening to the soothing sound of the filter gurgling away in the background.

It wouldn't be the first time she'd fallen asleep on the couch, wrapped in a shawl and wearing a risqué nightie that ought to be shared, but which she refused to deny herself simply because she had no one with which to share it.

Of course, reaching the fish in the small living room meant going past the even smaller office, a little utility room of space shared with her pantry shelves. She told herself she wouldn't check the computer...even as her feet took her there and her ass seated itself in the chair. The monitor flickered out of power-save mode; a few keystrokes logged her into the system—and then, into the Sentinel system.

Not that she was supposed to do any such thing.

She hunted around for activity. There weren't any big operations in play; no teams called up—nothing but background activity. That meant Sentinels on patrol, but mostly on their own terms, and the reports would trickle in according to the Sentinel and the situation.

So in the middle of the night, even with all these night-loving predators around her, she didn't expect to find much going on.

Whoa. Way to be wrong.

The phone action was off the scale. Messages, so far. She began to check them, frowning at the most recent listings, one call after another—to offices that varied from the most basic of building support services to the line that led directly to Dane Berger's office.

They all came from the same number.

Marlee didn't think twice. She accessed the last message, turning up her computer speakers as the file downloaded. She copied the number and started an identity and location trace on it.

"You don't know me," a woman's voice said, startling Marlee. She quickly adjusted the speaker volume.

"My name is Jet." Jet? Either she was a musician
wannabe or her parents had been leftover hippies.
Musician, Marlee decided from the voice. Low and
liquid, curling around the words in some odd way—
even the very faintest hint of a lisp. But not a baby-girl
lisp, not even close. Just a soft shirring of her consonants. "I am calling for Nick Carter."

Marlee baffled over that for a moment, since the
woman hadn't called Carter's number. Then she
realized...*on behalf of.* She was calling on behalf of
Carter. And given that Carter had been missing for a
day...Marlee came to complete attention, holding her
breath—not wanting to miss a single nuance.

"You should know he needs help. He needs healing.
He is in his home. And you should know—"

A background interruption, a man's voice growing
closer and more incredulous with each word. "Hey! Oh
my God! You're naked!"

"This is no surprise to me," the woman said to him,
and her voice held a new quality, one which made
Marlee wince on behalf of the intruder—even before
she processed what the man had said. *Naked.*

The woman could simply be a nudist. But in Marlee's
world, shapechangers were commonplace—and unless
they wore clothing of natural materials, they left it behind
when they shifted. Sentinels might wear a piece or two of
optional clothing, but they always wore enough shiftable
stuff to get by. So. Shapeshifter. But not a Sentinel.

"Ker-rist! Will you look at you? You don't even care,
do you? Are you looking for some, is that it?" The voice
sounded closer yet. The ogling behind it came through
loud and clear.

"I have no need of you," the woman told him.

Marlee leaned closer to the computer speakers, hoping the voice mail wouldn't cut out. It had no time limit, but any period of silence would disconnect the system.

"You sure as hell need *something,* baby. It might as well be—shee-it, just *look* at you—"

Marlee gathered, with a wry little smile, that the woman was pleasant to look upon.

The woman spoke into the phone, evidently ignoring her suitor. "You should know that I don't trust you. Any of you. So I have the brevis numbers from Nick Carter's phone, and I—" A sudden surprised sound, snarl-like. "You may not!"

"You gonna hang them out there in the open like that, you're gonna get touched." A smirk in that voice. "Now c'mon, baby—I can take care of you."

"No. You cannot. If you touch me again, I will hurt you."

Listen to her, Marlee thought at him, even though these events were an hour old. *Can't you hear it in her voice? The wild? The untamed?*

Marlee could.

To the phone, the woman said, "I am calling as many of you as he has in the phone."

But the man was slow. The man was stupid. "No, hey, c'mon—you see that trucker over there? If he drags you into that sleeper cab of his, you aren't ever gonna see daylight again. I'll take care of you—"

A loud clunk—the phone falling, banging into the side of the phone booth. The woman's feral snarl. A man's cry of sudden pain.

And then, of course, the voice mail cut off.

"No!" Marlee stared at the computer in outrage. After an instant of disbelief, she grabbed the mouse, quickly navigated back to the voice-mail list...found the call she'd just listened to, and then the one that had been placed before it. She clicked on the file link, jiggled her foot impatiently, and again stopped breathing as the message began to play—this one made to a care coordinator in the clinic who wouldn't have the faintest idea what to do with it.

"You don't know me," the woman said, that exotic way of speaking still in her voice, little concern or upset present. "My name is Jet."

Marlee stopped the playback. She pondered the message. *I don't trust you.*

Whoever this woman was, she knew. Brevis was compromised.

If these messages got through, then brevis would know, too. They would start looking. And if they were looking, they would find Marlee. If Gausto hadn't overstepped his intentions, if he hadn't gone too far...

But no, he'd done what she always feared. He'd broken their thin trust—enemies working toward the same goal—and he'd grabbed a moment to do exactly as he wanted. Using her, willing to expose her—willing to sacrifice her for this scheme of his.

So she couldn't have him looking.

On the other hand, if no one got these messages, then no one would know to go to Carter's...

He needs healing.

Gausto. What the hell had he done?

But Marlee wasn't ready for this. Not yet.

She copied the phone number down on the scrawl-filled scratch pad beside the computer, and she saved the sound file to her hard drive. Then, one by one, she deleted the voice messages from the Sentinel servers.

Jet stepped over the man down on the crumbling asphalt beside the worn gas station; he curled around his broken arm, moaning gently. The convenience store lights flickered low; no one inside had so much as glanced in her direction.

She opened her hand, letting the remainder of her gathered change trickle out on him. "Call for help," she suggested—and in those bare shadows, took back to the wolf, dimly aware of his fearful cry. She gave him the most disdainful of glances and loped away, back into the desert.

She'd done what she could. She'd left many messages. Surely one of those people would be the right person, even if one of them—or more—was the wrong person.

Alternating an easy lope and trot, she cut a trail more efficient than the road, feeling the pleasure of muscles loosening into movement and time. The night around her bloomed in sharp black and white, the light of a partial moon casting it into easy detail. She let her mind go, thinking of nothing…turning purely to the wolf, to the here and now. Every step, experiencing the full, heady sensations of the wolf.

Or trying to. But it wasn't the same. Not as long as her pack stayed prisoner. Not as long as they could scent the human of her. She was aware, ever aware, of how her thoughts had changed since that first change. Her very *being* had changed. The human clung to her through the wolf, complicating her thoughts, interfering with her existence.

Gausto had promised her an end to those things. A true return to what she'd been. And her people, free. This afternoon, she had forfeited that salvation—but not yet that of her pack. As the human-wolf, she could free them. She could escort them home, navigating dangers and following maps.

And then…she did not know.

She could not do that if she stayed with Nick Carter—if she allowed him to give her over to Brevis Southwest. If she traded Gausto for the Sentinels.

The sharp pain in her flank took her by surprise—renewed with vigor, cramping up her haunch and stifle and up through her ribs. She stumbled, plowing nose-first into the hard ground. Dignity offended, she rose for an quick hard shake, pawing her muzzle with her foot, and sneezed mightily. Then she trotted on.

Half a mile later, she went down again. This time she got up more cautiously, orienting herself…spotting Nick's house in the distance. Almost home.

Home? What was she thinking? Not if she wanted to help her pack. Not if she wanted what freedom was left to her.

And yet…

Home.

Nick blinked into the darkness. *Better.* He felt damp…sweating it out the amulet's poison, in spite of the air conditioning. And the strangely bitter scent on the air—that was him, too. *Sweating it out.* But he could do something about that.

He rolled out of bed on legs that felt rubbery, not bothering with lights, and headed for the master bath.

The shower spray hit him hard, not quite warmed up yet—shocked him awake. He turned his face to the water flow, letting it pour over him—rinsing away the stench of the Core. Letting it pound him while he tested himself…found his limits.

Hard limits. He still couldn't so much as reach out for Annorah, never mind detect power or personal trace. He couldn't feel the wards set around this house; he had to trust in them.

He couldn't rely on his uncanny ability to crumble amulets, filling them with small but precise reverberations of energy that tore them down from the inside out, leaving only so much dust in his hand.

Deaf and dumb. He was lucky he could still see through the night.

The water warmed; his muscles relaxed. He lathered up, hair and all, handmade wintergreen soap that cleared his head and went straight to his nose.

Jet.

What was he doing? What had he *done?* It had been indulgence to respond to her at the fairgrounds…to leap into her game of wolves-in-the-desert, giving in to that which she brought out in him. Falling so hard into what sprang up between them, profound and primal.

Walking right into Gausto's trap.

That he was here, in his home, spoke of Jet's nature and not Nick's good judgment. Pure damned luck, that had been.

Unless you saw through to the truth of her right from the start.

Nick shut his eyes against soap and roughly scrubbed the lather away. No point in softening it. He'd seen Jet;

he'd justified his decision to follow her. And maybe he'd been right, to a point. Until he'd let his response to her get in the way of his responsibilities.

That response to her remained alive and well, and very much evident here in the shower…very much wistful. "Get over it," he muttered to himself, and immediately made that impossible by thinking of Jet curled into him on the patio lounger, half-dressed and not the least bit concerned about it. Golden eyes beneath a tilted sweep of lash, body full of *sleek* and *power* and *wild,* an enigma of open heart and hidden places.

With this woman—this one woman—there was no need to hide the power and wild that rumbled constantly around inside him, hardly disguised by the veneer of civilization he so assiduously applied. Linen Prada suits, crisp haircut, sleek accoutrements.

As if he was really fooling anyone.

With Jet, he could drop all that. Whether wolf or human, he could be exactly what he was—and she matched it. Sensation enfolded him—memory grown large, her skin beneath his hands, her lips and teeth at his neck…

Nick opened his eyes, surprised to find they had been closed. Surprised to find himself leaning against the shower stall, water streaming down his face. He straightened, shook his head sharply—scattered droplets everywhere. Every part of him ached for release—for Jet's touch; Jet's body.

He turned the water off and reached for a towel.

Jet was the one thing he couldn't have.

The Sentinels came first. His responsibilities came first, here in a region ripe for problems after years of benign neglect—a region already quietly compromised from within, its missions failing on a regular basis, its field agents risking everything and more and more often coming in wounded, baffled…not understanding what had gone wrong.

This morning, Nick had given in to indulgence. One wolf to another, purely personal.

He'd nearly paid for it with his life.

No, face it straight. Brevis had nearly paid for it with many lives. Because it wouldn't have been a quick death for him. It would have been Fabron Gausto, playing with him and torturing him and taking him to the edge of death as many times as he could—all while sucking out as much information as he could. And Nick was realistic. A man could do his best, but under Core magics and Gausto's sadistic hand, he'd break—and break hard.

And probably never even know it.

No more indulgence for a brevis adjutant who had to keep his priorities straight—who couldn't risk being the weak link.

In the morning, he'd take Jet into town. She knew more about Gausto than anyone…and it was time to go after that bastard, once and for all.

Chapter 10

Almost home.

The thought came again, unbidden, as Jet lurched against stabbing pain. She yipped into the night, a bewildered cry; the wolf in confusion.

But the house was close; the scent of it came to her on the stirring night breeze. And Nick would know what beset her—for he was both human and wolf. His pale green eyes showed her instinct and wild forests and a hot, fervent response she thought the human in him tried to fight. He would understand. *He can help.*

She scented the interlopers too late. Not enough breeze, not the right angle…they'd waited off to the side, still and silent, and while on any other day she would have found them anyway, on this day, lurching erratically toward safety, she did not.

"Jet."

She staggered to a stop, whining under her breath—lifting a lip at them. They wore special night goggles, eschewing lights that would paint out their positions to the casual observer.

She could see *them* just fine. Two burly men, incongruous in their suits. Expensive suits, as beautifully cut as the linen pants Nick had worn but nowhere near the same beneath—no long leg and amazing ass and hard torso. Shorter men, stockier...beefier. Dark hair pulled back into tight pony tails, plenty of silver flash—a stud at the ear, silver rings and bracelets. As they moved closer she got a whiff of the patchouli the Core men favored.

She growled.

"Don't even bother," said the first man, and he certainly didn't seem concerned.

He should have. He should have looked at her the way a man looks at a growling wolf. He should have thought her completely capable of taking him in a single leap from where she stood.

That he didn't...told her to be wary.

Slowly, she circled them. Letting her heart slow and her breathing ease. Tail low, head low...but not submissively. *Stalking.* These men had come to Nick's house. They could not be allowed any closer.

Nick, still healing. Still pounding in her blood. Suddenly so important to her that she instantly discarded Gausto's first rule, his primary rule. *Never target his men.*

They should not have come into Nick's territory. It didn't matter that she intended to leave it herself. That made him no less important to her. No less vital.

These men would die now.

"Nice doggie," said the man.

"You must be kidding," muttered the second. "Have you seen her move?"

"No worries." The first, the shorter of them, held up his hand, a flat round object secured between thumb and forefinger. "Here. Proof." He took on an expression of concentration, enough to make Jet more wary yet.

But not wary enough.

Pain shot through her flank, twisting her so suddenly she flipped herself, biting at it, yelping *yi-yi-yi* and rolling in the pale, gritty soil. Only a few moments, with all of Nick's hounds suddenly howling in the background, and then it was gone—leaving her panting, dazed…and then instantly flinging herself at Shorty, stupid Shorty who'd gotten so close with such confidence.

Her jaws closed around his wrist; the amulet went flying. Shorty screamed in fear and bone crunched and blood filled her mouth, warm and salty and inexplicably tainted, but she let go only to whirl on the hand that ineffectively pummeled her, catching it in her teeth and closing down—small bones that had no chance against such power.

The other man gave a triumphant cry and even as Shorty stumbled back a few steps and fell, awkward and hitting hard, the pain arrowed through Jet's flank and took her down. Not so fiercely this time, not with their focus scrambled and hers intensified. *They should not have come here.* Enough so that she fell short of Shorty's throat; not enough so that she didn't try again.

But cold metal struck the side of her head—glancing, jarring her…she tumbled to the side and when she scrambled to her feet again, she found a gun barrel in her face. She froze.

The man faced her, crouching and awkward, jamming the gun at her until he saw she respected what it meant. He didn't even spare a glance at his comrade. Not at first. "Asshole," he grunted instead. "She's not *nice,* she's not a *doggie,* and she's not a *toy.*" Now he did glance, easing back a step. "Now get up."

Jet snarled softly under her breath as Shorty struggled to his feet without the use of his arms. His companion scooped up and held out the amulet, keeping his gun trained on Jet. "Take it."

Shorty looked down at his mangled arms—one hand a swollen mass, the other wrist broken and bleeding. "But—"

"You can use this thing better than I can. If she tries anything, then take her down."

Jet put herself between the men and the house. Drawing a line.

The man with the gun laughed, harsh and short. "That's what this is all about? Don't you worry about your precious Nick Carter, little bitch. That's not why we're here. Didn't he tell you we couldn't touch him here? Why do you think Gausto created you in the first place?"

To use. A tool. That had always been clear enough. But she'd never truly understood his limitations.

"But here's where you messed up." The man smiled, teeth white in the darkness. "Because we *can* touch *you.*"

"Now who's playing with her?" Shorty grunted, his voice full of pain. "Get it over with. I need a doctor."

His partner snorted. "What did you *think* would happen?" He himself kept a decent distance from Jet, the gun still pointed at her. She eyed that distance—and he must have seen the look. "Gausto wants you, little bitch, but he's not going to question me if I come back with your pelt. Not after what you just did to Arkady."

Jet slanted her ears, narrowed her eyes. Gausto was more likely to nail their hides to the wall right next to hers. But…she'd scared them. The tense fingers holding that gun…the smell of fear saturating the air. These things told her everything: this man would shoot her and deal with the consequences. So she sat on tensed haunches, but she sat. She listened.

"Smart little bitch," the man said. "Smart enough to know what we *really* want."

Yes. What Gausto had wanted all along—for Jet to reach Nick Carter in places where Gausto couldn't.

"You've still got a job to do." The man nodded at the house, where the hounds had settled—all but for Baroo's mournful howl of dismay ringing out over this tucked-away little valley. "We can't go in there. You can."

She just looked at him. If she went back, it wouldn't be for Gausto. It would be for herself. For what she had seen in Nick's eyes this day.

But Nick was Sentinel Brevis. And Jet had a pack to save.

Her reticence was clear enough. Impatience flashed across the man's blunt features. "Don't forget Gausto has the rest of your pack—and those other dogs, too. You don't do this, they're dead."

They're dead anyway. Unless Jet could free them herself. This day had given her the perspective to see that. To understand just how Gausto had manipulated her—telling her whatever lies necessary. Faced with

her innate and immutable honor, he had found ways to
soften his plans, to make it seem as though what she did
wasn't at all for the bad and was much for the good. But
everything he'd told her had been a lie—from his intentions for Nick to his plans for her pack.

She lolled her tongue out in an insouciant grin. It
meant the same in any language.

"Don't be an idiot," Shorty said. "Do you really think
the only thing he's got over you is a little pain?" His arm
trembled as he raised his hand, the wrist fragile and
bleeding—the amulet a threat.

Jet was ready for pain—but not for the abrupt inward
lurch, the distinct sensation that something tore her in two.
It passed through her, sending ripples of unease along her
spine. She lowered her head, glaring back at him. Silent
in suffering—fighting the impulse to pant her stress.

"That's showing her," the other man said.

"Screw you," said Shorty. "You think it's easy to
concentrate all ripped up like this?" And he scowled at
the amulet, an expression of deep effort, and—

Jet cried out, a wolf's echoing wail of anguish as the
pain ripped through her—not just her flank but her
entire being. It shuddered her perceptions out of phase,
shredding her very being—and suddenly her keening
voice was human, a more vulnerable sound, and her
front paws had turned to hands, braced against the hard
ground for only an instant before she collapsed to it,
sharp pebbles and sand grinding against sensitive skin.

Human. Human against her will, as Gausto had done
to her once before—but this time, human with no wolf
at all. Emptiness filled her; she floundered, searching,
hands clenching around dirt while all her strength went

to water and breath turned to a gasp. The world reeled around her; she barely heard cruel laughter. She barely felt the hard kick against her side, sending her sprawling against a cholla cactus. She choked on useless air and emotions so large they couldn't possibly fit in her body, boiling up to consume her. Another kick; she made no move to defend herself.

Because who she was…was gone.

Nick struggled with roiling claws of internalized poison, a hiss and steam of invading energies and murky images of strife. A snarl against his ears; a flash of gleaming white teeth; dogs howling. *A woman, wailing in the night.* A clash of muscle and bone, the snap of red-limned wards knotting into place, *a woman wailing in the night.* Corrupt Atrum Core power fizzling out in his hand, amulets gone to powder and ash. *A woman wailing—*

Nick jerked awake with a wild shout, braced upright in bed with his arms shaking and his heart pounding, and he didn't have the faintest idea why.

And still, abrupt alarm slammed home in his chest. *Jet.*

It made no sense. She slept, down at the other end of the hall. She'd returned to her own room and she slept.

And yet…

Jet.

"Stop that, you dickwad." The man's voice rang sharp and clear. "Give me that!" An outraged cry of pain and protest, and suddenly Jet flooded with completeness again. The wolf washed back in to fill the empty spaces, giving her back her nature, her strength, her very essence. And if she sobbed with relief, she nonetheless

snapped immediately back to awareness of her sur-
roundings, pinning down the location of the two men.

"What the hell—" Shorty said, sputtering with anger,
his two useless hands held protectively close to his chest.

"You dumbass idiot! What're you going to do, tell
Gausto you got so carried away with convincing her that
you broke her? 'Give her a taste of it,' he said. 'Explain
the situation.' That's *all*. She's got to be able to carry out
her orders!"

"No," Jet said, startling them both. She yanked a
cactus spine from the back of her arm and tossed it
away; she climbed to her feet and stood before them, un-
abashed at her nakedness. They stared, through night
goggles, their jaws momentarily slack.

"Shit," said the uninjured man. "Just—"

"Ker-ist," said Shorty.

"No," Jet said. "I will take no orders. Not from you.
Not from Gausto. Tell him he has this one chance to let
my pack go."

The uninjured man snorted. "Did you not understand
what we just did to you?"

"*I* just did to you," Shorty echoed.

The other man held up the amulet. "Did you think we
could only do it once? Don't you get it? Gausto put an
amulet inside you. And digging it out will trigger it
off—*permanently*."

"It changes nothing," Jet said.

"Little bitch, it changes *you*. Whenever we want. It
changes you completely. If the drozhar triggers it, you'll
never turn back into a wolf again. You'll never *feel* like
a wolf again. Your pack dies, and you die inside. Isn't
that right? Or did you *want* to be one of us?"

Jet growled deep. "I will never be one of *you.*"

"I would clap for you if I could," Shorty said. "Clap, clap, clap. Very noble. Now, you're going to finish what you started. You're going to take Carter down, and you're going to bring him back to Oro Valley." He shrugged. "And then Gausto will release your people and you can take them home."

Jet didn't believe it. The instant she had defied Gausto, she'd sacrificed herself. That they would even try to tell her otherwise meant not a single word they said could be trusted.

Except the part about what Gausto could do to her.

She believed that. She believed it utterly.

Nick staggered out of bed, lurched to the door frame, putting a hand out to catch himself. "Jet?" he said softly, and then cleared his throat. "Jet?"

And kicked himself for obsessing over her, when he was already paying the price for just that. For yearning for her, when indulgence had already gone so wrong. When the morning would mean leaving this game he'd let himself play, and taking her to brevis and—

Outside, the dogs kicked up an anxious howl, mellifluous tones ringing through the night, coming in clearly through the open door.

The open door.

"Don't even think," Shorty said, and his voice was tight with the pain and shock of what she'd done to him. "Don't even think that Nick Carter wants a piece of you after this. You think he cares why you did what you did? You think he trusts you?"

"What does she know?" the other man said. "She's a pet."

Shorty snorted at her. "He's going to take you in to his brevis offices and dump you off at their research labs. Maybe he'll make nice and stick you in one of those apartments they keep, but it'll be the same thing. You'll be a prisoner. If you think it's going to be different because he's your own kind, think again. He's Sentinel, little bitch. That's the only kind he cares about."

She wanted to growl at him. She couldn't quite muster it.

Deep in her heart, she believed it could be true.

After all, he'd been Sentinel all his life. They were his pack. She'd known him only for a day, and even if they'd taken that time in the desert...even if they'd wooed one another as wolves do, and drawn each other in with heated promises and powerful unspoken vows...

Well, she'd been the one to betray *him,* hadn't she? It didn't matter that those moments together still meant as much to her. Maybe they'd always meant more to her. She, after all, was the wolf from the heart up. Nick Carter had been born the human.

"Bring him to us," said Shorty. "If you want to live. If you want your pack to live. Bring him to us." He stopped, reeling slightly. "Dammit, Lyev, I need a doctor."

The other man relented, went to support his companion. But he didn't take the gun off Jet. "You heard him. Unless you want to live your life like...*that.*"

That. Writhing out the agony of being completely closed off from her wolf.

Forever.

Chapter 11

Jet let them leave. She stood numb and trembling, and she let them leave.

Forever.

As if she had any choice. Gausto would never let her go; he would never remove the amulet. She'd seen the gleam of hunger in his eyes during her training. He wanted what she had, and he'd do whatever it took to get it.

Forever.

So tempting, to run after them—to throw herself into submission and do just what Gausto wanted. To bring them Nick Carter. Surely they were right—he was human as much as wolf, and what had passed between them in the desert had not touched him as it had touched her. Even before she'd done what she'd been sent to do…so desperate to save her pack.

He'd had plenty of time to think about that. And unlike her, he had a lifetime of practice in navigating human ways. He knew how to protect that which was important to him. He knew how those things balanced in his life.

Jet knew nothing. She knew only emptiness and homesickness and the struggle to understand a world which had turned so suddenly strange.

"Please," she whispered after Gausto's men, knowing they couldn't possibly hear her—and that she wouldn't have said it if they could. They headed back for the dark lump of a sedan sitting off the side of the road— walking without grace through the uneven desert in their shiny shoes and expensive suits, one man now grudgingly helping the other.

Without taking her eyes from them, she reached for her wolf—her blessed wolf, the very heart of her. The response washed through her…a cool flush of pleasure flashing down her limbs and sweeping down her spine, and then she was on four feet and black-furred, night vision sharpening and nose drinking in the scents— sage and brittlebush and bird-of-paradise, warm caliche and even the horny toad dug in for the night not far away.

Gausto promised only betrayal. And Nick, in the end, would consider himself already betrayed.

Jet threw her head back for a single mournful howl of anguish, and flung herself into the night—wolf, and wolf alone.

Jet was gone. Nick swore, short and sharp, lurching out into the yard just as he was. No clothes, only flesh and alarm. The dogs already milled in distress; Baroo pressed his nose against Nick's leg.

They'd taken to Jet, all of them. They knew pack leadership when they saw it.

"You're safe," he told them, heading out the gate—out into the desert, not even sure if he could yet clothe himself in fur. As the gate latched behind him, a howl split the air, a fine line of sound slicing through the night in lilting minor key. Jet, calling to her missing pack...calling out into empty darkness.

It had the feel of farewell to it.

"Damn well think *not*," he said, grabbing for his elusive wolf. In the distance, a car motor ground smoothly to life; tires crunched and spun against nature's gravel.

The wolf slipped away from him. Still oppressed by the poison...still evasive. *"Damn well think not,"* he repeated, and dug in, hand wrapped around the black powdered steel of the gate. Sweat broke on his forehead, between his shoulder blades, and still he hunted himself, finding the threads of that other shape—refusing to let go. Pulling the wolf into existence in a way he'd never experienced, never even known he could. Not with the wolf always fighting so hard to break free.

She's out there. Jet is out there. Out there and running, if he didn't mistake that howl. He didn't know why. He did know that she was desperate—and that she would never simply leave her pack.

He would have said she wouldn't simply leave him, either. As little as he knew her—the details of her, the everyday things—he had nonetheless seen the grit of her. The soul. Laid bare, in a wolf's quick and easy assessment—in the space of a romp. Pure communication, unfettered by sly human half truths or double-talk, defining the profound nature of that which had sprung to life so quickly between them.

That which could not simply be discarded, not even with betrayal between them.

Not willing betrayal.

He'd seen that much in her golden eyes, even as the amulet had taken him down.

At that memory, the wolf in him steadied, built power...burst free, a shout turning into a quick hard snarl. Bitter Core workings wavered in the air, poison forced out and away and dissipating into the night.

Right back at you, Gausto.

Nick threw himself into a steady lope, following a scent trail so fresh and clear that his eyes could all but see it. But he didn't answer Jet's call. She'd decided to go; she wouldn't welcome him. He had no intention of telling her he was on his way.

Not that he needed to. She'd figure it out. And as fast as she was, he'd be hard-put to keep up with her at all.

Then don't.

He knew this territory. She didn't. She knew to skirt the edges of the city until she could find a place to cross I-10 between Oro Valley and Tucson. But she'd do as any wolf would, following the terrain—sticking to the natural paths created by the wild denizens of this area.

Nick knew those paths. But he also knew the terrain between—the shortcuts over rougher ground. And now he let his body settle into the rhythm of four feet and lolling tongue, hitting a small nameless wash that led to the Pantano, floundering briefly in that deep, soft sand, and scrambling back out the other side. Cut south and west and down through another—but he'd taken

miles from the looping path that Jet had likely struck—
a path that ran just alongside the high ground, and on
which she would have felt safe.

Nick found the path. He didn't have to wait long.

Jet trotted into view, a metronome of motion—emo-
tionally numbed, and not paying attention as she should.
And even when she saw him coming from above and
behind...three hard sprinting strides and he was upon
her, pacing her another two strides and then grabbing
hard at her ruff, taking her down. They rolled together,
thick fur protecting them from the cholla and prickly
pear until the thick base of a looming saguaro stopped
their struggle.

She snapped back at him, then, a desperate gesture.
He closed his jaws over her muzzle in alpha admonish-
ment—taking the chance that her wolf's nature would
respond so quickly, so instinctively, it would buy him
time. A moment, that's all—and he got it, long enough
to step over top her, and in the stepping...the change.
A hard change, and fast, pushing the energy out in ways
he'd never done before—taking another chance.

Jet yelped; she spasmed briefly beneath him—before
his shifting energies pushed out the change in her,
turning her from rangy furred wolf to long-legged and
smooth, the sweet and salty scent of exertion, sweet
and salty scent of tears, strong to a nose still sensitive
from the change.

"Damn," he said. "You're not *crying.*"

"Damn, I am *not,*" she told him, all but snapping the
words...but in a voice suspiciously free of its normal
mellifluous tone. But then, so very clearly crying,
dammit yes, she reached out—she outright grabbed

him. She pulled down his head to kiss him so fiercely that he immediately lost coherent thought, immersed in scent and soft skin and the utterly amazing sensation of lips both pliant and needy. Her fingers scraped through his hair, tugging at him; one long, strong leg hooked high behind his thigh.

He realized, in a dim corner of sanity, that he was about to take her right here in the desert, this wolf woman he'd known for such a short time—that he was about to take her hard.

That it was exactly what she wanted.

Even more dimly—somewhere beyond her lips and tongue and the crush of her breasts against his chest, all gathering a whirlpool of sensations so out of control as to head for out-of-body—he realized that her frantic need was less about *want* and more about desperation, a feral newborn woman cornered between circumstance and the very real bond that had sprung to life between them. Understanding and desire and mutual need—two souls alone, finding each other in the desert.

But mutual need didn't make the moment right.

Willpower, he had none of. If it was up to willpower, he'd bury himself in her hard and deep and fast, thrusting them both to clawing need and beyond. But it was not willpower that made him break off with a guttural gasp of physical disbelief. It was the equally fierce need to protect her, the knowledge that she floundered in a world that made little overall sense to her and that she reached out in grief as much as passion. *Trying to fill a void.*

So he pulled back from her kiss, torn by her noise of protest and his own fierce disbelieving groan. He rolled to his side to pull her in close, tucking her head into the hollow of his neck and shoulder and holding her tightly.

Tightly enough to make it clear: he had no intention of letting her go. Tightly enough so that he still ached to be inside her, nestling them together in a way that sent trembling rebellion through his body. She pushed her hips against him, so...utterly...perfect...

"Jet," he said, a strangled sound—barely a word at all. In that instant she understood—she was being held, not loved, and she resisted it.

But this moment wasn't about overpowering her simply to prove that he could. It was about changing where she was. Putting a stop to the frenetic and the fears. And yes...about claiming her.

She'd asked for him. She'd prodded him and demanded of him and now he told her *yes* in the most primal way possible—the way she'd understand the most deeply.

And she bit him.

She bit him hard, sinking her teeth into the muscle between neck and shoulder. He stiffened, capturing her in a blanketing hold, inexorable but not the least bit tight, enough strength behind it so it never needed to become that way. She fought him in silence, teeth bared, her breath gusting against the hot throb of teethmarks, a tiny grunt of effort escaping—

Until quite suddenly, she didn't.

She settled. Her panting eased; her breath came in small puffs against that same shoulder she'd bitten.

Into that calm and silence, he murmured, "Good, now?"

She thought about it; she nodded. Nick eased his hold, relaxing onto the harsh ground. She, too, slowly relaxed, accepting this new kind of contact. Not sexual, not hot. Not defiant, not grabbing or needy—because he was right *there*, already giving her what she needed. Instead of easing away, she gave the ragged throb of his shoulder a solicitous lick.

Warm and cool, intimate and gentle…it thrilled him all the way down to his toes. She settled against his erection, accepting the moment.

He supposed he could consider it progress. Certain parts of his body called it otherwise. He rested his face briefly against her head—glossy hair short and wild, caressing his face. "What happened?"

A hesitation. "They said you would imprison me. That you could not forgive me." Her voice had never sounded so *other,* with the faint blending of one syllable into another, the melody behind it.

"They?" he repeated sharply. "Gausto's people were here?"

"I think I brought them," she said. She glanced over her shoulder, looking down toward the gleaming, rounded shape of her ass.

Nick couldn't make sense of it. He went back to her initial words, said, *"Forgive* you? For what, being tortured by the Core?"

She licked his shoulder again; it took him unaware, and he pushed himself against her with a quiet rush of breath. She flexed to meet him, completely natural and unselfconscious, and said, "He did not call it torture. He said he was doing me a favor, to make me more than what I had been."

"Mind games." Anger surged hot in his chest. As woman she was exquisite; as wolf she had nonetheless been whole. "Jet, Gausto lied to you, he manipulated you, he threatened you and those you love, and he bullied you—all while you had no context for what he wanted from you. The amazing thing is that you broke from him anyway. I'm alive because of you."

She whispered, "But you have been so very sick because of me."

"Because of *Gausto,* dammit."

She gave a little alto growl into his collarbone, and he laughed, short and a little dark. "Lest I forget who you are," he noted. *What you are.* "And how, exactly, do you think you brought them here?"

"Those men said he put an amulet inside me," she said, and sniffed into his neck, burrowing a little closer as the cold night air closed in around them—their sweat drying, their muscles cooling. "Gausto won't be happy. I'm not supposed to hurt them." And then, "I'm not sure about that man at the gas station. I don't think Gausto would care about him. He would care about drawing attention. *Be one of them,* he told me. *Don't give them anything to look at.*"

Nick snorted. How could anyone with eyes *not* look at Jet? But then her words penetrated more deeply. "What gas station?" he asked. *"When?"*

So she told him. In the unusual voice to which he could listen forever, she told him of her run to the gas station, of acquiring coins most expeditiously, of defending herself against the man who had grabbed her. She told him of calling brevis from numbers instantly memorized from his phone, and didn't give him time to wonder if she had an eidetic memory or if it was simply a skill a wolf would have—a wolf who had to remember every experience of her life in order to survive.

She told him of Gausto's men, and of her fears for
him. She took his hand and ran it down along her side,
to the scar just beneath her final rib and the sleek muscle
there. A scar divoted the flesh, short and deep. "I thought
it was from the dart, when they first captured me," she
said. "It was…a weapon, as much as dart. But Gausto…
he put something inside me when they took out the dart."

"Son of a bitch," Nick breathed. "That *son of a*—"
But he cut himself short, for she was tensing up again.
Not frightened—not of him. Not *physically* frightened.
But overwhelmed, perhaps. Ready to shift and return to
her wolf's world.

For an instant, he wondered if it might not be better
that way. Let her turn back…let her run. Let her be free
of it all while he dealt with Gausto—and kept the man
too busy to find her. And when that was over, he would
no longer have the means to look for her—to follow his
amulet connection.

Nick would make certain of that. If Gausto hadn't
already guessed what so very few people knew—Nick's
ability to short out most amulets with a targeted surge
of just the right energy—he'd damned well know it
before this was over.

And then Jet said, "It does more than just find me. It
takes away who I am." She took a short, sudden breath.
"When I find him, I will take away who *he* is." A simple
statement, said quietly. But Nick heard the difference in
her voice—the alto throatiness gone hard, the complete
focus on her own words. More than just a wolf bitch,
now. A wolf bitch with a mission and a grudge and with
deep intent.

After so many heinous crimes committed, so many

of both Sentinel and Core laws broken, so many good Sentinels hurt... Where before Nick had been patient, biding his time—waiting for Gausto to cross that one, final, irrevocable line...

Now he was done waiting.

"Tell me," he said, teeth clenched enough so the words came hard, "that doesn't mean what I think it means. *It takes away who you are.*"

"It is agony," she said, so quietly the words hardly registered. "I would tear out his throat for it."

So quietly that anyone listening carelessly might not have heard the intent in her voice.

He held her more closely against the encroaching cold of the night, blanketing her with his body. Still aroused, but with a different kind of ferocity. His immediate impulse—to protect her from that experience— gave way before understanding.

He didn't need to protect this woman from anything.

She growled slightly, a surprised sound. *Too tight.* Nick forced himself to ease up. He forced himself to think sensibly. Jet didn't need his protection; she didn't want his world. She wanted to free her pack and return to what she'd known.

And he had no room for a personal vendetta. Not when brevis was likely rocked by his absence...vulnerable. Because Dane Berger was no leader, not any longer. Out of touch, distracted...he would try his best, but he'd been leaning too hard on Nick for too long to be of any real use. And those who had resented Nick's assumption of leadership in the void left by the aging consul...they wouldn't hesitate to take advantage of the situation—inserting influence, stirring up trouble.

Creating a mess that Nick would have to clean up before he could get back to the business of dealing with Gausto.

After a single day.

Imagine what it would be like if he indulged himself, if he took another day, or another on top of that—

Gausto would end up dead, that's what. And Nick would then have the time to clean up whatever had happened in brevis.

Unless he didn't. Unless one day was all it would take for things to go too wrong to fix. Sentinels could die in a day, if the Core was ready to pounce.

Nick reached for Annorah. A long shot, that—the middle of the night. But she would wake, if the mental knock was strong enough. And suddenly—now that he was back to himself, the last of the amulet's poisons flushed away by the energy surge of his shift to the wolf— he had to know how things were. He had to tell them what he'd learned—warn them of Gausto, who—having made his move—would now strike hard, breaking written and unwritten rules of their cold war pact with the Core.

But Annorah didn't respond. Annorah felt strangely… *absent.* His call should have had the sense of a pebble tossed into water—tiny ripples of reaction, of impact.

There was nothing.

"We need to get back to the house," he said, suddenly not even sure they'd be safe there—even though the Septs Prince would surely execute Gausto for breaking that final rule of engagement. "We need to get out of the open."

She made a noise of protest—not wanting to be pulled off her own path.

"You can't stay out here," he told her.

She pushed back from him—rolling gracefully to

her knees, and up to her feet. Bare feet in front of his face, bare toes wiggling in the gritty sand. "I make up my own mind."

He found his feet just as swiftly as she. Cold air crowded him. "This battle has been raging for generations beyond count, Jet. What happens next is beyond what you or I want or care about. We do what we have to. We do what's good for the *world*."

"If I want my pack to live," she murmured, and they didn't sound like her words. More like words she'd been told...words she was repeating. Words that had sudden meaning for her. She straightened, her eyes an eerie whiskey-tinged gleam in the darkness. *"I,"* she told him, a warning in her tone, "do what is good for my pack."

Chapter 12

Marlee sat at her cubicle, a thumbnail drive clutched in her hand.

Audio files. Voice mail .wav files, saved from the previous night.

Before she'd deleted the originals from the system.

A woman none of them knew, trying to help a man that brevis had not only come to know, but to fiercely support.

Most of them.

Not everyone on Berger's staff. They'd sensed Carter's assumption of the consul's role in the wake of Berger's preoccupation and distraction. They resented it. They made no effort to smooth the way for Carter, no matter if his needs were great or small.

And now, she knew, some of them had done worse.

She wasn't alone here in brevis, working under Gausto's hand.

She might even be the least of them. Kept in the dark, used for her limited, stated goals—keeping the balance.

What if she'd been the one messing up the balance all along?

Without the Sentinels, she suddenly realized—clutching that thumbnail drive so very tightly, seeing it clearly now—the Core would run amock. They might think much of themselves, these field Sentinels who assumed so much of this organization's power—but they filled a role. They might well cross the line to arrogance, and they might mess with people's lives in ways they shouldn't.

But so had she.

And so suddenly she wasn't sitting in her cubicle, the stressed problem-solving tones of her department in high pitch all around her, but heading to the community room in Nick Carter's section—below the apartments, separate from the consul's section of that floor. Most Sentinels thought the consul and adjutant worked closely together, one commanding the other—but when Carter had arrived nearly two years earlier, Berger had shown little interest.

And Carter had shown no hesitation. Almost instantly brevis became more active, starting with the small things—patrols more frequent, reports coming in regularly—data gathered and information sources established. From the murky awareness that the Core was in the area and doing their own thing—with the assumption that if that thing went out of bounds, the Sentinels would learn of it and stop it—to the more proactive strategy of mapping activity, logging incidents…putting people in place to get in the Core's way.

The beginning of the end for Gausto.

Come to think of it, the beginning of the requests

from Gausto that had made Marlee less comfortable. Interfering with Dolan Treviño's *adveho* earlier this year…that had been hellishly ticklish stuff, and only Gausto's assurances that it would inconvenience, not truly harm Treviño, convinced her to do it at all. And Gausto had been telling the truth, hadn't he, because Treviño had been just fine. Misusing the *adveho* system, most likely—that Sentinel Mayday, spread across the miles through an intense mental message made possible by skill and training. Only to be used in life-or-death situations.

It had been easier to misdirect the mail going out to Joe Ryan—the reminders that his reports were late, warning of Core activity in the area. Because if he had been doing his job, his reports would have been in on time. If he'd been doing his job, he would already have known about that Core activity. He had deserved to bear the consequences of his arrogance, his willingness to mess with the power of the San Francisco Peaks.

Although somehow he seemed not only to have avoided that, but to have gotten under the skin of Lyn Maines, the one woman Marlee thought she could trust to ferret out problems like Joe Ryan in the first place.

Compared to her past *favors*—messages gone astray, information lost or delayed, inconsequential tidbits passed along to Gausto…

This thing with Nick Carter suddenly seemed big.

Especially when she walked into the community room—ostensibly to use the very nice espresso machine there, but in truth to assess just this—and instantly saw from their expressions that he was still missing.

That palpable discontent in Dolan Treviño—black

jaguar clothed in attitude, startling blue eyes in black Irish coloring, startlingly handsome lines in his features and body—didn't mean anything. Standard Treviño. To find it in Meghan Lawrence…that meant something. Faint freckles, the tough, lean figure of a working ranch hand, dark brown hair slipping from its ponytail and eyes worried in sharp features. Meghan was nice; Meghan got along with just about everyone. She didn't brood.

Generally.

Nor did Joe Ryan, whatever else Marlee thought of him. A big man, standing by the window and looking out as though he hoped to see something other than the city on the other side. Rugged in body, casual in dress—nothing like Lyn Maines, who stood beside him all neatly tucked together, her worry just as tucked away.

Maks sat on the couch—built like Ryan, his green eyes more intense, his hair a dark gleaming chestnut with streaks of white that the unwitting might take for gray and not signs of the tiger within.

As one, they looked at her in the doorway. No doubt they'd used their superpower hearing to detect her footsteps on approach. Their murmur of conversation cut short; their expressions were neither welcoming or hostile.

Marlee tightened her hand around the thumbnail drive. Now. Now was the time to tell them. To hand over this thumbnail drive and the files it contained. She didn't have to confess to everything. She could tell them she'd had trouble sleeping, that she'd been keeping an eye on things. That in the wake of its malfunctions the day before, the system had been floundering and she'd just barely saved these files before it had gone down.

But they would smell her lies. They'd pursue and dig. They'd never believe her denials, and they'd be right.

And yet...Nick Carter was out there. In the cold. Exposed because of her actions, and with Gausto after him. Marlee was sure of it by now. She could put the pieces together as well as any field Sentinel—and at the moment, she was the only one who *had* all the pieces. Marlee closed her eyes, trying to think past the sudden panic that closed off her throat, tightening down her chest.

"Marlee?" Maks said, and his concern sounded genuine. Of course it would be Maks. Caring, for all his hands could do to a person. The one who might just have noticed Marlee's reaction to him if he considered her anything other than *not*-Sentinel.

And that was the whole point, wasn't it? The Sentinels had forgotten they were indeed human. Not entitled, not God-gifted with the power to use others, all unknowing, as playing pieces.

Marlee knew what it was like to be one of those playing pieces. She'd known since childhood. She'd known their hubris...she'd known they needed to be controlled.

And so Marlee slipped the thumbnail drive smoothly into her pocket. "Hi, Maks," she said, suddenly calm. "Any news?"

As if she didn't already know.

But as she reached for the tiny cup that would hold the espresso, their attention went elsewhere altogether—to the doorway, where, in short order, Annorah staggered in.

"Annorah!" Maks sprang to his feet—and instantly

faltered, which was the reason he was still here. Strong, robust, and recovered from the incident that had nearly killed his team in Flagstaff—except for those inexplicable moments during which he wasn't. Ryan put a hand on his shoulder, steadying him; Lyn and Meghan moved quickly to Annorah as she reeled into the doorway.

Marlee just stood there in shock. This wasn't her doing—but it was someone's.

"What the fu—?" Treviño, of course. Easily the most raw of them, the most outspoken. And in this case, clearly voicing the thoughts of the other men.

"Drugged," Annorah said thickly, as they guided her to a chair. "Last night…"

"Marlee." Maks looked over at her—directly at her. A rarity. "The coffee."

Practically a speech for Maks. After a startled hesitation, she popped the espresso serving pod into place and pressed the start button, and less than a minute later she handed the foamy beverage to Meghan, who took it to Annorah and steadied her hands as she brought the little cup to her mouth.

Marlee made another for herself, and by that time Annorah's expression was starting to clear. She looked down at the short-sleeved pajama top and a pair of boy boxers over her rounded shape and womanly hips. "Crap," she said. "Where's my bathrobe? *And what happened?* Isn't there any security in this building at all?"

Marlee had a sudden image of Berger's executive assistant. Barely blooded at all—but damned good at his job and apparently good at what he was doing for

Gausto as well. Security wouldn't be any use against one such as him.

Security, she imagined, *hadn't* been any use against him.

What the hell was Gausto thinking, to interfere with Sentinels here within brevis? Did he really think it would go unnoticed? Did he really think the Sentinels wouldn't respond?

And then she had a scarier thought.

What if he didn't care, because he knew it would be too late by the time anyone did?

And there was Maks, peeling off his flannel shirt to drape over Annorah's shoulders, tight black T-shirt beneath. Annorah clutched the shirt with a nod of thanks, and almost instantly cried, "Whoa! Whoa! Shut up! Everyone *shut up!*"

Treviño swore for them all—knowing, as did even Marlee, what had happened. *Communications.* Supplicants inside Annorah's mind, crying for attention. Internalized switchboard operator, hailing frequencies suddenly open. Her eyes went distant as her expression shifted into dismay, and alarm, and fear. And then a gasp, and she clutched Mak's shirt close around herself, crying, "Stop, *stop!* I have to—" and shook her head, emerging from her inner world back to the community room.

"What's going on?" Lyn asked. Lyn, who'd been there when Annorah screwed up in Flagstaff, hurting Ryan so badly; Lyn had less patience for her now, but at the same time...more understanding.

"Everything," Annorah said, her voice barely making it above a whisper and yet somehow sounding

like a shout. "They've been trying to get through…all night. *Adveho vigilia*…gone unheard. *Monitio,* not passed along. I can't begin to untangle…" Tears filled her eyes. "They're hurt out there, Lyn. I know you don't think much of me after…" She risked a glance at Ryan, who seemed to withhold comment with effort. "But I would never leave them out there alone like this…"

The room broke into a sudden babble of conversation. Annorah choked, "This is no coincidence! Not when I was drugged…when I couldn't help…."

Several dead, it sounded like. They got that much out of her. Several more wounded, with remote backup needed—out on the rim of the Grand Canyon, up by the Four Corners, south near the Mexican border at Los Cruces. Sentinels led away from safety, Sentinels ambushed with amulet workings they'd had no sense of until far, far too late.

"Stealth workings?" Lyn said, coming to complete, alert attention. "Are these people who should have detected Core trace?"

Annorah nodded, but she held up a hand, forestalling further discussion while she quickly attended some other message, shuttling information around. "What do I do?" she asked when she emerged again, despair in her voice. "Someone needs to authorize rescue, *now.* I can't reach the consul—I can never reach him, that's why Nick has taken over so much of operations in the first place. I don't know, maybe I can reach his exec—"

"No!" Marlee cried—and snapped her mouth closed in horror. *What have I done?*

But if they all snapped to focus on her, it didn't last

any longer than a moment. For that's when Annorah cried, "Nick!" and her face blossomed with relief. "I have Nick!"

Nick!

Annorah's shout in his mind sent Nick ducking away, sending back an instant wordless snarl of reprimand.

Sorry, she returned, her inner voice practically sobbing with relief. *We're just so happy to hear from you—*

We? Nick kept an eye on Jet as she prowled his great room—high ceilings, tile accents, a couple of sky-lights—and plenty of room for a restless wolf to pace among the sparse furniture in premorning light. Restless and barely here at all. *I do what is good for my pack.*

Your primaries, Annorah said, and then added, *Not counting Michael and Shea and Ruger and—*

Those still in the brevis clinic.

Ryan and Lyn, he said. *Treviño?*

Yes, she told him. Good. He'd need Treviño in on this, hard and dark and ready to act. He needed them all. And maybe he let his relief leak out, for Annorah said, *Nick, are you all right? You don't feel—*

I got ambushed, Nick told her shortly. He didn't mention Jet. He wasn't ready for that yet. He hadn't decided if it was because he didn't want to muddy the waters or if he wanted to protect her or if he simply wanted to keep her all to himself. *Trust no one,* he told her. *No one outside my primaries. There are new workings in play—undetectable amulets—perfected—*

Yes! she responded, with enough enthusiasm to alert him. It wasn't a new concept to her, and that wasn't good—although he'd seen hints of them for months, he'd kept them under wraps. After a moment she returned with, *Stealth amulets, Lyn calls them. She's been trying to pin them down since you sent her to Flagstaff—but she doesn't have anything yet.*

Nick held a moment's silence, eyeing Jet. If anyone knew…

Then again, Jet could be surrounded by them and not have any idea of the significance. There was nothing to gain by revealing her. Not yet.

Nick?

Here.

Whatever's going down, it's big. You weren't the only one to go down yesterday. We… More hesitation. *We lost field agents last night. We might lose more. We need—*

Lyn is there, he interrupted her, trying to hide the sick impact of her words. *She's my second, as of right now.* This was far beyond what his exec could handle—a fine man, but not field status and not even in the office yet. *I should have done that a month ago.*

But… Her thoughts stuttered to a halt, faltered onward. *Aren't you…aren't you coming in?*

He couldn't quite say it—that in spite of the obvious crisis, the obvious need…that in fact, he wasn't.

If he was at brevis, he was predictable. He was responding to pattern. He was in a mode that Gausto knew well and for which he had no doubt prepared.

Those were all reasons…if not the determining factor.

For if he was at brevis, then Jet would also be on her own. If he was at brevis, he'd have to answer questions. He'd get tied up in meetings and brevis politicking and procedures.

If he was at brevis, Jet would be alone.

And he knew she wouldn't stay. Not when she'd barely come in from the desert in the first place.

He gathered his mental composure, replacing barriers around those things that he didn't want Annorah to see. He told her again, *Trust no one.*

"Trust no one."

Annorah said it out loud, with a blink of surprise—with despair in her voice and fear in her eyes. "He's not coming in. And he's hiding something from me."

"He knows something," Treviño said simply—sharp blue eyes catching them all up in his gaze. "He's learning it the hard way—sometimes you just have to do things yourself."

"Trust no one," Meghan repeated, her open features gone somber. "It's as big as we thought, then."

Trust no one, Marlee thought, and set aside the half-empty espresso cup with trembling hands.

She wondered when they'd figure out that Carter meant her.

Nick was back.

Jet saw it immediately; she stopped her prowling, her toes pressed against the cool saltillo tile and the strong desert sage and sand scent of Nick all around her, imbued in this oversized t-shirt he'd given her. Her back prickled with the cactus spines he'd pulled from her skin; her flank ached with what Gausto's embedded amulet had wrought.

Take it out, and lose the wolf forever.

He'd been gone, somehow, in his head—pale green eyes distant, expression reflecting the difficult nature of the conversation he'd warned her he was about to have.

Leave it in, and lose her freedom forever.

So much depended on this man. He who would now leave for the city. For his brevis.

"I wish—" she said suddenly, and then hesitated.

Those didn't seem to be the words he'd expected. He, too, had pulled on quick clothing—cutoff jeans. They left his legs free, feet as bare as hers, muscle raising highlight and shadow in the single light he'd bothered to turn on. She'd run and romped beside him as a magnificent wolf, assessing him with her wolf's eyes. Now these human eyes saw him very differently—long lines, lean muscle, sparse, crisp body hair as hoarfrost as that on his head. As with the wolf, straight, strong features.

She ran a hand over her nose. Her wolf nose wasn't quite level in plane—just the slightest of elegant curves. She found the same on her human face. And now, when she looked at him, she found the tension easing from his body and a hint of a smile on a face too easily prone to fierce. She dropped her hand. "I wish we could just be wolf," she said, finishing those words. Not thinking about them, just saying them. "I wish we were back together in the desert where we met. None of this. I...you..."

And then, apparently, she'd run out of words. Maybe Gausto had never given her those words in the first place, or maybe such words simply didn't exist. How could she say the joy she'd felt at his presence, the instant awareness of what two unique beings—both wolf, both human—could mean to one another?

Instant trust, because she knew how to read him.

Instant respect, because she saw what he was as both man and wolf.

Instant *want,* because her body could see these things too.

Instant longing, because she'd become just human enough to comprehend what it would mean to be with this man.

No wolf was meant to be alone.

Not Jet. Not Nick Carter.

The wistful expression crossed his face so quickly she almost missed it. And then he looked away. "Gausto's been busy."

Jet frowned. "I don't understand."

He got to his feet—and now, while she stood quiet and still, he was the one who moved restlessly around the room. Resting his hand on the back of a chair; touching the couch. Hesitating to scent the air—or so it seemed. Jet thought he was looking deeper.

This was the Nick she'd first met on the fairgrounds. Strong again. Powerful. So much of him hidden from her, and so much revealed at the same time. She had no idea what he was thinking...but she could see what he *was.* She took a step closer, stopped herself.

He noticed, of course—because this was the Nick who would notice everything. "Yesterday. Last night. He went after my people."

Jet felt the dread of that. "Because you..."

He interrupted her with a sharp lift of his head, a direct glance. "Because I was out of it. He'd planned to have me, but...*out of it* must have been good enough. He jammed up communications, and he—" His jaw tightened on the words; he looked away from her.

Jet took a careful breath. Careful, because it was hard to breathe at all. "You have to help them."

Because that's what he was. A leader. Not like Gausto, with strutting and threats and power plays, but a leader who cared for his people. She'd seen it out there in the desert, sparring with his wolf. She'd seen it in the way he responded to her even this evening.

And because Jet, too, knew that responsibility, she knew he had no choice. And so the words meant even more, came even harder, when she said fiercely, "I *wish—*"

He met her gaze. Looked at her a long, strong moment—looked at her in a way that managed to suck all the breath from her body.

"There is," she said steadily, "so very much I don't understand. I just know what *is.*"

"Better than almost anyone else," he agreed. He hesitated, and seemed to struggle with…she wasn't sure. Circumstances. Himself. He took a deep breath, jaw working. "You see very clearly. Uncluttered." He took a step closer to her, conflict evident in the hand that closed too tightly over the chair currently between them. "I need that."

"You—" She stopped on that startling thought. She would not have said this man needed anything. "Me?"

"You," he said, a single rough-edged word.

The shirt moved against her bare skin; air stirred across her bare bottom. "You talked to your people," she said, reminding them both. "They need your help."

He didn't look away from her. Steady, that gaze. Her skin tightened down; she felt the pull of him. The impulse to move closer came strongly—but not stronger than the future rushing down.

He would go to them now. He would take her—*try* to take her—with him.

"They needed me last night," he said, an unreadable gleam in his eyes, pale green and all wolf. "Today, they can do without me. Because what they need—what *I* need—is to get to the bottom of this. With you."

The startlement lasted only an instant. She grabbed up his words, and she took that step. "You're not going." Not returning to the city, not taking her in.

He shook his head again, and his expression—set in that groomed face with its groomed hair and thin veneer of civilization—had never looked more wild. More ready. "We're doing this together."

"Your pack?"

"They're doing what they have to. I'm doing what I have to. And you—*Jet*. You're part of that, too."

"Am I?" she asked. Challenging him, in her way. "After I tried to take you down?"

He smiled, with those wild eyes. "But you couldn't do it, could you?"

"I chose not to." Still challenging, if only in the subtle posture of her shoulders, the intensity of her eye. "I'll save my pack in my own way, that I trust."

"Exactly." Another step closer. "And I do *this* my own way." His hands tightened into brief fists; for that instant, she glimpsed a vulnerability—an uncertainty. Only an instant, before conviction returned. "This is the only way to help you…to put brevis back together. The best way to stop Gausto. He won't expect it. He thinks of me as a suit and tie and leather briefcase. He forgets what I *am*."

She bared her teeth at him, briefly. "Who *we* are."

His voice bottomed out. "Are we?"

"Uncluttered," she reminded him, and stepped

closer. He stiffened—holding back, because his human mind was so very cluttered, that was easy to see. Wanting her, wanting to do what was right, unable to see clearly that those things could be one and the same. For now. For always, regardless of what happened after. What choices they made.

No, Gausto's lackeys had not known this man. She had been foolish to listen to them in the desert, stricken and reeling with what they had just done to her.

But they had not known him, while Jet...

Jet knew this man.

Chapter 13

*U*ncluttered.

The gift of Jet: a new concept. What brevis wanted of him didn't necessarily define what he should do. And this new uncluttered heart...it could see that fact clearly.

Who the hell knew?

Jet, barely clothed in the first shirt Nick could grab—material too thin to hide the detail of her body, draping to show hints of athletic curve beneath proud shoulders—Jet knew. Jet, fierce and proud, not intimidated by Gausto or by her situation. Outnumbered in a strange land, without resources...without true knowledge of this aspect of herself.

But Jet knew what she wanted, that too was clear.

She looked at him with the morning light spreading over her shoulders and glinting off her crisp black hair, whiskey gold eyes catching the diffuse waking sun so that the glow seemed to come from within. . "We do this together."

His words, but repeated back at him with a difference in intent. Nick held his ground as she came right up to him, bare feet silent on the tile—stopped only inches away and then studied his face.

Just as she'd done the first time they met, only then her gaze had been impulsive...inscrutable. This time, it held heat. She stood so close, so barely not touching him...so *there*. Her body, her scent, her warmth. The very tickle of her presence. She wasn't Sentinel; she had no sweeping trace, no reaching power.

But she had presence, and it touched him—his heart kicking up into overdrive, his skin tightening to a startlingly sensitive degree. He should have said something, but found himself stricken dumb. He should have stopped her...

But he didn't want to.

She leaned closer; her breath washed over his neck. He closed his eyes, so lost in that simple sensation that he could only clench his hands into fists and just barely hold himself back.

The Sentinels were his people. But Jet...

Jet was his pack.

And she knew it.

Mine, now. Ours. Jet nuzzled him; his breath hitched. She licked at the edge of his jaw; he stopped breathing altogether.

Her hands found his body, molding themselves to the long, lean muscle covering his ribs, flattening at the planes of his chest. She rubbed lightly across flat nipples, watching his face—his eyes closed, and his expression might have been pain.

But probably not.

He didn't reach for her. He still held himself in that control. Maybe he didn't know how to free himself.

Jet knew. Things human were still new and strange—but instinct lay close to the surface, and Jet knew how to do instinct. She let her hands find their own way, happy at the open snap of the shorts. She let her body press up against his, aching for the touch of his skin.

"Jet," he said, a strained whisper.

She reached into his shorts, running her hands along the smooth flesh of his buttocks—tense unto trembling, so tight, so perfect for pulling him closer. He made a desperate noise as their bodies pressed close, and Jet wrapped one leg around him, pulling them even closer—and still he didn't reach for her, so she let herself arch back, pleasuring in the stretch, in the trust of leaving herself so open to him—in the heightened angle of where they met through his shorts. Either she'd fall, or—

He caught her. One hand hooked behind her back, he held her with no effort at all, and the other hand landed under the shirt on the flat of her stomach...possessing her. Jet arched into that, too. "See?" she whispered. "Be free."

"You don't want that," he said harshly. "You don't know what—"

But Jet knew. She pulled herself upright, an effortless motion, found they'd half dislodged his shorts... took advantage of it, swiftly untwining her leg and just as swiftly tugging that clothing away. And then she touched him, held him...stroked him.

"Jet—" He would have stopped her. Barely breathing, every muscle clenched and trembling with response, and he would have stopped her.

She stopped him, instead. "I *do* want," she said. "And I know it. So do you." She laughed, a little breathless—all that heat sparking around inside her, all the aching emptiness and need. "I have been a wolf with wolves, Nick Carter. Do you think I cannot handle a man?"

He growled, deep in his chest; he jerked her in close and threaded his fingers through her hair and kissed her—and if at first she wasn't sure about mouth and lips and tongue, she never doubted that she wanted more of it. As fiercely as he came at her, she drove back at him, grabbing at his shoulders, his arms, his back…it only inflamed him, and this time when she arched back from him, he took the invitation, pushing the oversize T-shirt out of the way so his hands could have her skin—and this time, when she cried out her need, he was the one who grabbed her tighter, pushing against her in ways that made her vision recede to nothing but darkness and sparks.

She lost her language, then—she made a pleading sound, pleasure and exquisite need tangled together. They stumbled a few steps and ended up on the floor, and his hands whispered over her skin, stroked her body—drew from her such intensity of feeling that she quite suddenly knew she'd been wrong. She couldn't handle this at all. She had no *idea*—

The want drove her. She tugged at him, twisting within his hold. Hands and knees, as close as she could get to the way it should be.

He froze; for an instant of breathless *no, no, no, don't*

go she thought she'd done the wrong thing, something to make him think again, and take him back to the place where he forgot how to be free—but with a harsh sound, he hooked a hand around her hip, tumbling her to her side—just rough enough so she resisted it, a snarl of protest and a lunge forward. Just as fast, he pulled her to him, tugging her in tight—his breath at the side of her neck, his teeth at her shoulder…his hand splaying low just where all her ferocity curled into *oh, please*—

She cried out, all protest forgotten, all thought fled. And then he found her ready and he took her from behind and she keened with it, astonished and startled at the feel of him within her. His breath came hard, his teeth resting against her skin, and she snarled protest as he withdrew—she reached behind, her hands scrabbling against his buttocks, urging *oh, please* and then crying out pleasure when he filled her again, his grunt in her ear sounding like pain but so very far from it. And again, and again, while all the sensations built and tightened and sent Jet keening into demand and joy with every thrust, reveling as his breath came harsher and less controlled until a sound of pure deep pleasure finally broke free. Only chance, then, as they moved and clawed and thrust, that her hand found opportunity between them, reaching him—stroking.

He made a surprised noise. A beyond endurance noise, a primal noise, and he embraced her close and tight as he drove wildly from behind, hands just where they needed to be, touching her just so, and Jet—

She—

Oh, please—

A wild cry, as her body came apart around her—

even as he grabbed her close and hard, jerking into her, his fingers gone splayed and stiff, astonishment in his voice.

They trembled through the aftershocks of it into another pleasure altogether. Still close, still tight, still entwined, his body wrapped around hers and his panting breath at the back of her head, his hands still intimate and possessive— and her hands over his, keeping them that way.

Still touching her. Still claiming her. Still holding a body that would never, ever be the same.

Not, Jet realized suddenly, *free.* No longer free in the slightest.

Completely, totally, irrevocably bound.

Free.

Nick took the deepest of breaths, his skin brushing Jet's with the movement.

Free, finally, to do what needed to be done. Not without responsibility…but months of preparation had given him people to depend on. Lyn would handle brevis—Lyn *could* handle brevis. She, among all of them, would know who could be trusted and who couldn't.

While Nick himself suddenly understood Dolan Treviño's willingness to go rogue in the field, his tendency to stray far outside the parameters of his assignments. Because right here, right now, Nick should contact Annorah again; he should try his cell service, check the phone…drive down the road to use the same pay phone Jet had used the night before.

Except…

Annorah. He reached out to her without thinking, following up on sudden realization. For Jet had splashed an overload of messages across brevis the night before. And yet...

Nick? She sounded distracted. Not surprising. *You okay?*

Fine, he said, keeping his thoughts as private as possible—keeping from her the sense of Jet still encompassing him, her warm bottom tucked up against him, their legs tangled...her lips and teeth nibbling at the sensitive skin at the inside of his wrist, making his fingers twitch with pleasure. *Annorah, have you heard of any messages left on my behalf last night?*

Her brief silence tasted baffled, and it was all he needed to know. *Do you want me to check on it?*

No. Triage your time. That's answer enough.

Because brevis should have been buzzing with it. Listening to each other's messages, realizing the same woman had left them all, realizing she wasn't on the Sentinel roster. The moment he reached Annorah, there should have been questions.

And that meant brevis communications were still compromised.

And that meant he had no idea how deep it went; it meant he couldn't tell Annorah anything else. It meant communications were *completely* compromised. Trusting Annorah and Lyn meant nothing if someone had the means to eavesdrop on their conversations—and over this distance, it wasn't unheard of, no matter Annorah's skill.

They were on their own. No calling for backup, no warning brevis what he knew, what he had in mind. No heading into Tucson; if Gausto found out—and he *would* find out—he'd take it out on Jet. He still had that amulet.

And if Nick didn't show up at Gausto's place, then...
he'd take that out on Jet as well.

Jet licked the inside of his elbow—a tender-fierce
gesture, possessive as hell. "Who was that?"

His hand had been on its way along her hip, cupping
the curve of her, reveling in soft skin and sleek muscle—
but now it stilled. "You heard that?"

"You," she said. "Talking to someone."

"You shouldn't—" he started—but stopped. Shouldn't
what? Have been able to hear his exchange with Annorah?
Right. Shouldn't *exist,* for that matter. Wouldn't have, if
Gausto hadn't toyed with her very nature.

There was no telling how many ways it had
changed her.

When a Sentinel had his or her first sexual encounter
with another Sentinel, it changed everything. *Initiation,* it
was called, and in that one moment, an individual's powers
achieved fruition...and new powers sometimes bloomed.

But Jet was no Sentinel. Jet wasn't even close. And
Nick had felt nothing of initiation in their encounter, or
in her calm aftermath.

Nick put some attention back to his hand. Jet shifted
into the touch, gorgeous ass settling against him; for an
instant, he lost his train of thought. His body had no such
problem—given what it wanted, it now only wanted
more. She murmured surprise as he grew hard, still
within her, and tipped her hips into the sensation.

He stopped her. "Heart," he said, "I'm trying to
have a brain."

Her silence came puzzled.

"I can't think when you move like that," he told her.
"No more than you can think if I do *this.*" So soft, so

ready…she shifted her leg for him, utterly unselfconscious, and that in turn caressed the entire length of him, and he in turn thrust into the renewed pressure, and Jet moaned, and—

"Hell," Nick said desperately. He clamped a hand on her hip; he clenched his legs and butt, resting his forehead on her shoulder. "Could you…" he said, and grasped at scattering but important concepts, teeth gritted as Jet gently spasmed around him, squirming ever so slightly. "Could you hear us this morning? Right after we—*ah*—got back?"

"Nothing," Jet said, breathless. Breathless and something else—he didn't have to see her expression to know it held that same wild child mix of determination and playfulness he'd glimpsed upon her invitation to romp only the day before.

He closed his eyes. *Think.* Surely he could think. All he had to do here was pull away from her— "This," he said. *Can you hear this?*

"Can you feel *this?*" she responded, doing something with inner muscles that wrenched a gargling noise from him, and again he quivered, and suddenly found his hand down at her soft self, holding her as she held him, fingers gentle and insistent and seeking entrance made impossible because he only encountered himself, already filling her and damn, she moved against him and she knew what she was doing, *exactly* what she was doing, only the tiniest whisper of pressure when any more would have—*damn*—

"I—" he said, and had no idea why. "We—" *Control. Surely he could—*

"I can hear you," she whispered, and clenched around him.

"*I*—"

"*We*," she said fiercely, and did it again.

"*Jet*—"

"*We*," she said, high and breathless and hell, yes, she did it *again*.

And Nick shouted harsh surrender, and gave in to the *we*.

Chapter 14

Nick sat at the table over a cup of coffee, damp from a shower and listening to Jet croon to herself in the guest shower down the short hall, a carefree song with a feral edge.

Brevis was under attack, and he had taken a time-out for not one but two quickies on the living room floor.

Brevis was under attack, and Nick not only wasn't there to help, he had no intention of returning to that compromised situation.

He rummaged around inside himself, looking for the guilt...not finding it.

I'm doing what's right.

For himself, for Jet...even for brevis.

Harder to look away from what he'd done with a woman who didn't even know what it was to be a woman. Not a virgin, no—her previous life hadn't left her one. But not a *person* long enough to know what sex meant to her or what she even wanted it to mean to her. Just someone with a healthy appetite who knew what she wanted and how to get it and who should have been able to depend on him for restraint.

From the shower, she called, "Do you want to do it again?"

No!

Silence. No movement under that water. Hurt.

Yes, dammit! He gusted a sigh out onto the coffee, stirring the dark surface. *But not now. Now, we have to deal with Gausto.*

The water shut off. "Now, we deal with Gausto," she agreed, shoving the shower curtain aside. In short order, she walked into the kitchen, scrubbing the towel over her hair, gloriously naked.

Nick resigned himself to a permanent hard-on.

She could hear him; she couldn't make herself heard. What else they had, Nick couldn't tell. Given time, they'd figure some of it out for themselves. But for the moment what resonated between them was the rich, deep satisfaction of their lovemaking…and the craving for more.

Jet moved around the kitchen without care, though her skin pebbled with goose bumps and her breasts drew up tight. "No wonder this body needs clothes," she said. "Not enough fur."

Wouldn't she just be surprised to learn how hard most women worked to remove every bit of excess hair.

"Will we kill him?" she asked, reaching for her own mug, and for the carton of mixed berry juice in the refrigerator. In spite of their time together, the morning was still only starting, sun-hot sage and cactus and creosote just barely scenting the air.

Her casual attitude startled him. "We shouldn't," he said. Gausto answered to his Septs Prince, the continent-wide leader who had done little more than slap his hand so far, giving him chance after chance to redeem himself. Nick understood it now, finally—that the Septs Prince wanted these things done, these chances taken… he wanted the big wins that Gausto was always promising him, the advantages gained.

He just didn't want to take the risks to get them.

So until Gausto crossed that final line, the prince had been finding a hell of a lot of advantage to letting Gausto take all the risks while the prince repeatedly disavowed him.

Jet gave him a look that said she'd picked up on a good part of his thoughts. "Maybe later, then," she suggested, intent in her gaze.

"Maybe," Nick agreed, and a deep part of him meant it. Within the past year, Gausto had cost the Brevis Southwest too many losses. No one yet even knew the cost of the previous evening.

Because Gausto had *wanted.* He wanted the Liber Nex; he'd come away with his personal ability to use Core workings forever muzzled. He'd wanted the power held in the San Francisco Peaks of Flagstaff; he'd barely escaped the mountain, bleeding and damaged. Now he wanted…what?

As far as Nick knew, this latest assault had one main objective: to take out Nick himself.

While doing as much harm as possible along the

way, of course, because why not take advantage of circumstances?

"You say maybe," Jet said, putting aside the empty mug of the juice she'd finished in swift order, her slender throat moving with each deep swallow, "and you think about *yes* and *no*."

"It's complicated," Nick said. He gestured with a tip of his head and she considered him, amber-gold eyes holding such contemplative expression that Nick took it as warning—a mistake, to assume her straightforward. A mistake to assume anything about her at all, except for the truths she freely offered.

A gift, that she consented to come to him at that gesture, to stand before him as he rose and put a knuckle under her chin and contemplated her features—not soft features, not tender or delicate, but strong bones and exotic angles not the least bit overwhelmed by amazing eyes, large and tipped and thickly lashed. She eyed him back in the same fashion, no more self-conscious about her nudity than she'd been to start with, and Nick shook his head ever so slightly, unconscious betrayal of his amazement in her. He had to close his eyes to take in the enormity of it—this wolf before him, become brilliantly, beautifully human—and when he opened them, he let a hint of a grin take the corner of his mouth and he kissed the fruit juice away from her upper lip.

"Clothes," he told her. "And then I have an idea about Gausto."

She watched his mouth a long moment before responding; she touched her lower lip, as if contemplating the memory of sensations there. Then she headed for the back bedroom, her easy, athletic strides unaf-

fected by her exposed condition. Without bothering to
turn back and throw the words over her shoulder, she
said, "Does it involve killing him?"

He absorbed the low undertone of her voice. The
intent there.

Jet, it seemed, had made her own decisions about
how to handle Gausto's incursions on her pack.

"It's complicated," he said again. "We have certain
hunting rules. Gausto has broken them, but it would be
best if we didn't."

Jet made a disgruntled sound. She disappeared into
the bedroom, and Nick stood in the kitchen nook feeling
unaccountably alone.

He took a deep breath, straightening his shoulders;
stretching his spine. He scrubbed hands over his face
and through his hair, hunting the layers he normally
held in place—between himself and the world, himself
and other people, himself and...himself.

It hit him with a spark of shock that he didn't have
to do that for her. That she not only knew what he was,
but she reveled in it. A slow, quiet grin made his chest
feel lighter than it had in a long time.

Sentinels dead, brevis in disarray, Nick himself
unable to help, and here he was with a grin in his heart.

From the bedroom, Jet made a profoundly startled
noise—a pained noise. Nick flung his foolish grin aside.
"Jet!" But he'd only taken one swift step when it hit him,
the merest echo of what she felt as she cried out again
and lightning ripped through his body and sent him
down. *What the—?* More than pain—a bereft and empty
sorrow, a gaping absence of—

Self.

Jet wailed the *ki-yi-yi* of wolf fear and pain and loss and suddenly he knew, breaking through the unexpected impact of it all to crawl forward, up to his feet and then running—staggering, bouncing off a wall or two and never quite making it upright before he slung around the corner into the guest bedroom and tumbled back down beside Jet.

Gausto. Gausto and his amulet and his threats. He'd told Jet to bring Nick in; he was making sure she didn't forget—didn't think him incapable of following through on his threats. And now, even as the pain faded, as Jet quit jerking in agony and the echoes of it slipped away from Nick's body, she curled up around herself and sobbed like a heartbroken child—her wild ferocity abruptly gutted, her self-sufficiency destroyed.

Nick pulled her into his lap, warm skin reassuring against warm skin, and wrapped his arms around her, and rocked her gently while she clung to him and mourned even that brief absence of her wolf. Dazed himself by what he'd felt in those moments, his own thinking stripped down to the bare core.

The Septs Prince had had his chance to stop this man; he hadn't done it.

Now Nick would.

"Where are you?" Marlee muttered, typing furiously into the instant messaging window. Furiously, because she had only a moment here by herself, while the others put their heads together over the recent security breaches—hunting Marlee, if they but knew it, and leaving her out of the hunt itself simply out of habit.

Typing furiously, indeed; typing at all because she

was desperate. She was in the middle of it, she was in far, far over her head, and she hadn't heard from Gausto.

Because she was beginning to suspect that she wouldn't.

Used...and used...and used. For years, used. And now discarded?

Unfamiliar footsteps made her whirl in the office chair; she was beyond pretending her nerves weren't stretched to the limit. But then, it hardly mattered. After the previous night, they were all on edge. It was only natural that they'd all be affected.

All of them except Dane Berger's executive administrator, apparently. He still looked too slick, too groomed. Where Nick Carter always looked like a man about to break free of the constraints of civilization that he placed on himself, this man looked like someone trying to be what he wasn't. Reaching, rather than restraining.

And therefore dangerous in an entirely different way.

"You've got the look of someone about to fold," he said.

She found herself on her feet. "I was right! You—" She stopped herself, shook her head. No point in that. Not exactly, anyway. "What did you *do* last night? Do you think they're not going to realize that Annorah was drugged?"

"Of course they will." He shrugged. "And who made that last pot of coffee in Carter's community room yesterday at the end of the day? Knowing that some of the others would be working late?"

His words landed cold and hard in the pit of her stomach. "But I didn't—and I wasn't there to see who would drink what!"

He waved her protest away with a manicured hand.

"Doesn't matter. Put it together with all of this—" a gesture at her cubicle space "—and it'll be enough."

"But *why?*"

A raised eyebrow, supercilious and even cruel. "My dear, surely you can see they're going to need a scapegoat. Much better to direct them at only one of us. And you and your second thoughts…did you think they wouldn't be noticed? You were well-groomed, but you've outlived your usefulness."

"My—" For an instant, she was speechless. "I've been working *for* something all this time. A better balance—a more equal way of doing things—"

"Yes, yes," he told her, standing there in the doorway in his overly fussy lightweight tan suit and his limp, too-fashionable hair and his plucked brows and looking down his nose at her—sensible attire, her feet in flats and her Scooby-Doo lunch box peeking out the edge of her cubicle. "The thing is, my dear, we want so much more. So sad for you!"

And he left.

Jet looked at the full-length mirror in the guest bedroom. There she was. Human. By choice, for the moment, but perhaps not always.

Her image glared back at her—an unforgiving expression, paired with a stance that barely fell short of belligerent. Angry at Gausto, angry at this new world she found herself in, angry to be caught up in this conflict between two factions that had nothing to do with her life.

Hadn't had anything to do with her life. Now…it had become her life.

The clothes weren't as fresh as they'd been the day before, but she'd spent enough time not wearing them at all…they'd aired nicely overnight. All black, in spite of the hot sun—because it suited her. Mere leather slippers of shoes on her feet, because that suited her, too. Smooth flesh, faintly tanned; long legs and curves and breasts she hadn't quite gotten used to having at all except that they seemed so important to this body.

So important to Nick, to judge by the amount of attention he gave them.

Human now. That was fine. Her choice, at the moment.

Human always?

Never her choice.

Nick came up behind her, meeting her gaze in the mirror. "Feeling better?"

"Angry," she said. "Feeling angry."

His mouth quirked, ever so briefly. "I see that." Still looking at her through the mirror instead of directly, he passed a thumb over her damp cheekbone. Her eyes shone more then; her nose was a little red, and her cheeks, too. She touched her lips, confirming what she saw—still plump, still wildly kissed.

She narrowed her eyes at her image. With the slightest lift of that plump-kissed lip, she growled at herself.

Nick raised his brows. "What was that for?"

"Reminder," she told him. "Warning. This crying thing…it happens. But it doesn't stop what has to be done."

"Ahh, Jet." He stepped up against her back; he enfolded her defiance into his embrace from behind. And though she could feel that he was again aroused against her, that didn't seem to be what this particular embrace was about. Not as his hand spread across her belly and pulled her in, the other arm encompassing her shoulders; his head nestled in beside hers. He nuzzled aside her naturally short, crisp hair and kissed her neck.

"What?" She twisted to look at him directly instead of finding his gaze in the mirror.

He laughed, muffling it with the ticklish hollow of her neck. "You move me, Heart. That's all." He released her, and turned her away from the mirror. "About what has to be done—"

"I'm going back," she said firmly. "You will not turn me away from his throat again."

"Unless," he said, a hard edge into his low voice, "I get there first."

She stiffened. *"We,"* she told him.

Something glinted in that pale green gaze. "Yes." And then he seemed to give himself an infinitesimal shake—bringing himself back to this moment. "But not like that." He didn't have to explain what *that* meant. They both knew what Gausto deserved, and that it involved teeth and ripping flesh.

She frowned, stepping back from him just enough so his hands fell away.

"Jet," he said. "He's got an amulet linked to the one inside you. He's got people who will pick up some of his work where he left it off—and we can't kill them all."

"We can try." All too easy to bring to mind certain of Gausto's men—those who had poked and prodded her upon arrival as wolf, those who had jeered her those first days as woman, those who had put hands on her—

No, come to think of it…those two hadn't come back. She didn't know if she'd crippled them or if Gausto had sent them elsewhere.

"It's...*complicated*," he said, and his jaw hardened in brief frustration. "He's hurting my people, Jet. *Stealth amulets.* If the rest of the Core doesn't know about them, they will soon. So I need to find information. Samples. *Something* that will help us formulate a defense. Especially while brevis is compromised."

"And we can't do that if we run straight at them," Jet said, reluctant in that conclusion—but seeing it clearly all the same.

He shook his head. "You need to take me in," he told her.

She stared at him in shock. "No!"

He stood his ground—physically, and with the energy of his intent. "Just as Gausto asked."

She narrowed her eyes. "No. That is not being *we*."

He laughed—short, without humor. "It can be. If we work together. It's the only chance we have to get everything we need out of it. The amulet he's using on you, your pack's freedom, intel on the new stealth techniques he's using against us. And Gausto himself." He hesitated. "Jet, I've been dealing with this man for a long time. With his family, with his people. I know how to do this."

"You!" she said, and her emotions careened unfamiliar and wild. "Have you been captive in this den of his? Have you been his *experiment?* Have you watched what makes him feel important and seen his expression when another of you dies?"

"None of those things," he told her, and instead of reeling back from her sudden intensity, he stepped right up into it. "That's why *I need you*." He hesitated long enough for that to get through the churning sensations in her chest, the floundering thoughts—memories tangled with intent. "I know how to approach it, Jet. You know how to handle the fine points once we get there. If you take me in, you're still in the position to do that. Gausto may think he has me, but it'll be our way to have *him*."

She kept her narrowed gaze on him, unconvinced—too horrified at the thought of turning him over to Gausto to see past it. "He wants to hurt you. I heard what he told his prince—his dominant. He has no retribution, only hate. He has no justice, only cruelty." She looked at him in sudden surprise. "I wouldn't have known that before spending time with you. The differences."

"Jet—"

She hadn't expected to see him nonplused. "He doesn't use the same patterns we do, wolf. He is twisted."

"Jet," he said again. And then, eyes closed briefly as he took a deep breath, only to open them and pin her with pale green alpha honesty. "That's why I need you. That's why we have to do this thing. Because of what he is. For so many reasons, we have to stop him. And this is how."

She growled again, the noise slipping out of her in spite of herself. "We free my pack."

"Yes." He met her gaze straight on.

"We take his power over my wolf."

"Yes."

"We find how he hides his amulets from you."

"Yes."

"And your people can't help."

"We can't *go* to them for help," he said. "There are some I trust…but I can't reach them without exposing us to those I don't."

"So we do this alone."

The slightest shake of his head. His eyes glittered hard—intent and readiness. *"Together."*

"Together," Jet agreed. She waited long enough for him to see her acquiescence, her own readiness. "Tell me your how."

But she didn't wait so long that he could see beyond it to the resistance—the part of her determined that Gausto would never get his hands on this man—this *wolf*—of hers.

For Gausto, in all he had so callously done with and to her, for all he had killed her pack members...he had also cherished them—in his own way, for his own means.

Jet had a good idea what he would do to one whom he called enemy.

Marlee stared at her keyboard, her heart pounding. *I wasn't wrong. I had good reason for everything I did.*

But maybe Gausto had been the wrong partner.

Because maybe, if the strong-blooded Sentinels needed some balance, their mission was nonetheless a valid one. And their opinion of the Core...

Probably not too far off the mark.

And so Marlee had been working with a man who had done just as she should have expected...if her thoughts hadn't been so full of fear and resentment that she grasped for any opportunity to make herself feel better.

She couldn't even say when it had started. So young, with the little strong-blood who hadn't yet learned his own strength. The badly broken bone she'd gotten for his failure—the betrayal she'd felt when he hadn't been punished. Extra training, that's all he'd gotten, while everyone made so sure he knew it wasn't punishment, simply necessity.

Marlee, at four years old, thought that a few hours in time-out would have been fair. Even learning, later, that the boy had been restricted from running for the same amount of time she'd been in the leg cast…it hadn't seemed enough.

She frowned, thinking about that. Six weeks of no running…to an active boy, it was indeed a significant punishment. How he must have chafed! And he certainly would have understood what it meant to be injured and mundanely human—something all the strong-bloods had trouble grasping as children, when they healed so fast themselves.

So why…? *Why* did she think of that time as though the boy hadn't been punished?

It doesn't seem fair, does it? That's what the nurse had said to her—a brevis employee, another light of blood like herself. A woman checking her toes for swelling and proper circulation while the boy played with his friends—for he still played freely, if not allowed to run. And Marlee the child, wounded and hurting, sorry for herself and feeling unprotected, less important…

Marlee had agreed.

But now that she thought about it, she hadn't started feeling those things until after this woman started her daily after school follow-up care.

Scowling at the keyboard, she forced herself to think back through all the resentment and childhood hurt, back to right after it had happened. In the hospital… right before she'd been allowed back to school…before the nurse had taken up her care in the Sentinel after school training program.

She'd had ice cream. She'd had attention. She'd been... Special.

And yet somehow, once she'd spoken to that nurse, she'd never felt special again. Reassurance from her parents meant nothing. Smiles from her teachers, nothing. It seemed there was always someone in the background, whispering in her ear—the unfairness of it, the entitled attitude of the Sentinel children, the way they used their abilities to get what they wanted. And eventually, Marlee had seen enough and heard enough that she didn't need those whispering adult voices in her ear.

She'd become her own.

You were well-groomed, her unwanted visitor had just said.

Surely not. Surely she hadn't been targeted at *four years old,* vulnerable because of the accident. Surely her life hadn't been *orchestrated.*

But when she thought of Gausto—how he'd treated her, so full of manners and respect and pleasantries...so very grateful to her. Right up until these last couple of days.

Because now he wasn't trying to fool her any longer.

"Did you not think I'd figure it out this fast?" she asked her keyboard and the silent instant messaging interface. "Or did you just think I couldn't do anything about it once I did?"

Either way, he'd been wrong.

Chapter 15

Nick wore Gausto's second amulet.

Even dead and deactivated—as dead as he could make it—it burned cold against his skin. To truly nullify it would have meant destroying it, and that would have defeated the purpose entirely.

Jet hadn't wanted to use it at all. Hadn't wanted to pull it out of her bike saddlebags, or to trigger it, or to lay it gently in his hand.

But he'd been ready for it this time. And what Gausto didn't know…it could definitely hurt him.

For Nick could kill amulets. Even this one, given the right circumstances.

"I still don't like it." Jet pulled off her helmet in Gausto's wide circle of a driveway. He'd gone without one, ensconced behind her on the bike, his hands on the narrow sweep of her waist and her firmly rounded bottom snugged up between his thighs. Forty minutes north and into Oro Valley, past gated driveways and expensive homes carved into the sere, dry sides of the Tortolito Mountain formations and onto the winding dirt road that led them to this particular expensive home, set back on plenty of acreage with mountain ridges curving around it. Private. Distant. Dangerous.

"It's the only way," Nick told her, not for the first time. "He has to believe I'm under your control. Let him think you used this thing." If it wasn't blistering his flesh, it sure as hell felt like it. "He might believe you could overpower me in the wake of that first amulet, but—"

"Yes, yes," she interrupted. "But not that you would ride the bike with me. I *know*." But she scowled, pushing the kickstand into place and settling the bike against it.

"Hey." He stilled, and it brought her gaze to him. He couldn't do what he wanted to do—he couldn't take her in his arms and tell her everything would damned well be all right. Not with Gausto's men watching...and not when it might be a lie.

So he held his gaze steady, and he held his body quiet. The driveway curved around them, nature buffered from Gausto's activity. A road runner scooted off to the side, raptorlike, and gave them an accusing look before disappearing into the xeriscaping. When she finally relaxed, quieting her wolf, he split his attention.

Annorah, he called, seeing the flicker in Jet's eyes that reminded him she, too, could perceive his communications.

Annorah's response came delayed but eager. *Nick? What's happening?*

He shook his head—not a physical gesture, but an internal sensation that Annorah would recognize. *No details. I'm sure of it. Brevis is compromised.*

You don't think someone's figured out how to tap in—! Her thought disappeared in a huff at the very notion, but she was back soon enough. *Not with me. I'd know.* And then, at his silence, annoyance filtered through. *If you aren't going to tell me anything, why did you call? And are you sick? You don't feel right.*

I'll tell you this, Nick said, watching Jet's eyes widen. *I'm doing exactly what Joe Ryan tried to do in Flagstaff. And I'm going to stay open—you can trace me down.* No one with a tap would be able to do that—it took direct connection, and Annorah's skill. *You know who you trust. Tell only them.*

Don't you just make it all sound easy, Annorah grumbled. *Nick, I don't—*

You'll figure it out.

"Come with me," Jet said roughly, suddenly. She tossed her leather jacket across the bike, grabbing Nick's arm and hauling him toward the house—toward the two Core guards who had emerged from the shadows of the big blocky adobe house to scowl at them. Typical Core muscle, with black hair slicked back, silver jewelry in abundance, and olive skin flushed under the heat of the Tucson sun. Jet didn't hesitate, striding along with her hand above his elbow.

"What's going on?" one of the men demanded, one hand resting inside his suit jacket. So subtle.

"Gausto told me to bring this man," Jet said flatly,

steadying Nick as he put some sway into his movement. "You are in my way."

They exchanged a glance between them; she bared teeth in a subtle expression, every nuance of her posture proclaiming herself beyond their authority—shoulders back, body held tall and proud, gaze directly pinning theirs.

He didn't think they'd linger in her path.

And they didn't, stepping aside to let her pass—if not without a shared leer that Jet pretended not to see.

Nick barely managed the same. Protective anger swelled behind his facade, threatening to break out into the wolf right then and there. Take them down, for the implication of what they'd do if they had the chance.

Get a grip. Jet was depending on him. The Sentinels were depending on him. Even Jet's pack was depending on him.

The walkway curved around the house, splitting off to a showy front entrance—Jet ignored it—and around to the shadows of the rear entry. A camera tucked away into a high corner, trained on the doorway; Gausto had taken no chances with this new hideaway. Unlike the rented facilities outside Sonoita, unlike the hotel room of Flagstaff...this was the home base they hadn't been able to find.

I hope you're paying attention, he told Annorah, following Jet to the door in puppet mode.

Joe Ryan, Annorah said promptly. *I get it. I think. He—* Gone.

Just like that, gone.

The amulet-driven protective workings around the building kicked in, flooding over Nick with a surge of tainted energies. Stolen energies, stored energies...

trapped and decaying energies always yearning to find their way back to their natural state. The amulets hid this place much as wards protected Nick's home. Gausto might know where Nick lived, but he had no way to discern what went on within the property—and no way to penetrate the area with any hostile workings. Not so much as a probe.

Jet glanced at him, her eyes gone wary.

Gausto has protections on this place, he said, fighting a sudden surge in the burning amulet—cool braided leather cord, cold-hot metal, cruel, cruel intent. *It's why we couldn't find it before now.* And then, on second thought, *You* can *still hear me?*

She didn't do anything so blatant as nod; just the slightest tip of her chin. Her expression, if anything, looked more determined than ever. As she reached for the door, she glanced at the camera and around them— and managed, with that single eloquent expression, to convey her concern: if Gausto might somehow tap into Annorah's communications, then why not those between the two of them?

In other words, maybe he'd better shut up.

Nick kept his grin from showing up—mostly. Just a twitch at the corners of his mouth, the camera ever in mind. *I'm not truly sending. You're picking up.* But even so…. *I'll keep it quiet,* he told her. He didn't dare raise active personal wards in this environment—Gausto no doubt had detection in place for such things.

The amulet bit at him, sending the long hallway reeling; only Jet kept him upright. Down the hall, past a small room with an open door from which wafted Jet-scent, past a bathroom…past several closed doors.

Nick's sense of direction told him they'd gone beyond
the house and into the hill behind it; when Jet took him
down a half flight of stairs, he was sure of it.

The air grew thicker...muskier. Dog and wolf,
mingled in close quarters. Sick animals...unhappy
animals. Jet stopped outside the door set at the foot of
those stairs, reaching for the pad beside the door—a
palm scanner, flashing bright lime-neon and LED red
lights turned Christmas tree green at the calm pressure
of her hand, clicking the door open. Did Gausto really
trust her so much?

More likely, he trusted in his own power and control.
Overconfident.

And then she opened the door.

Not just a house. A Frankenstein lab of modern
proportions.

A huge room, cavernously large. A kennel area lined
the entire back wall; individual kennels were positioned
sporadically around the side walls. Metal exam tables,
surgical spotlights, instrument bays...Nick set his jaw
and held his tongue.

Jet had less success. She stiffened beside him, her
fingers tightening down on his arm, a pained noise
escaping her throat.

Harder than holding himself back from protecting her
outside, this was. The urge to pull her into his arms—

But she wouldn't want that. She was a fighter, his Jet.
A hunter. She neither needed nor wanted coddling. And
now a low sound vibrated in her chest.

No wonder. It took everything Nick had to maintain
his distant expression as the full stench of the place hit
him—antiseptic mixed with pungent Core workings,

hardly indistinguishable from the scent of illness and infection permeating the place.

The wolves, crammed into close quarters and dull of fur and eye, nonetheless watched Jet with a keen and eager eye. They might not understand what had befallen them here, but they knew she was one of them. They knew she could be trusted.

The other creatures here didn't fare even as well. A few purebred dogs—a Great Dane, a Bernese Mountain Dog, a Kuvasz—all depressed and thin, circling desolately in dirty, cramped kennels. Man's best friend, languishing in isolation and callous circumstances.

On the other side of the room, the kennels held...

Nick wasn't sure. Couldn't make visual sense of it at first, and then didn't want to. Limbs and fur and human skin; fingers here, distorted joints there. A giant tongue lolling out of a marginally human face, another face so jumbled that even identifying the basic features proved impossible. From this side of the room came the stench. Twisted beings, unable to function...unable to survive. And yet unable to die mercifully without help.

Jet sent him a hard glance; he realized he'd lost his impassive mien—that he'd straightened, metaphorical hackles raised and a growl vibrating deeply in his own chest. Her glance shot right, then left—alerting him to the presence of two men. Assistants, guards...hard to tell. Instead of suits they wore black workout pants and snug black polo shirts—the Core had a color theme, all right—and they looked entirely capable of providing muscle where it was needed.

And then there was Gausto. Turning away from one of the kennels with a smaller man by his side, both in lab coats—not all that imposing after all. The smaller man held himself with much deference; for all he had classic Core coloring and presentation, he emanated none of the arrogance, none of the confidence...none of the outright cruelty. His movement was more of a scuttle than a walk, and Nick instantly pegged him as a Core tech nerd.

Because Gausto can't handle the workings himself. Not any longer. Not after Meghan Lawrence had tricked him into a warded cage at his own command. Coyote's daughter, indeed. Grim satisfaction tried to find its way to his expression; he forced that part of himself more deeply inside.

"Jet," Gausto said, moving to the center of the room—there, by the metal table with drain gutters around the outside edges, stains on the concrete floor. "I am not pleased that I had to send messengers to you."

"I was confused," Jet admitted without hesitation. But she stood before him without deference—subtle postural cues he didn't seem to be able to read, although he looked at her with a faintly dissatisfied frown—and something more. Possessiveness. *Greed.* He came toward them, his gait uneven and his movement...Nick would have called it pained. Lyn had left her marks on him after all, there on the top of the San Francisco Peaks. Ocelot fury. *Good.*

"Eduard," Gausto said, so casually, "Please make sure our protégé understands her situation."

His assistant blinked—looked as though he might protest—but instead quickly looked away, dipping his hand into one of the many pockets of his unusual lab coat.

Nick felt the impact of it from the inside out as Jet cried out, crumpling to the hard floor with a boneless grace. He almost dove for her. He almost broke cover and doomed them both, gathering her up in his arms to tremble out her pain. He almost leaped upon the smaller man, ripping the triggering amulet away and destroying it with a single targeted blast of power—resonating energies, applied just so.

But no. To save them both—to save her pack, to stop the attack on the Sentinels—he couldn't do so much as glare. She writhed a futile attempt to escape, and the best he could do—the very best he could damned well do—was to let himself falter and fall to his knees beside her, one hand coincidentally landing on her torso where he could squeeze, ever so gently. *I'm here.* He risked it. *I'm with you.*

Damned useless.

Hang in there, Jet.

But Gausto raised an abrupt hand, and Eduard the amulet tech relaxed, and Jet's agony faded from Nick's body. She stilled—if only long enough to gather herself, ready to twist and launch and—

Nick closed his hand—only an instant of pressure, and Jet checked herself.

But Gausto had seen that fleeting defiance. He might not realize how deep it had been, or how close he'd come to fighting off alpha bitch revenge, but he'd sensed it. "Ah," he said, his eyes heavy-lidded and his face holding something suspiciously like satisfaction, "you *don't* understand, do you? Not quite yet." He jerked his head at Nick, and the two men strode in to take his arms, jerking him to his feet.

Let it happen, he told himself, keeping his gaze from meeting Jet's—all too afraid of what he'd trigger within her. He kept himself unresisting in their rough hands; kept himself from turning loose on these two, whose evident skills would nonetheless never stand up to a Sentinel in full action.

Not even one under the pounding assault of a largely nullified amulet with the remnants of his lover's agony still washing through his body.

"He should have been wolf." Gausto moved up to Nick, the halting nature of his gait more evident than it had been. Nick hoped it hurt like hell. "He should have been completely subdued wolf. Not this walking puppet."

Jet's voice came thick. She sat straighter with caution. Cement dust coated her shirt and dulled her hair. "He resisted," she said simply. "This is how it worked. So I brought him."

Gausto released a thoughtful huff of air. "I suppose you did well at that. It really is a shame, then, that I can no longer trust you."

Jet glowered. "I did as you asked."

Gausto laughed—dark, and again with that gleam of possessiveness. "I had to insist, didn't I? You defied me. All those hard-learned lessons…how quickly you forgot them." He shook his head; silver jewelry flashed in the harsh overhead lights. "I should have realized, of course. Once on your own, you reverted to true nature." He turned to his assistant. "That's the challenge, you see. The dogs…they don't quite have what it takes to go out and handle a complicated task. And my little wolf bitch…untamed, in spite of all the time we spent together."

Jet flashed him a dark look, making it clear enough what she thought of *all that time.* "Then let me go," she said, her voice low and somehow full of threat. "Let all of us go. We are of no use to you."

Gausto's smile invoked another snarl down deep inside Nick. Easier to hide it this time, with the amulet spilling its diluted poison into his system—harder to hide his alarm at that realization. They'd thought the thing more inert than this.

Gausto didn't notice…too tied up in his satisfaction. "I'm afraid you misunderstand, Jet, my dear. You are, in fact, plenty of use to me. You see, it occurred to me, somewhere about the time he—" and he pointed to a lump of fur and flesh that had no discernible identity at all "—resisted so strongly that he did *that* to himself…I might be going at this the wrong way. Taking dumb animals and applying intricate workings…so many variables. But if I swap the transformation around…" He let his words trail off, raising his eyebrows with meaning, opening his arms in a *there you are* gesture.

Jet scowled at him without understanding.

But Nick understood. Nick understood plenty. Gausto thought he'd done it: the Atrum Core Holy Grail. He thought he'd developed a working that would reliably transform human to animal.

"I see you don't follow me." Gausto's focus on Jet went beyond paternal. "Possibly you consider me power-crippled—but when it comes to the workings I want to apply to myself, I'm far from out of practice— didn't you realize?"

"I did not think about it," Jet said, her disdain coming through.

"Ah, there it is again. Defiance. Trying to think on your own. It's a pity you won't have that chance." He gave her a paternal smile, a satisfied expression. "The truth is—I don't need you any longer, my dear Jet, because very soon, I can *become* you."

Jet recoiled, deeply offended. "You cannot," she snarled at him. "Release me. Release *him.* Then you will see the difference!"

"Ah, yes," he said. "Lessons to relearn." He waved a hand toward one of the empty kennels. "Put her there for now, and then prepare her room."

One of Nick's attendants broke off and went to Jet, his faint hesitation telling its own story. She rose to her feet on her own—took a single, reluctant step toward her prison. Gausto added, "And strap this one to the table. Time for a chat."

Nick stiffened in spite of himself. Once he was on that table…

He risked a quick glance at Jet. So many reasons to be here…*free her people…free her of the amulet…find information on the stealth amulets.* But they'd be lucky to leave at all, never mind with any of those things accomplished. Cut off from brevis—*I should have known*—faced with experiments gone far beyond what he'd imagined—*I should have known*—they'd played this deception about as far as it would go.

This was my *idea,* he shot at her, a quick burst with such hard energy that she stumbled, and Eduard, startled, slapped at his many amulet pockets, where something had no doubt reacted. Gausto's eyes instantly narrowed, his attention shooting in on Nick. *Don't you forget it. My idea!*

She stared back at him without comprehension—but when Nick moved, she responded with gleeful ferocity anyway. For when Nick moved—

He *moved.*

He jerked the amulet free of his neck, closing his hand around it—completing its destruction and flinging away the remaining crumbs of metal. He turned on the man beside him, a human snarl on his lips and all his wolf's strength drawn from within—the man was fast, he was trained...he was good. But he couldn't beat the reflexes of a wolf, a palm-strike to center chest—hard enough to break bone.

To stop a heart.

The man went down in a heap, and by then Jet had leaped for her escort, taking the change in midleap so he winced away from flashing blue energy an instant before black paws slammed into his chest, taking him down before powerful jaws. His collarbone cracked; his head slammed back into concrete.

And Jet, more than just wolf, instantly whirled from him, knowing as well as Nick that their only recourse lay in speed—and in stopping the man who could take them both down.

Not Gausto.

They turned on Eduard. Gausto staggered backward as Eduard screamed high and thin and turned to flee—one futile step before Nick snagged his arm, slung him around, and went for not the man, but the coat—ripping it open, ripping it down off Eduard's shoulders. Jet snagged material with her teeth on the way by, finishing the process—slinging the coat and its many amulets into the very far corner of the vast room and then whirling to set herself in guard, head low and tail stiff and golden eyes shining with determination.

Eduard dove a hand into a voluminous pants pocket,

withdrawing it to spill coins and keys and paper clips across the floor, a clatter lost in the sudden cacophony from the kennels—wolves howling excitement, the dogs roused to barking, the distorted creatures wailing in what might have been hope. Nick snatched his wrist, closing his grip tight—breaking bone without remorse. He caught the man's terrified gaze and held it, snarling with threat—with intent. *Submit or die.*

"My God," Eduard gasped. "He is right! You cannot be allowed—"

Screw this. Nick slammed a precise strike to the man's temple; Eduard dropped like a rock. And then, because *time, time* with Gausto crying alarm and backup surely on the way, he ran for the kennels. "Keep the coat," he told Jet, fumbling with the first latch. "The control amulet is inside. My people will work it out." *Yes!* The first door opened; Nick swung it wide, ignoring Gausto's howl, his scrabbling at surgical supplies. A risk, but...*no time...*

The second door...the latch was gummed and damaged from the wolves' attempts to chew it through. Nick fumbled with it, sparing a quick glance at Jet. *Once they're out, see if you can get them out. Keep them together. I'll find you. We'll keep them safe—*

The gun's muted hydraulic *thwp* didn't come unexpected—neither did the hot slam into his shoulder. Nick gritted his teeth, sprang the latch—sprang aside. Wolves poured out—snarling, snapping—warning Nick off.

No warning needed. He staggered to the final kennel door, knowing he wouldn't make it to free the dogs— already swearing to return and tear this place down, his shoulder burning hellfire. A glance showed him Gausto in flight, clawing for the top of one of the dog kennels. *Go,* he told Jet. *Go with them. Get them outside. I'll be right behind you.* Sentinels…damned hard to kill.

One of the reasons the Core worked so hard at it.

Jet hesitated, the coat in her teeth, haunches coiled and ready and trembling. *Get out of here!* he shouted at her, loudly enough to break through the chaos and uncertainty. *Before they use that amulet against you somehow—*

It was enough. Snarling conflict, Jet sprinted for the door, gathering the attention of her milling pack as she nudged it open. First one, then another…slipping away as Gausto shouted profanities at them.

Just this final kennel door to go and the captive wolves were already whining after their pack members, staring with fierce intensity at the exit. Just this one more…

But the third latch resisted him. He couldn't see just why. Blood splatted at his feet—his own. His movements, slow and thick…his mind, slow and thick. *Go,* he told Jet. *Find them a spot. Go back to my place…use my phone…call for…call for…*

Too thick to send, those thoughts. He staggered back against the stout wire of the kennel, thinking, finally, to slap at his shoulder. Dull surprise fell leaden in his chest at the thick barrel beneath his questing fingers. *Trank…*

Couldn't even finish out the word in his thoughts. Just the vague realization that Gausto had made a weapon of it, doing damage and pumping the drugs at the same time. Blood crept down his arm in a steady stream; the chaos around him receded into a dull, slow gray fog…

But only until he felt a cold, questing nose…a gentle tongue on his cheek, followed by the rough nip of teeth. He didn't recall his descent to the floor—only realized that his knees and elbows and shoulder hurt from the impact. "Coming," he told Jet in a mumble, and then realized—*Jet*—and dragged his head up to find her there, crouching low and submissive but insistent, her teeth exposed with worry. "Oh, *hell.*"

A shout in the background; a clang of noise. *"Go,"* he said. "I mean it. They'll come for…"

They'll come for…

They'll…

Jet growled, grabbed his wrist from the floor by his head—on the floor again—and tugged. Not gentle.

And then she spasmed, her teeth closing down hard, powerful jaws grinding. Change energies flashed high and hard as her agony twisted them both; the electric blue-white of it engulfed them, for that brief instant melding them into an echo of determined thought. *I won't let them catch you I won't leave without you save yourself!*

But it was too late for them both.

Chapter 16

Marlee walked past the espresso machine in the community room. With her hands shaking this much, she hardly needed an intense shot of caffeine.

But if Anthony Warner, executive assistant and professional sneak, thought he'd be able to reach Gausto today, he was sadly mistaken.

Hacking the phone system had been easy; Gausto had already put her through those paces. Hacking the exec's computer had been even easier—she was here to fix the network; she certainly knew how to break it.

Not coincidentally, there was also an abnormal amount of cell phone interference currently in play around the building. As if an organization like the Sentinels didn't have cell phone jammers, and as if Marlee didn't know how to find them. Inconvenient for everyone else in the building, but then again…the important stuff was coming through Annorah and her crew.

And still, her hands shook. Because eventually, someone would figure it out. Eventually, the finger would point at Marlee.

Eventually, she'd have to explain.

She headed for the refrigerator with its bottles of stress tea.

"I'm telling you, it's everywhere." That was Lyn's voice, frustrated. "But it's too subtle. Except for those first, definite traces—oh. Marlee." That last as she came around the corner, and although Lyn didn't outwardly reflect her ocelot with anything other than a natural smudge of liner around large brown eyes, at that instant, everything about her shouted *huntress*—from her instant intensity to the tension in her strong, petite form. Marlee, one hand on the open refrigerator door and a bottle of tea in the other, fumbled the tea.

Joe Ryan came right behind Lyn, and if he waited for Marlee to set the tea on the counter, it was a brief respite. "What she means is, we were looking for you."

We. All of them, coming into the room. Joe Ryan, who had misused his unimaginable control over the earth's natural power flows. Dolan Treviño, whom no one ever trusted to do as told. Meghan, who could create such powerful wards that the *aeternus contego* she'd placed on Gausto had crippled him for life. Quiet, strong Maks, chafing in his final days of convalescence here.

Exactly the kind of overconfident, overreaching Sentinels Marlee had been working against.

And yet suddenly, they seemed like the only chance Nick Carter had.

Maybe the only chance this entire brevis region had, with reports of ambush and wounded Sentinels still trickling in from the night.

They filled the room, those five Sentinels. Marlee slipped a hand into her pocket, fingering the thumbnail drive. It didn't tell them anything they didn't already know, not since Carter had contacted Annorah. But it still represented everything gone wrong with Marlee.

Joe reached beside her, took the tea, popped the metal screw top, and handed back the hefty glass bottle. "You see, the Core's been using stealth amulets and stealth workings. It's a new thing…we've been trying to figure them out for a while. Almost meant the end of me up on the mountain, in fact—that's how they tied my trace to power there. Made me look like the problem."

Marlee's eyes widened slightly in spite of herself. She hadn't realized…hadn't been privy to those reports. But now that he said it…

It quite suddenly made perfect sense.

He had horrifying, frightening power…but he hadn't been dirty at all.

Ryan seemed to see it in her. He raised one eyebrow over a dusky hazel eye…a cougar's eye. "The thing is, Lyn *can* detect them." He glanced at Lyn, then, the faintest smile at the corner of his mouth.

"The thing is," Lyn said dryly, her nose faintly wrinkled, "you stink of them."

Marlee startled. She clutched that cold tea bottle. "I—I *what?*" She had no amulets. She would never touch an amulet. She would never allow Core workings to be placed upon her. She put a hand flat to her chest, as though she would suddenly detect something.

"What—?" she asked, looking down at herself. "What are they—?"

Lyn started to shake her head—but broke off the gesture, turning to the doorway. "Annorah," she said, and an instant later, running footsteps on carpet reached Marlee's ears and Annorah herself spun through the doorway, catching her balance on the frame. "Oh, God," she said, too breathless for coherent speech. "You're all here. I just—I didn't know what to do—he said communications aren't safe...trust no one—" and her eyes cut to Marlee.

"We're taking control of the situation now," Lyn interrupted. "No more super wards, no more skulking around following trace when we're pretending we're not. No more pretending all this sneezing is allergies, either."

Marlee looked at her in surprise—remembering, quite suddenly, the spate of sneezing Lyn had gone through in the hall outside the IT room. Not dust after all. *You stink of them.* She would have backed away from herself if she could. Oh, God. What had Gausto done to her?

"Relax," Meghan said, not unkindly. "We would have done something right away if it was harmful. And I warded you days ago against further influence."

Meghan, hanging around her computer station. Just chatting. Right.

"You don't understand," Annorah said. "He called me. He's in the thick of something and we got cut off *and we need to find him.*" She barely stopped for breath, forging ahead—wild-eyed, utterly devoted to this man and his cause and his brevis, and Marlee felt a stirring of unfamiliar shame.

"Carter takes pretty good care of himself," Treviño noted, his dark tone utterly characteristic.

"No! That's just it! He said he was doing what Joe did on the Peaks and seemed to think we could find him that way and I think he wants us to find him that way, but I was *there* and I still don't know what that means or how we can—"

It was Maks who acted, striding across the room to take Annorah's head between his hands and look into her eyes and hold her there. He didn't say anything...he often didn't say anything. A sudden stab of cold, sharp envy took Marlee's breath away...made so much clear to her. How much she wanted what she couldn't have, in so many ways. How much she'd let that color her decisions. After a moment, Annorah took a deep, sudden breath, closed her eyes, and let it out slowly. "Okay," she said. "I can think now. I'm okay." She clasped her hands around Maks's wrists, squeezing them in gratitude, and he stepped away.

"No thinking necessary," Ryan said dryly. "I know exactly what he's talking about. He's going to the source, damn him."

"The source," Marlee repeated, words faint from all the shocks of the past few minutes.

But Treviño knew. "Gausto."

"Gausto," Lyn agreed.

And if Maks said nothing, the look on his face was enough.

Some of Annorah's panic returned. "But I didn't have time to trace him. I only know he's north of the city."

Ryan didn't hesitate. "It's more than we had. You can get us close. Lyn can track Nick's trace. And if they've disturbed the power flow, I can follow it." He looked at Dolan. "We're enough for a team, all of us."

"Maks isn't cleared," Meghan said, sending a worried look at the big man—another one of those moments that made Marlee aware, all over again, that she stood on the outside looking in—but it was suddenly a wistful awareness.

Because she'd begun to wonder how much she'd put herself there to begin with.

Lyn's peremptory response startled Marlee back to the here and now. "I went through Nick's IN basket this morning. Maks is good."

Even Maks gave her a look of surprise at that. Lyn amended, "He's good *enough.* Call it an executive decision and I'll take the blame when Medical blows up on us."

And if Meghan looked worried and Lyn looked a little grim, Maks himself sported a sudden grin.

Annorah's sudden frustration came through loud and clear. "I can't believe he thinks someone is listening— *reporting*—to Gausto."

Lyn glanced at Marlee, then dismissed her. Not Marlee, with her weak blood. Of course not. "There's too damn much trace built up these past couple of days, even with the stealth. There's no way I can pin it down…I'm drowning in the damn stuff." Her voice reflected it, hoarse with irritation.

"Put the place on lockdown," Dolan growled, looking at Marlee—obviously including her in the category of things to be locked down. "There's someone else at work here. She can't have done it all."

There it was. The first finger, pointed. But no one greeted it with surprise. Dully, through the roaring in her ears and the faint gray layer over her vision, Marlee realized that they not only knew, but they'd *known*.

"Shut the place down," Maks agreed, speaking up for the first time. "We can't let word of this get out to Gausto."

The prospect turned the room grim. Brevis had enough troubles right now…shutting it down would leave so many of the field Sentinels out in the cold; it would make it difficult to bring in the support they might need to care for their wounded.

It would keep Annorah and her people from communicating outside the building—from letting any of the others know what was going on. Annorah looked as though she might cry at the prospect—but she offered no protest.

Marlee closed her eyes. Only moments before, in this empty room, she'd realized it: eventually, she'd have to explain.

Eventually was *now*.

"We don't have to go to lockdown," she said, opening her eyes to discover she had their complete attention—sharp gazes, a small group of elite hunters all focused on her. She forced her voice steady, her thumb stroking over the small keychain drive in her pocket—drawing strength from the determination she'd heard in the voice of the woman who'd left her messages for Marlee to find. "The man you want is Anthony."

Chapter 17

Jet grasped at the pieces of herself. Layered in icy-slick pain, her thoughts scattered…wolf patterns shoved into human mind, wolf senses shoved into human body. Silent cries of protest whirled into confusion; an anguished cry of pain echoed in her mind.

Finally, a familiar sensation settled within her. *Breathing.* She left all else behind, focusing on that panting gasp of air. Slowly it settled—still strained, still rapid—and then it evolved, turning into a pattern of comfort. Sharp, deep breath in…slower release, with effort behind it. A low moan, barely audible.

It carried her through the confusion and the pain, and then it sustained her.

Until metal clanged beside her head, jerking her to a new awareness. Eyes, human. Hands, shoving herself away from the noise…human. Human alone.

"Shut the hell *up!*" an annoyed male voice snapped as Jet blinked the cavernous workroom into focus. Kennel doors, swinging ajar—and three wolves still trapped in the final section. Jet didn't know their names; they'd needed no names in the wild. They'd simply known each other. The pale bitch who'd joined them the season before their capture, the tawny youngster from the litter after Jet's, the muddy gray bitch whom Jet thought of as *aunt* but who was no relation at all. They milled in their small space, miserable and anxious.

On the floor, a dead wolf, too many tricked-up darts sticking out of his body.

Jet's brother.

Several of Gausto's men moved at the end of the room. They all showed signs of damage—bloodied skin, ragged clothing. The men they'd attacked were being tended—one rolling in pain, one pronounced dead. At the ominous exam table and adjacent rolling cart of instruments, the submissive lab assistant stood pale and shocky, being tended by the woman who had once seen to Jet's own early needs—black hair drawn back in a severe ponytail, black suit tailored tight to her generous curves. A short woman with the same complexion as Gausto, the same penchant for silver jewelry; her fingers flashed with rings under the exam light, but her touch was swift and sure as she plucked an amulet from the table and placed it around the man's neck, murmuring instructions to him.

Gausto stalked the room, his temper boiling big enough to fill the entire space—a phone at his ear and a snap in his voice. Orders, demands...setting things to right. Sending out hunters. The words settled in through her ears and sifted out to make sense in her head. *We*

can't have anyone wondering how a damned pack of
wolves came out of nowhere. Take care of them!

And then she realized she wasn't alone, and she
forgot that she was caged. *Nick.* Her mouth opened; her
voice and tongue and lips wouldn't quite form the word.
She responded with instinct, dropping to nudge him—
and remembered again that she had no muzzle, no
scenting nose…and withdrew.

Nick. She'd meant to save him. To drag him out of
this place over her back, if she had to. But she hadn't
known that one of Gausto's people, upon finding the
coat she'd dropped, would know which amulet controlled her. Or how to use it.

Nick. He sprawled against the far bars of the cage,
limp where they'd flung him—askew and boneless,
muscle relaxed and tendon not so much as twitching. A
trickle of sweat ran down his temple above a face paled
in shock; that wayward forelock splashed over his brow.
Blood soaked his broadcloth shirt and puddled over the
concrete floor.

Gausto knew how to hurt. Those barbed tranquilizers, close range…this one had gone deeply into Nick.
Had been yanked with a careless hand.

On hands and knees, she made her way to him,
ignoring those outside. She knew from experience…they
would do what they would. Until they approached this
prison again, they were of no consequence to her.

"Nick," she said, and this time her voice worked.
She touched his arm, his hair, his face. *Almost made it.*
Her pack free, the amulet in her possession…missing
only the badly needed information about the stealth
workings. "I'm sorry." She tried to feel *of* him—

inwardly, that sense of his thoughts that had struck her without warning since they'd come together that morning—and found nothing. Gone, when Gausto had yanked away the deepest part of her being.

Weak. Without her strength, without her heart. Only what she had learned of herself in her brief time of freedom with this man. For he'd been hers from the moment he accepted her invitation at the fairgrounds— the moment they'd shed human skin and human manners and flung themselves into the wolf and into the desert. Deeper than the amulet she'd triggered on him, deeper than her unwilling alliance with the Core, deep enough so that he hid her from his own people.

Mine.

She laid her head on his arm and watched Gausto through slitted eyes—and realized then that some part of her hadn't yet given up. Some foolish, leftover defiance remained. Her three sisters still needed freedom. And if she couldn't stop Gausto outright, maybe she could—somehow—slow him down.

Nick shifted; she raised her head. "Be careful," she said, barely a murmur—not for Gausto's ears. "You are hurt."

Pale green eyes showed dazed through half-raised lids; he rolled to his side with a surprised grunt of pain, uncoordinated at best.

"Drugs," she said, close to his ear. "Be still. They wear off." He quieted under her hand, his breathing hitching with his internal struggle. Jet crouched beside him...not just being, but being with him.

Gausto hardly spared them a glance. Supervising the speedy restoration of his work space, exchanging a few pointed words with his assistant, exchanging a few even more pointed words with one of the men who had accosted Jet in the desert—a man now taking the blame for letting them in. The man snuck a glare at Jet within her prison; Jet lifted her head and showed her teeth in a feral smile.

Nick took a sudden deep breath, and all his vulnerability somehow went with it. He stilled; he pulled away from her without moving at all. No longer sharing himself with her. In that single moment, Jet went from being with him and being part of something back to...

Just being, after all.

She made a small sound of protest.

He pushed himself upright, moving as though he'd never been drugged at all, or as though bright blood didn't well freshly against his shirt. Insouciant, sitting against the stout bars of their prison. "Gausto," he said, and his voice was clear and loud, and those pale green eyes were clear and bright, and they hadn't once looked at Jet.

Gausto broke away from berating his staff. "Carter. How nice to see you functional."

Nick smiled in a way that Jet recognized as threat. A show of teeth. "Hard to kill, aren't we?"

"If you think that was my intent, you were mistaken, though I admit a certain carelessness." Gausto moved closer, gesturing vaguely at the bloody floor. "But then, I know the punishment your kind can absorb. In fact, you went down more easily than I expected."

The amulet. It *had* affected him. Jet had known it, had seen it in him—even if he had waved it off. She opened her mouth—and Nick cut her off. Didn't look at her, didn't acknowledge her, simply...spoke right over her.

"It's been an off kind of day," he admitted. "But you know…" he shrugged. "I'm feeling much better now. And I won't be alone here for long."

Gausto smiled. "You may allow yourself to think that, if it sustains you. But I have dampers in place around this property—so of course you haven't made contact with your brevis. No one knows where you are. In fact, I believe they just barely know you were alive as of this morning."

Jet glowered at him, but Nick only lifted a shoulder, apparently without concern. Even though he'd been right. A leak within brevis; a strong one. *Trust no one.*

"Truly," Gausto said, "this whole show of yours was pretty much pointless." His ruddy anger had faded; satisfaction took its place. He glanced at Jet with a lidded and proprietary gaze. "I still have a few pets to play with, if I even need them." He nodded at the nearest cage— took a few stilted steps closer to the distorted creature within, his hand caressing the bars. "This man failed me early this morning—Jet no doubt recognizes him. His active resistance to the working was a significant error on his part—he need not have turned out this way. But he is the still first non-Sentinel human to turn wolf."

Jet *hadn't* recognized him…but she did now. There, in the mass of wolf haunches and gray fur and limp tail and a distorted face that wasn't one thing or the other, she found hands. Familiar hands. Wounded hand, wounded wrist. She recoiled.

Nick's attention wandered to the sight, wandered away. Disinterested. Distinctly unimpressed. "Congratulations."

Gausto ignored the slight. He stroked a thoughtful thumb over his lower lip, nodding. "You, of course, have gained nothing. A few wolves freed? They won't last the week. But you've lost your freedom, and soon enough you'll wish you had lost your life. Your new bitch—" was that *hurt,* briefly shadowing his eyes? "—already wishes the same for herself, I believe."

Nick's dismissive glance evoked a deep, twisting pain within Jet—a wound that threatened to topple her, bereft as she was of wolf and self. He propped up one casual knee, resting his arm on it. "She had nothing to do with this. She's nothing more than what you said. A tool." His smile came dark, along with another little shrug. Jet's astonishment burst out in a little growl. And when Nick raised an eyebrow at it, she realized suddenly...was he *laughing* at her? Or was it pure condescension?

Gausto's lips thinned...but only for an instant; he abruptly shook his head. "She came back for you, Carter—hadn't you noticed?"

Nick snorted; a wince flashed across his features, barely perceptible. Gausto didn't seem to notice at all; he turned briefly away to receive a murmured report from the woman, nodding shortly to her. Nick said, "She's a wild animal, Gausto. She just *reacted.* Or did you think yourself such a Pygmalion that you'd created a perfect thinking woman?" He snorted again; sweat had gathered at his temple. "You're an arrogant son of a bitch, I'll give you that much. No, she didn't have any idea I was using her to get into this place."

Gausto's eyes narrowed; he gave Jet a good long look. Jet—impotently human, aching and hollow and empty and listening to her new and chosen pack disown her to the enemy—growled back.

Nick snorted again in response; it seemed to leave

him breathless, but then in the next instant he was as strong as he'd ever been—strong enough to worry Gausto like a wolf worries prey. "Good God, look at her. She doesn't care that she's stark naked, or that your men ogle her at every opportunity. Or you, in case you thought I hadn't noticed. But she's just an *animal*." His fingers worked the small wood buttons of his dark broadcloth shirt; he jerked it off his arms and wadded it into a bundle and threw it not *to* Jet, but at her.

She let it fall to the floor. She saw the involuntary flutter of muscle and pain and she saw his face pale and she knew, as well as she knew anything, that he was indeed hurt, he was somehow covering what the drugs had done, what the deeply impaled barbed dart had done…what the amulet had done. But for that moment, the silent cry of concern flailing around inside her went numb. For the moment, without moving, she withdrew; she became only herself again.

She'd been wrong to worry about losing him.

He'd never been hers.

Chapter 18

Marlee followed them through the executive office floor. Not all of them—Meghan and Treviño headed to the ops department to gather up gear for what they intended to be a strafingly sudden strike.

"Nick appointed me in his stead," Lyn had said. "And he said *trust no one*. So hell, no, we're not going through any channels. I don't even want the gear requisitions on paper."

Marlee must have stared in surprise, for Lyn gave her a wry little smile, plenty of self-awareness in her expression. "Didn't expect it of someone as rule-bound as I am?"

Marlee had tried to find a response, only to be waved off. "Never mind," Lyn had told her. "Neither did I. But here we are." And then she'd led the way to find Anthony—and the closer they got to his office, the more

Lyn's expression flickered. Until at last, outside his office, Ryan and Max at her back and Marlee along simply because they didn't have anything else to do with her, she sneezed.

Ryan shot her a sympathetic look as she wiped beneath her eyes, and then she stepped up to the door and gave it a matter-of-fact series of raps.

Anthony's muffled response came with irritation; after a minute, he opened the door, already talking. "It took you long enough," he said. "I don't know why you can't fix the phones centrally—" and then he realized he wasn't talking to tech support at all. His expression flickered with poorly concealed disdain, and then he smiled. "Ms. Maines," he said. "Mr. Ryan." And he nodded at Maks, who stood back slightly. If he saw Marlee, hanging back in the hallway, he showed no sign of it. "How can I help you? The consul's schedule is full for the day—"

"Is he in on it?" Maks interrupted—so congenial that even Marlee missed his meaning at first—until she realized that Maks had simply gone right for the throat.

If Anthony understood it, he pretended not to. "Excuse me?"

Lyn turned impatient. "Dane Berger," she said. "The consul. Boar, Sentinel...leader. Is he in on whatever you've got going with Gausto?"

Anthony opened his mouth, the protest already clear in his frown. And then he did see Marlee, and his lips thinned, and a faint flush rode his cheeks and neck. "Marlee, Marlee, Marlee. What have you been up to?"

"The thing is," Marlee heard herself say, "I'm not entirely sure any longer." She stepped closer. "I thought

I was doing the right thing. I thought I was ensuring balance. But now I don't think that's what was happening at all. All the little things I did, over the years…they were much more than I thought, weren't they?"

"You flatter yourself," Anthony said, the curl of a sneer on his lips.

But the other three were looking at her, startled. Lyn voiced it for them. "Over the *years?*"

"The e-mails I should have gotten from Carter," Ryan said, realizing it—warming to it. "And Dean— *don't* tell me you had anything to do with my partner's death in Vegas."

"No," she said. "Nonono, I would never—just little things. I mean, I thought."

"Dolan's *monitio,*" Lyn said suddenly. "The one he sent when the Core attacked him on Meghan's land."

Panic fluttered in Marlee's throat. "No, I swear, that wasn't me! I wouldn't interfere with a *monitio* even if I could—" not with the Sentinel's silent Mayday, rarely heard and always critical "—and I can't!"

Maybe the truth of it was there in her voice. They turned from her back to Anthony; the man gave a sullen shrug, slim shoulders beneath a designer brand shirt. Perfectly turned out, perfectly capable of presenting just the obsequious, overgroomed image that kept the consul—that kept any of them—from taking him too seriously. "Dean Seacrest covered for your shortcomings all your life, Ryan. I guess he paid for it."

Ryan didn't give any warning. From Mr. Affable to strength and power and threat, all in a single breath. And in the next—

"*Joe,*" Lyn snapped, putting herself between the

two men. "He probably knows about the clerk who sold Dean out."

Marlee got the impression they were the only words that might have mattered. Ryan pulled himself up—took a deliberate step back. But he didn't take his hard gaze off Anthony...and Anthony, finally, began to squirm.

"You didn't do it for the balance at all, did you?" Marlee realized. Not if he was, somehow, blocking *monitios*. "You did it for what you thought you could get out of it."

"Of course he did," Lyn said. "Didn't you?"

"No—I—*no!*"

"Consul probably put him up to it," Ryan observed, confusing Marlee—the consul had nothing to gain from working with the Core; they could offer him no more power than he'd already enjoyed these past years. "There's no way he could pull off half of what's gone on here." He exchanged a glance with Maks, a nod. "Yeah. We need to find Berger."

Anthony snorted. "That doddering old man? For *years* I've—" his voice cut off as Ryan exchanged a grin with Lyn. *Berger, cleared.* Anthony's mouth twisted on an unvoiced curse; he glared at Marlee. "You bitch," he said. "You'll pay for this."

And Marlee said, "I know."

Nick closed his eyes as they came and took Jet away. Affecting boredom, hiding weakness. Still trying to control his breathing—taking everything he had to keep his hand from creeping over to grasp his arm, easing the ache in the muscle behind. Below his shoulder, high in the lats—he'd been lucky. Lots of flesh to tear, lots of blood to bleed...no joint to destroy.

Of course, Gausto wasn't through with him yet.

Nor with Jet, to judge by the collar he now secured around her neck. She stood before him with her head up, her shoulders back—wearing Nick's bloodied shirt in a gesture that felt more like defiance than acquiescence. *Wearing it in spite of me, to be clothed at all.* It had been his intent—and his great relief when she'd slipped it on.

Light chains dangled from the collar—token chains, too short for control, but long enough to hit her chest as she moved. Amulets shone dully, clinking against the links. And in spite of her brave posture, there was something missing from her presence—some powerful, crucial piece.

Satisfied, Gausto caressed her jaw—a strangely lingering touch—and stepped back. He said, "Jet, my most excellent pet. I need to know what you saw at Carter's home. What you learned."

Nick thought of the phone numbers she'd so instantly memorized—and what else she'd so casually had access to—and closed his eyes. If she wanted to, she could slash Sentinel security wide-open. Maybe not such a good idea, alienating her.

Just trying to keep you safe, Heart.

But he knew she couldn't hear him. Not any longer.

"Jet," Gausto said at her continued silence. "Little bitch. You know how this goes. You know I'll get what I want. You can either have what you want, too, or you can pay the price of resisting me." He eyed her. "Or didn't you realize that I can give it all back? You can be yourself again."

Jet regarded him with steady dignity, there with the

shirttails of his bloody shirt just barely covering her ass; her athlete's legs looked impossibly long and lean as they emerged beneath. "Show me."

Gausto looked over at his assistant and lifted his chin slightly. The smaller man clutched possessively at the lab coat of many pockets, although the pocket contents were now mainly spread out over the exam table. The woman who'd been tending him shot Gausto an annoyed look, but she stepped back with submissive body language and said nothing. And while the chaos continued around them—shouting and slamming doors from outside the room, the clatter of industrial pail and mop, even some hammering—the man went unerringly to the correct amulet, and touching it with two reverent fingers—

And suddenly Jet seemed just a little taller. Just a little more proud. Strength filled her in visible measure, and she looked at Gausto with defiance boiling unto fury.

Nick felt it from her. Not the clear, pure sharing he might get from another Sentinel who had opened to him, but something deeper…something more profound. As much a part of him as he'd ever been a part of himself. And if he felt *her*…

Jet! he said, surprised by how hard it was. Her back might have stiffened faintly; he tried again. *Heart—*

But then Gausto said, "You see?" gestured to the lab assistant, and the man again touched the amulet, dull stamped metal turned malignant with workings, and Jet doubled over with a cry.

But she didn't fall, and she didn't cry out. She slowly straightened, and if she was again less than she had been that moment earlier, she was still magnificent.

Nick had no idea if she'd heard him. She hadn't so much as twitched at the sound of him.

"Unfortunately for you, my pet," Gausto said, "you've never been able to hide what you're thinking. Not from me. Remember that. Vasilisa will escort you to your room now, and see to it that you clothe yourself. You will ponder your offenses there—and wait for this conversation to continue. And Jet—" He smiled thinly at her, "Don't underestimate her. You will behave yourself, or she will punish you. And I believe she holds a grudge."

The woman looked at Jet and smiled, lipstick suddenly looking far too starkly red and her expression full of cruel dare. Her hand trailed along the arm of the lab assistant, making the reason for her grudge all too clear, and she picked up a short, weighted leather whip from the instrument table.

Just play it quiet, Nick told Jet, knowing she couldn't hear him…unable to stop himself from trying. *My people will be here.*

He hoped. He wished.

For there was no telling if anyone at brevis had truly understood what he'd been trying to say to Annorah. *Follow the problem to the source.* Or, if they had, that they could then locate this place. He had no doubt it was shielded and under dampers, just as Gausto had claimed. And while he had faith in Lyn, he also knew she had to be within a certain distance to detect such obscured trace.

If Gausto had used their stealth technique, she'd damned well have to be right on top of them.

Gausto said, "Vasilisa, we'll be quite busy here this afternoon. On your way back, please bring a cache of the quiet blanks. Hurry, if you will." So casually spoken, the request held a world of menace behind it.

Vasilisa hastened to respond, reaching Jet with no-nonsense stride of high boot heels against concrete—taking her arm in a less-than-gentle grip and wrenching her around to leave.

Play it quiet, Nick told her, trying to keep the desperation from his thoughts—trying to keep the effort from his face. *My people* will *be here. Jet. Trying to keep you safe, Jet—*

Jet didn't even look at him as the woman led her out.

Nick jerked to sudden attention at Gausto's voice, grunting at the pain the movement brought—realizing then that he'd drifted away. The workroom had gone quiet, aside from Gausto's unexpected voice—a cell phone voice, the kind used by clueless people in public places talking about their intimate doings, their surgeries, their recent intestinal upsets, or their sexual indiscretions…as if no one else would notice, or perhaps as if everyone else should care.

In this case, Nick cared. Nick cared greatly.

It wasn't often he had the chance to eavesdrop on a conversation between the Septs Prince and one of his misbehaving drozhars.

"Completely under control," he was saying—and anyone dropping by at just that moment might conclude the same. The workroom was back to status quo—clean, tidy, and relatively quiet. Only the occasional whine from the three remaining wolves…the occasional moan from the creatures who had once been human or wolf. The dogs had gone silent…too worn for any continuing protest. There was only Eduard's battered appearance—and that, too, was much improved by Vasilisa's ministrations. "The night's operations are still playing out, but they are so far a great success. My preparations were painstaking, my prince—the Sentinels were caught unaware."

When had his eyes closed? Nick forced them open again. Gausto stood in the middle of the cavernous room, legs braced, eyes on the ceiling as he spoke. "I took every precaution. Even if they catch my inside woman, they can't trace her. I used the quiet workings with every contact. No, no—she's utterly reliable. I've been grooming her since childhood—one of my very first. She has no idea—no, she thinks it's her idea to work with us. But she knows nothing." A moment of listening, of nodding. "Yes, my prince—Anthony has more skills and complete dedication. But I felt it better not to risk exposing him."

Anthony.

Anthony?

Nick lost his focus on Gausto, too startled by that news—too full of self-recrimination. *Right under my nose.* The consul's exec.

"Berger," Gausto was saying, words with such derision behind them that they pushed through Nick's thoughts. "That fool. He didn't have a clue. Not even after the last adjutant didn't survive finding Anthony at work." A pause. "I don't see any way to cover our involvement with Carter's death. But why bother? He came to me…he meant me harm." There was smug satisfaction in that voice, as it took truth and spun out a story. "I have no idea what provoked him, but of course my men defended me." Then, more matter-of-factly, "We'll make sure the condition of the body supports that story."

Well, *that* was only to be expected. But it wasn't what Nick desperately wanted to hear from this conversation. He wanted to know more about the *operations* instigated during the night. He wanted to know what was still in play, what had happened to his Sentinels, who had survived.

Who hadn't.

Gausto wasn't the least accommodating. "Yes, my prince. Regular reports. Once I twist what I can out of—" A pause. Nick watched Gausto through slitted eyes, saw his countenance change, his mouth tightening and his brows drawing down. None of that was reflected in his voice. "I understand. I'll...keep it simple."

Nick didn't need translation for that. The Septs Prince had just laid down the law. *Don't play with your food. Get it done.*

A clang on the kennel bars jerked him to alertness; he sucked in breath at a slash of pain, biting back on the growl that wanted out so badly. He opened his eyes to Gausto—the phone gone, the man intent on his prize.

He'd lost time again.

"Time to talk." Gausto inserted a key into the lock that held this kennel secure—a prison that had, unlike the others, always been meant to hold human as well as animal. The door swung wide in invitation.

Options. Not great. Staying here until he regained some strength wouldn't be allowed. Emerging into that workroom...

Well, nothing good would come of it.

"You're going to die, of course," Gausto said. If he

showed regret, Nick was certain it came from the directives to *keep it simple.* An uncomplicated death.

In a way, ironically appropriate. It was Jet, after all, who had pared away all the complications of his life and given him what was important. Jet, whom Gausto had made.

Maybe a little of that growl made its way to Nick's throat after all. "Of course."

"Consider yourself lucky." Disgruntled resentment showed in the turn of Gausto's mouth. "It'll only be as bad as you make it."

"I'll remember that," Nick said, without moving.

"You realize, of course, that your cooperation is almost incidental at this point. What I've accomplished here…" Gausto shrugged, as if it hardly needed to be said. Behind him, the lab assistant glanced over, and the look on his face said it all: Gausto was taking credit for his work. "The truth is, I've done what I wanted. I've slashed through your brevis. I've got a man safe on the inside. Marlee's usefulness may be at an end, but she's served her purpose."

Marlee Cerrosa? Nondescript, full-bodied, pretty features and a sense of permanent hesitation? Light of Sentinel blood—worked down in tech support.

Tech support. With the skills and aptitude to cause the troublesome internal systems issues they'd experienced since Nick had come on as adjutant.

Marlee Cerrosa. Damn.

"Truly, this conversation of ours is one to which you'll want to pay attention." Gausto's face held a mixture of amusement and annoyance; Nick realized he'd faded away again. "You may even find it advantageous to participate."

Nick shook off the entangling fog. "Blame yourself. If you wanted clever repartee, you should have gone light on the juice."

"Probably true." Gausto's regret seemed real. "I was relying on that inconvenient Sentinel bounce-back."

So was I.

"Of course, there was the amulet. What did you do to it, exactly? That's the first question. Then we'll get into your current field Sentinels, your plans for the Core, and other such things."

"No," Nick said. "We won't."

Gausto gave the exam table a meaningful glance. "Did I not explain clearly enough how much my prince wants you dead and disposed of?"

"Clear," Nick said. "Not convincing." He looked past Gausto to where Eduard had laid out his stash of amulets on the other table, smoothing the defining thongs and ribbons, sorting and touching them all. For the first time, he saw the mini-amulets about which Sentinel specialists had speculated.

Gausto followed his gaze. "Ah," he said. "The right series of intention amulets combined with the correct stored energy, all invoked with the correct timing and imprinted on the final piece…it's an art." He scowled at Nick, quite suddenly. "An art your people took away from me, requiring me to rely on those with lesser imagination."

The lab tech stiffened infinitesimally, never pausing in his task.

"But you made the stealth amulets anyway," Nick guessed.

Gausto laughed. "Do you really think you're going

to get all the answers, just because you're about to die? Give me some credit. We'll play this hard and fast, and *then* you'll die."

We'll see about that. Nick scraped around inside himself, looking for reserves. Preparing himself. "And Jet?"

"Jet," Gausto said, "is mine."

Nick lost control of his voice, of the snarl in it. "You've gutted her."

"Don't worry about Jet." He pulled an amulet from his pocket, stroking his thumb over it in a reverent fashion. "She's earned a place here—she was the first step to this masterpiece. With this, the Sentinels will lose what little advantage they ever had over us."

He means it. He believes it.

The most dangerous of zealots.

"Come then," Gausto said. He gestured, and two men peeled away from their position at the door, instantly responsive. "I want to know how you overcame my amulets."

You can't be serious. Marlee had said it out loud once; now it rang in her head—over and over and over. As she struggled into a flak jacket. As she was outfitted with a stun gun and admonished not to put herself in a position where she'd have to use it. As Meghan pulled a pair of lightweight sneakers from the ops outfitting closet and shoved them at her.

It was her own fault. She'd answered their question— the one she'd been dreading. The *why did you do it.*

"Because I'm afraid of you!" she'd finally shouted at them. And once her mouth was open, it stayed open—

revealing her fear of their strength, her awareness of how they abused it.

"Fine," Lyn had said. "Then maybe it's time you came out to see how things really happen in the field."

There had been some protest, of course. Ryan, saying she'd get hurt. Treviño, saying she'd get in the way. Maks, saying nothing...but saying it with a scowl. And then Meghan, exchanging a look with Lyn and slowly nodding.

And Lyn, intractable.

She'd been serious, all right. Serious enough so Marlee now huddled in the middle seat of the hybrid SUV as they headed north on I-10. Lyn commanded, "Take this exit!" and Treviño made an unflappable shift through two lanes of traffic to do it, and Ryan said, "Nothing's moving, but it's doing that *wrong*," and Maks looked grimly satisfied.

Marlee could only guess that Nick had kicked off enough amulet activity to make Gausto's formerly hidden home base evident.

You can't be serious.

But Lyn had been. And she still was.

Marlee just hoped it wouldn't be deadly.

Vasilisa's fingers felt like claws in Jet's arm; the hallway moved too quickly around them. Her eyes didn't perceive as they had when wolf...her legs felt strangely absent, as if any call for action would result in no response at all. From wolf to wolf-human to human alone...

Three different existences, and the only one that felt right was the one that tied her to Nick.

The man who had just dismissed her.

But he'd tried to say something to her in the workroom, in those brief moments she was wolf—she was sure of it. And then Gausto had taken the wolf away, and she'd felt nothing.

But she was *sure*—

No. I want *to be sure of it.*

Maybe that was okay, too.

Maybe a wolf whose world had been changed so many times, in so many ways, had to believe in what pulled at her heart.

Believe in me. Believe in Nick.

Humans had strange ways. She wouldn't try to understand them right now. She would simply do what was right, when it was right.

Vasilisa snatched the chains that hung from Jet's new collar, jerking them. "Pay attention, little bitch." She hefted a long leather whip with a weighted flap on the end. "You made a mistake when you hurt my Eduard—or don't you see that the drozhar *rewards* me with this duty?"

Even without her wolf, Jet knew how to shadow prey. She fell in beside Vasilisa, anticipating rather than following, movements smooth and predatorial and not the least bit submissive. Vasilisa, foolish one, did not note the difference.

She took Jet down past her bare little room and through a door into a hall where Jet had never been, one that felt like a part of the main house. Inside the high-ceilinged room she entered, she shoved Jet away and went swiftly to the two-door wooden cabinet against the wall. Opulent wood, opulent furnishings...all dark, rich colors and textured walls and thick carpet with an oriental carpet layered over. As Jet moved to follow her—*shadow her*—Vasilisa shoved her back. "Wait there."

Jet felt the loss of herself a little too keenly to growl. But she narrowed her eyes in a way that any human should have noted.

And maybe Vasilisa did, at that. She used a key to open the cabinet, targeting a single drawer of the many and withdrawing from that a heavy pouch before relocking the cabinet. "Eduard deserves the same respect you show the drozhar," she said, with a significance that let Jet know this was why she was in this room—to learn this thing. "*He* is the one who has developed the new amulets for which the drozhar takes credit. In the future, you will remember that."

What Jet would remember was that these amulets were significant. And that Gausto had asked Vasilisa to bring *quiet blanks*.

Stealth amulets, before the workings were placed.

She'd looked at them a little too hard; a little too long. Startlingly hot pain streaked along her arm; the sharp smack of it made her jump.

"Now, do you understand?" Vasilisa drew the flat, heavy end of the stick gently down Jet's arm—over the torn spot she'd just made in Nick's shirt, her voice smug. "Your respect and obedience is expected at all times."

And Jet said nothing, absorbing the pain…absorbing the situation.

Vasilisa's first mistake had been hitting her. But her second was to take Jet's silence as acquiescence.

Because Jet might be missing her wolf, but it became clearer—every second, every minute—that she was nonetheless still very much herself.

Vasilisa gestured at the door, giving Jet no time to respond before shoving her at it, her mouth flattened by a grim little smile. She'd liked that first taste of power, it seemed. Enough to shove Jet again when they turned back into the basement, and again as they approached the door to Jet's room.

And then Jet had had enough. She turned.

The whip cracked down sharply on her shoulder; she growled deep, and rejoiced to feel it in her chest and soul. The part of her that no man, no woman, no Core amulet, could ever take away.

And this woman had not earned her respect; had not proven herself dominant. Had not shown she could handle any part of the wolf.

Vasilisa must have seen it in Jet—in her eyes, in her face. Alarm flashed; the whip flashed. Jet raised her shoulders and crouched ever so slightly, eyeing Vasilisa from beneath tipped and lowered brow, and for an instant they stood frozen—Vasilisa's hand drawn back for another blow, Jet balanced between obedience and defiance, a growl still in her throat.

And then Nick cried out. A sound full of agony and defiance both, a sound wrenched from an unwilling body, long and drawn and choked at the end. The sound of a man far beyond what any should ever endure.

Fear flickered across Vasilisa's face.

And then Nick cried out.

Indecision no more.

Cold liquid splashed in his face and down his shoulders; Nick sputtered, choking. More than water—bitter, stinging, creeping into cuts and bruises and flaring to fiery life as it pooled beneath his back. He couldn't lift his head to clear his nose and mouth; inexorable restraint pulled at his throat, a thin band of cold metal stapling him down to this cold table.

The exam table.

He twisted his head aside, desperate for a clear breath; the onslaught stopped and a bucket clanged to the floor.

"Did no one ever teach you it's rude to pass out during a conversation?" Gausto asked.

Dolan Treviño had faced this man. Meghan Lawrence. Joe Ryan and Lyn Maines.

And Nick had sent them out to do it. He could damn well take his turn. He blinked his eyes open, squinting against the light that fractured off drops on his lashes. Gausto, looming above him. The exam table beneath him. His blood, still oozing out to mix with the tainted water, clammy at his bare back. Thin metal restraints at his neck, his wrists, his ankles, biting into flesh.

Restraints not made for Sentinel strength.

"Pay attention," Gausto snapped. He dangled an amulet between them—reminder and threat. "And consider telling me just how you defeated my workings these past two days. Those workings were developed specifically for you...matched to you. There's no way you simply shook them off."

No. Nothing simple about it.

"If your Sentinels have developed a new ward—"

You'd know all about that, wouldn't you? But Nick didn't say it out loud. Didn't remind Gausto of how Meghan Lawrence had trapped him, permanently warding him from the use of power—and at his own command, although he hadn't realized it at the time.

Then again, he didn't need to say it out loud. His face must have shown it. Gausto's brows grew thunderous and close; his mouth tightened. *"How,"* he said, and dropped the amulet on Nick's bare stomach.

Nick meant to curse at him, to snarl defiance. He meant to give Gausto a personal demonstration of *how,* right before he broke free and ended the man's life. But instead his head snapped back. His back bowed and his thighs strained and his wrists jerked against their restraints; the agony of internal fire spun through his limbs and gathered in his belly and shot up through his voice, a straining, gargled cry against clenched teeth.

Gausto stroked him with that hot-cold metal, trailing it gently down his stomach as Nick twisted away, gasping for air against the choking restraint at his throat. His fingers scrabbled against metal, clawing for relief; his eyes rolled back. Oblivion sucked at him.

Gausto leaned down to his ear. "Yes," he murmured, an oily caress of sound. "Even a Sentinel dies." And he smiled.

Jet staggered down the hallway, the whip in hand, the chains around her collar slapping skin with her movement. Blood trickled down her cheek and a welt raised just beneath her eye…but it was the only new blow Vasilisa had landed.

Maybe she would live. But Jet didn't think so.

A man shouted at her from the end of the hallway, startled to see her there—heading for her at a jog.

She ignored him. Through these doors, that's all she cared about. Through the doors and into this room where Nick cried out in raw agony, no longer sounding quite sane.

In that instant, she pictured the room as it had been before she'd been taken away. The cabinets within, the rolling carts of supplies and food, the shelving. The wolf had seen this place too many times to ever forget it.

Wolf or not, she was ready. Just Jet. *Ready.*

She slipped through the door, instantly upending the nearest set of shelves—pulling them down in front of the door. She gave no heed to the shouting from those now blocked out, her attention wholly occupied by Gausto's stage of torture.

That, she saw. *That,* she snarled at. Ignoring Eduard's startled shout, she heaved down another set of shelves to block the door, fury fueled—but she never took her eyes off Gausto.

Off Nick.

Nick, torso gleaming with moisture, floor splashed and puddled around the exam table. Nick, straining against the metal bonds of that table, body strung impossibly tight, only his heels and shoulders touching the table at all. Voice harsh and cracking and raw.

Yes, he'd rejected her. Repudiated her. Insulted her and scorned her.

But Jet knew what was right.

Right was how she felt when this man touched her. Right was how she felt when she was with him. Right was what he was trying to do with his world…fighting the Core, fixing the bad things…even looking out for those simple-headed dogs.

Right was what two wolves had seen in each other those very first moments they'd met.

By then Gausto had turned to her; Nick went limp, his cry choked off, his breathing ragged...his head lolling to the side.

"Jet!" Gausto cried, both accusation and command— both ignored. For Jet never so much as hesitated—and Gausto's trank pistol lay where her memory had placed it, sitting on top of a rolling work surface also holding an open lab notebook, a scalpel, and a stained towel. Her hand closed around it—an unwieldy breech-loading thing with a long barrel. Gausto had often bragged on it—how even normal darts had a small explosive charge to inject the drug upon impact and how his were heavy-loaded; how a dart in the wrong place could break bone. How the small expanding broadheads dug in, ensuring drug delivery— because unlike most, Gausto wasn't particularly concerned for the welfare of those on the receiving end of his pistol.

But he was concerned for his own welfare. No doubt about that, with his scowl drawing down hard at the sight of her. Eduard eased away from the exam table, sliding a hand over a few amulets from the second table.

Jet slammed the weighted whip against the rolling work station; wood cracked beneath the blow, and Eduard jumped. She pointed at him. "You. Stay back. Put those amulets away and stay back."

He held his hands up, empty; he backed away. It wasn't what she had said, but she let it go for the moment. He'd have to separate the amulets—now in his pocket— before he could use them, and she'd see it coming.

"Jet," Gausto said. "What have you done with Vasilisa?"

But simply Jet pointed the gun at him—steady, without qualm. "Move away from Nick."

"After how he used you?" Gausto shook his head. "You still need me, Jet. I can save you from those like him. I can save you from yourself."

"Move away from him." And then, because Nick hadn't so much as twitched. "If you have killed him, you will die, too." Her voice broke slightly, but steadied.

Gausto made a disparaging noise. "Dear Jet, your hero has but fainted. Nothing more." He lifted the amulet. "I can get his attention for you—"

Jet snarled, but she checked herself—she knew a feint when she saw it. A verbal human feint, but a feint nonetheless, designed to prod her into hasty action.

Eduard's composure proved less sturdy; he took another step back. "Drozhar!"

"Steady, Eduard," Gausto said, his tone a threat.

"Get into the cage." Jet pointed with the whip.

"Only one shot, Jet, and two of us. I have no doubt you can take one of us down—and it will be painful, but not fatal. And then what of the other of us?"

"I know where the blood flows," she informed him. "I know all the places it comes close to the surface. I know where your breath flows, and how to stop it. I have known those things since long before I ever met you."

"Drozhar…" Eduard glanced at the cage, his meaning clear.

"Be still, Eduard. Or did you really think I had left myself without a weapo—*no!*"

He'd been careless, he'd made assumptions, he hadn't kept his distance, and Nick—

Not so fainted after all.

The amulet, torturous and threatening, brushed past Nick's hand; he snatched it out of the air, making a fist around it—closing down hard. Eduard shouted in alarm as power flashed through the room—visible power, too big to contain—it blasted past Jet, singeing against her skin; it made Gausto stagger backward. It whitened the room and reverberated around them, leaving Jet tingly and her ears hollow and her vision momentarily washed out.

When Nick opened his hand, hot ash trickled out.

Gausto swore, grabbing the cage for support. "No one can—" But he wasn't so stunned that his hand didn't dip inside his jacket, heading for what surely would be another weapon.

But Jet was already moving. Her feet slapped lightly over concrete; she ignored the trank pistol and set herself at Gausto. His hand cleared his jacket; his gun cleared his jacket—but then she'd slammed him, shoulder-checking him with wolfish ease...spinning him into the open kennel door. The gun clattered across the floor, caroming out of sight; the trank pistol did the same.

Behind her came Nick's great shout of effort; she clanged the kennel door closed, couldn't lock it... snatched a leash from the dog kennel, swiftly wrapping it around the door bars. It wouldn't stop him, but it would slow him...and then *she* would stop him.

When she whirled, she discovered Nick with one hand free, the metal restraint blackened by power; he'd bent aside the restraint at his throat as well. And now Eduard's coat hung from his outstretched hand, the exam table teetering in the wake of his effort to snatch the man himself—he who had thrown himself at an obscured exit Jet had not even known existed. Half-height door, set low, obscured by stone facing.

Eduard...tail between his legs, running. She let him go. She threw herself at the table—threw herself over Nick, settling the table down. She kissed his jaw; she kissed his mouth. He gasped, "Jet—"

And she said fiercely, "I don't care. You don't have to want me. It doesn't change what I feel."

"I tried to tell you—I tried to reach you—"

She drew back to look at him, ready to demand explanations. But she found the answers ready for her—right there, pale green eyes holding her gaze—full of his want, full of regret, full of apology. Pain lingered there, as well, and she knew she couldn't stay here, reveling in his gaze.

She slid back to the floor, yanking the borrowed shirt down to cover her bare bottom—mindful of Gausto in ways she had not been before. "We must escape this place." She pulled the restraint pins at his ankles as he fumbled to free his remaining hand and sat, rubbing red wrists. "We release my sisters and then we run."

"Escape," Gausto snorted, standing back from the cage door in disdain. "That's not going to happen. Maybe if you could both take your wolf forms—but oh, that's right. You can't do that, Jet, can you? Did you plan to run the desert in bare feet? Or did you think the motorcycle is still where you left it?"

Jet had no idea. "I don't know. It doesn't matter. Any chance is better than being here." But she caught the grim look in Nick's eye, and dread tightened over her matter-of-fact determination.

"Backup from brevis is out there," he said. "We won't be alone for long."

Gausto crossed his arms, leaned back against the bars...crossed one ankle casually over the other. "I would well know if that were the case."

"The consul's office doesn't know my teams," Nick told Jet.

"Anthony makes it his business to know." Unperturbed, Gausto merely shrugged.

Jet moved in close to Nick. "We need the wolf," she said, voice low. "If we are to survive until your people find us...and beyond, when we can find my pack." Scattered in the unfamiliar hills, waiting for her call. She put a hand to her low back, just above her hip. Over the scar. Her own voice came dimly to her ears. "You must cut it out."

His expression came on incredulous and hard.

The suggestion amused Gausto, however. "Oh, yes," he said. "Let's try that. Never mind that such interference will trigger the amulet permanently. Let's talk about how deep it is."

Jet ignored him; to her relief, so did Nick. He swung his legs over the side of the exam table—legs that in wolf form would have carried him endless miles or driven him in short, tremendous bursts of power, but which in this moment buckled as his feet hit the floor. His eyes widened; his knuckles whitened around the edge of the exam table.

She understood, then. What that first amulet had done to him...what the drugs had done to him...what Gausto had done to him...

But mostly, what he had taken out of himself to destroy that last amulet. That incredible surge of power—so strong that even Jet, blind to him without her wolf, had felt it.

Her face must have shown her dismay. He shook his head, a mere shift of his chin. "We'll make it," he told her. "There are teams coming."

Marlee looked at the stun gun in her hand. "That's *it?*"

"That's all you get," Lyn agreed.

"But—they use *guns.*"

"They do." More agreement, so congenial, as they disembarked the SUV and Treviño went back to flip the tailgate up, pulling out not the impressive and manly weapons Marlee had hoped for, but small field binoculars and belted water bottle packs. They'd gotten close…but now they'd travel on foot, because the property they'd found was gated and fenced.

"And wards…they won't stop a bullet?" Marlee shot an uneasy look around the gathering.

"Meghan warded us heavily," Treviño said, brusque as ever, handing her a water bottle belt. "We're safe from workings. But bullets are what they are."

"That's why the flak vest," Lyn reminded her, buckling on her own water. She settled the twin bottles into balance at her hips and gave Marlee a patient look. "It's not *safe,* Marlee. No one ever said it was. And the Core is always happy to harvest your dying energy for a special amulet or two."

"But the detente accord—" The agreement, both spoken and unspoken, that said they would take no action that might reveal either faction to the world at large. Their Prime Directive.

She should have known they would just laugh.

* * *

Jet leaned in close, her breath warm on Nick's chilled skin. Behind her, the pounding at the door changed to a syncopated slam, complete with shouted threats. "We need to be the wolf. *Both* of us."

His hand closed over the smooth skin of her flank, tightening there, his thumb resting just over her hip, his fingers settling in above the base of her spine. Cut into that, hunting for an unknown lump of metal? If he hadn't already been in a cold sweat, the thought of it would have brought it out.

And yet…

She was right.

"Do that, and she'll never see wolf-form again," Gausto said, with evident satisfaction.

Jet's hands tightened on his arms—pulling him closer. "He does not always tell the truth," she whispered in his ear. The brush of her lips against the side of his face drew his skin tight; the thought of what she was asking sent cold hard dread down his spine.

Knowing she was right…

He closed his eyes, struggling with it.

Gausto couldn't resist; the kennel must have felt as much refuge as cage. A smug sneer lifted his lip. "Don't tell me you can live with doing that to her."

Could he live with himself if he didn't?

The door shook and rattled beneath the onslaught; soon enough it would come awry on the hinges, and Gausto's minions would pour into this place. If they were to have any chance at all…

Ah, Jet.

"Come closer, Heart," he said to her, as if she

wasn't already pressed against him from top to bottom. "This is going to hurt."

A huge dog streaked away to the side of the house on which Marlee closed in, bringing up the rear of their small expedition and already limp from the heat and double-time approach. She clutched Maks's arm—but only long enough to realize what she'd done. "Did you see?"

In response, Maks merely jerked his chin off the left, and then slightly ahead of them. Marlee didn't get it at first…until then, suddenly, she did and wished she hadn't.

The first wolf might have been Nick Carter. She'd never seen him as wolf, after all, so what would she know? But the second…and the third…and then were they surrounded? She made a small, strangled noise.

So preoccupied was she with the wolves that she didn't notice when Treviño slipped away—and might not have noticed him returning if he hadn't spoken on approach. "Two of them, tromping around after the wolves. They're down."

Marlee bit down on a gasp. "You didn't—"

Annoyance flickered over his features—already so imposingly dark, with his black clothes and black hair and piercing blue eyes and most of all the constant brooding vibes. "Stun gun, Marlee. That's what they're for."

"And these." Lyn held up an odd little sheaf of tabs, splitting some from the group to hand to Treviño. "The stun guns take them down, these little chill tabs keep them down. Transdermal sedation. We won't be dealing with the same guys twice."

"Whatever's up with the wolves, those guys weren't

dressed for hunting or tracking," Treviño told her. "Something's taken them by surprise."

"Nick." Lyn smiled in grim satisfaction. But an instant later she stiffened, looking immediately to Ryan—who nodded.

"Annorah's cut off," he told Marlee. "We're on our own."

Jet drew a sharp breath; she came willingly into Nick's embrace. She may have thought he meant to comfort her before going to work on her—right then and there, in this chamber of horrors—but she found out otherwise when his arms snugged her in tight and kept her that way. For an instant, she tensed, fighting it—but then relaxed against him. Giving herself to him. Gausto said something from his prison—an alarmed tone, going toward demand. Nick didn't even bother to decipher words. He didn't bother with the slamming at the door, either.

But he took the time to center himself, pulling in his thoughts and his focus. He didn't know if he could do this; he didn't even know if it could be *done*. He damned sure didn't know if could be done by a man who'd already expended every reserve to destroy that last diabolical amulet.

An amulet dedicated to causing pain. As if there weren't enough ordinary ways to do that already.

Jet stirred in his arms, her unease palpable. He kissed the top of her head. "I need a moment, Heart. I'm played out."

Her fingers tightened into the muscle of his back, so careful to avoid the shoulder that burned and throbbed.

"You need." Her voice came muffled against the side of his neck where she'd tucked her face. She licked the join of his neck and shoulder, a small and tender gesture. "Take from me," she said, as Gausto sputtered some protest in the background; the cage bar rattled. "You can do that?"

He couldn't. Few of them could.

"Think of me," she said. "Think of us. Think of running in the desert. Think of this morning. Maybe I am still enough."

"Heart," he said, "you will *always* be enough."

"Stay with us!" Lyn snapped. "It isn't safe to separate!"

"It's not safe anywhere!" Marlee wailed, cowering in the hallway of the house into which they'd bludgeoned their way.

She thought she'd understood about the Sentinels. She thought she'd known.

She'd been wrong.

The strength she'd just seen…the quickness. The efficiency, working as a team to locate the guard between them and the house entrance, the brutal expertise with which they dispatched him.

He'd barely seen them coming. He'd certainly never had a chance to raise the gun he'd held.

Two more went down in the early hallway, their bullets discharged into the wall and one across Maks, which only seemed to annoy him. Just a scratch, he'd said, glancing down at his arm and the deep furrow that bled freely but indeed didn't seem to slow him down.

It took a lot to slow a Sentinel down. She'd heard that—heard them joking. She suddenly had a new appreciation for those words.

Maks had put himself in the path of that bullet to protect Marlee.

Now he ranged out ahead with Treviño, while Lyn sneezed in a violent cluster and wiped her eyes clear of tears, and Ryan went distant and puzzled, returning his vague attention to them to say, "There's something going on, but I can't…" and then he went distant again.

"Is he okay?" Marlee asked, aghast to see him so vulnerable here in the enemy's den.

"I'm shielding for him." Lyn's tone might be dry, but her affection was clear. "He'll be back in a moment, unless there's something really big going on—and we frankly don't expect it. The Core doesn't have that ability."

"Usually," Ryan muttered, taking a few steps down the hall as the other two men fell in before him, covering him. But though the hall was longer than it should have been—longer than the house allowed, literally dug into the hillside backing it—it only took a moment before he came to the short stairs and the doorway the two downed men had been struggling with. "In here," he said. "Something."

"Out *here*." Treviño grabbed Marlee, pushing her back against the wall. "I knew we shouldn't have brought her."

And then she saw that Gausto had a whole small army pouring in at the end of the hallway. With guns. And bullets. And twitchy trigger fingers.

Stun guns. Knock-out drugs. No-kill policies. Whose great idea was *that?*

Gunfire sounded from the hallway beyond the jumbled shelves and closed door—and if the pounding ceased, the ruckus multiplied. Gausto smirked; it colored his words. "If you let me out of here before they break through, I might be lenient with you. Otherwise, you can damned well expect the worst."

Nick ignored him. Jet was the one who mattered now. If he could give her back her wolf, they might just—barely—make it out of here.

He closed out the chaos of the hallway—the filtered screams, the solid thump of something slamming against the wall. He balanced himself, setting his feet more widely, coiling his thin remaining power—drawing it out from every corner of himself, gathering it…ready to strike. Connecting them as strongly as he could, absorbing every facet of her—her hair brushing against his bare shoulder, her breath against his neck, the tiny cool spot she'd so recently licked. Her body pressed against his—breasts firm, abdomen toned and tight against his, hips curving under his hands, legs very nearly twined between his. He shut away the burn and throb of a wound laced with whatever Gausto had put on that tranquilizer dart-turned-weapon, and felt only Jet.

She must have realized, at the last minute, that he had no intention of using a scalpel. She startled as he found the scar on her back, focusing on it—finding what was within, matching it, pulling up the energy to counter it.

To destroy it. Knowing the miniature conflagration the process often triggered…not knowing what it would do to her. He whispered again, "This is going to hurt."

And then he went for it.

Jet stiffened; she lost the air in her lungs, a warm gust against his collarbone. He steeled himself—he *forced* himself. Going for it. Going *after* it, a wolf after prey.

She jerked; her fingers clamped into his bare arms, biting deep…she jerked again, crying out.

Going for it…

All his efforts, all his energy. Because if he didn't manage it, then neither of them was going anywhere. Gausto would win. *Driving down through the muffling interference of her flesh, getting his teeth into the metal and its corrupted power—*

Jet threw her head back and screamed.

Oh, my God, Marlee cried—inside her head, out loud into the chaos—she had no idea. She crouched down in the corner by the door, making herself as small as she could, the stun gun thrust out before her as if it would stop a bullet or even as if it would stop one of Gausto's men. *Change,* change *already!*

And quite abruptly realized what she'd demanded, silently or not. *Change, so you can use your full Sentinel strength against them.* Change, so they could take advantage of the strength and skills for which she'd resented them all these years. Change, so they could even the odds—so they could maintain their no-kill directive without *being* killed.

But Treviño had gone down already—a vest shot, leaving him stunned and then leaving him mad, lurching for cover. Ryan was tucked in at the open doorway halfway down the hall—how he'd made it there, Marlee wasn't sure. Lyn and Maks covered as best they could, laying down a few shots with a semiautomatic taken from one of the downed men…and a few shots was all it had.

From behind the door beside her came a haunting scream, full of agony and fear. *A woman's scream.* Lyn jerked around to look at the door in alarm, exposing herself—Maks pulled her back to the dubious cover behind his own body.

Nothing kept Gausto's men back but their fear of the Sentinels; nothing kept them from steady fire but their fear of return fire. But they'd realized there would be nothing more than sporadic plinking; they'd realized the team had not shifted.

They'd gotten bolder.

"Change!" Marlee shrieked, very much out loud. "Would you just *freakin' change already!*"

Resistance. The amulet within Jet fought back. Well-crafted, well-protected…a strong working. Gausto shouted at him—railing for freedom, scrabbling at the hard-tied kennel door…just plain trying to break his concentration.

Not now. Nick held to the amulet, pouring power into it, keeping Jet close as she twisted against him, one scream leading into another, no room for more than a sobbing breath between—not until she gave a deep, gasping groan and went suddenly limp. Dead weight and he just as suddenly wasn't strong enough to carry the both of them, desperately juggling his grasp on her with his attention on the amulet with his attempt to make their descent a gentle one—feeling some last gasp of himself strike out at the amulet as he took them down.

Cold, hard floor; warm, scented Jet; gunfire in the hallway and shouts of fear, something new slamming up against the door. Limp and utter emptiness and still that thin veneer of resistance remaining. *Just a little more…*

He dredged it up from somewhere…his soul, perhaps.
His own wolf. His heart.

The amulet shuddered within Jet. Jet shuddered
around it. She gulped air, a convulsive breath; she
thrashed briefly in his grip.

And this time her cry was of triumph.

But Nick could barely hear it any longer.

Marlee blinked at the speed with which they did it.
With Ryan glancing back at Treviño "—Hell, yes!—"
and Lyn's expression taking on a sudden resolute determination—Lyn, who had left Gausto with his recent
and permanent limp.

As for Maks…he simply did it. Pulled free the Velcro
on his flak vest, a quick series of jerks and the garment
hadn't even hit the tiled floor before he pulsed in blue-
white light, a crescendo of gathered lightning that
stabbed through the hall until Marlee had to turn her
face away, eyes closed—and even then, the cascade of
flares kept her blinded for what seemed like a deadly
long moment.

But it blinded their Core opponents, too. And they
knew as well as Marlee what it meant. Cursing, the
sound of scrabbling…they were pulling back.

Marlee opened her eyes with trepidation. Maks filled
the hallway directly before her, massive Siberian with
vibrant striping and silent presence. Lyn, quick and
nimble in her gloriously spotted ocelot, darted around
him and down the hall; Ryan gazed back at Marlee with
dusky green eyes, wise eyes, and she knew she was
being told to stay put.

Treviño didn't so much as bother to look her way.

Heavy-boned jaguar, already on the hunt, padding down the hall at a silent trot that nonetheless resonated strength and power.

But Maks didn't follow. For from beyond the doorway—a door battered and damaged and nearly pulled off its hinges—the woman screamed again.

No, not that. Not quite a scream. A shout, a cry—something feral and soul-deep and full of welcoming victory. Maks looked at that door, great gold-green eyes an eerie reflection of his human's golden brown, and Marlee must have been crazy because she quite clearly understood his intent, scrambling out of his way.

And Maks took on the door.

The shouting, the gunfire, the heavy assault against the door behind the shelf barriers she'd made, Gausto's shouts of rage as he rattled the cage door...Jet heard it all and cared about none of it.

Here, in Nick's arms, she was herself again. Tangled on the floor, her back on fire and her body still twitching from the power Nick had poured into her, she was nonetheless herself. Complete and secure, exultation swelling into a howl at the back of her throat.

It burst free, sweet to her own ears—a song from her deepest wolf.

But celebration didn't last long. Not with Nick so still beside her, beneath her; his hands fell slack from her hips. She nudged him, a hand on his arm, and shook him when the nudge didn't work.

His head lolled on the stained concrete; his eyes fluttered open, making a brief attempt to focus before they rolled back again.

He was all right. She had to believe that. He had given of himself, given *everything* of himself, but he would be all right.

The door shuddered, a rending sound, and shifted in the frame. The shelves blocking it groaned.

"Let me out, Jet—I can help him. In exchange for my freedom." Gausto's voice had taken on a desperate tone. There, behind the bars he clutched, the cage still lashed closed, he looked a battered and broken figure. Lamed in body, crippled in power...he could no longer hurt them. "You were never spiteful, Jet. Release me, or they'll kill me!"

Jet's gaze flickered to the besieged door. Nick had shown none of the ruthlessness that Gausto had once assigned to him; she did not expect it from his people, should they prevail. And Gausto's minions had never defied him. *Kill* him? "I don't think they will," she told him simply. Not for the sake of doing it. "You are safer in there."

"Bitch!" Gausto railed at her. "Pretending to be human! You gave yourself to him, didn't you? You were *mine,* Jet, you had no right—! *Mine!*" Words failed him into sputtering, saliva gathering at the corners of his mouth, his knuckles white around the bars of the cage. He grasped at composure, managed to snarl, "If you think I'm helpless in here, you're laughable. I have amulets—"

Which he could use only on himself. Jet turned away—turned back to Nick. Stroked the side of his face—and realized that his breathing came shallow and erratic. Sudden panic gripped her. What had he done? She prodded him; she poked him. He didn't so much as stir. Behind her the door groaned and the shelves shifted and her time ran out. He'd done this so they could turn to wolf and escape, and yet…here they were.

Still trapped.

"Nick," she said, low and urgent—running her hands along his body as if she might find some answer there, bending down to nip along his collarbone, letting the wolf take charge. *"Nick—"* But no, there was nothing, nothing at all.

Because it is all inside me. And now she was whole, she was complete and fulfilled and strong and *free,* and she didn't need what he'd given her any longer.

He couldn't take it. And she had no idea how to give it back.

And the door groaned and the shelves shifted and Gausto's words beat nonsensically at her ears and on impulse she bent to Nick and kissed him, thinking of the way they'd touched each other—the way it had felt to change beside him, shared energies sweeping through them. She reached for the intent of the change without making it—hovering there, with the energies triggered, the faint flicker of blue-white lightning tracing around her and through him.

"What are you *doing?*" Gausto demanded, panic in his own voice. "What the hell are you *doing?*"

As if she even knew.

But she knew the pliancy of Nick's lips beneath hers, the hard muscle and bone beneath her hands. She knew that moment of touching him, intertwining energies that had not, perhaps, ever been meant to intertwine. She held herself there, in that place, and she *pushed* herself at him. Blindly, ignorantly…bluntly.

No question as to whether she reached him; he jerked

as though snake-bitten. His eyes opened, wide and startled; pale green stared back at her from so very close; his mouth froze beneath hers. She *pushed* again—his eyes widened; his body jerked, arching slightly. His breath gusted out to mingle with hers. And she *pushed,* and he gasped a surprised noise and she *pushed* and he cried out, carrying her right up off the ground as his body tightened—and then before she could do it again, up came his hands to cradle her head—fiercely, possessively—and his mouth came back to life, owning her.

That much, she also knew.

He kissed her with fervent intensity, until she let the edge of the change die back, leaving her fully human with wolf within; she forgot the cold, stained concrete and Gausto's raging and the conflict beyond the door—

Until a hard impact on the door knocked the top hinge askew and Gausto cursed soundly. Nick broke away from her, and if it felt abrupt, he softened it with the lingering hand at the side of her face, gentle when the rest of him had gone hard and alert. "There's no point in that," he said, and his voice rasped, strained by agony under Gausto's hands. Jet twisted to see, and found Gausto pulling an amulet from his pocket.

"You underestimate me if you think I'm going to be caged by your kind." Gausto's hand closed over the amulet; the other rested at the leather-tied cage door, where the tight knot on the outside of the bars had resisted his efforts to work it loose. He looked directly at Jet. "You can still come with me. We have our differences, but I value you. I will protect you. I *made* you, Jet. No one understands you better than I do."

Jet sat up, Nick's shirt askew around her, and she

narrowed her eyes at Gausto. "You are mistaken," she said. "You don't understand me at all. You never have. And after what I have seen of you, I will stop you at any price."

"Good." Gausto sneered a smile at her. "Because that's what you'll have to pay." He stepped back from the cage door, holding the amulet up. Jet only knew he'd activated it when Nick reacted, climbing halfway to his feet—his back smeared with bloody streaks and his legs uncertain, but no hesitation on his face. Only alarm.

And behind the crush of shelves, a huge, reaching paw pushed briefly through the space at the edge of the crumpling door, gold and orange and white. Jet gave it a startled growl of surprise, but Gausto only looked even more resolute. He shrugged out of his suit coat; he unbuttoned his shirt, still holding the amulet. "Do you feel it?" he asked Nick, unbuckling his belt. "It comes up a little slow, but I'll still be out of here before—*ah!*—small price, that pain…" He put the amulet around his neck as the huge orange and gold paw raked shrieking claws across metal, and he smiled at Nick—a terrible smile, all teeth and hard, cold gaze. It didn't waver, even as he jerked, losing breath; when he straightened, he stepped out of his pants, tossing them away; he stepped out of his boxers and stood tall, with no attempt to hide his stirring erection. "Nothing personal," he told them. "The workings have their own mind."

"Don't do this." Nick made no attempt to rise fully; he'd put himself in front of Jet, who still fought the lingering burn deep inside her back. "Those are my people—you'll face all of us. But it's not too late to—"

Gausto laughed. "Too late for *you*," he said, and then he had only an instant's warning—enough for uncer-

tainty to flicker over his face, and then his eyes snapped
open wide and his head snapped back and his arms
flung away from his sides and his entire body sounded
a silent scream, a puppet held aloft and dangling. A
black wave of power trumpeted out from his body; from
the hallway, a great beast snarled in startled alarm. Nick
ducked his head, one hand out to shield his eyes, the
other reaching back to Jet. Waves and concentric waves
of black power oscillated from Gausto, coming faster
and faster—raising the hair on his head even as it raised
him to full arousal, his eyes open incredulously wide
and his voice spiraling in an upward cry.

Fear forced its way out Jet's throat. She grabbed
Nick's hand, held it hard—made herself watch as the
power throbbed to a climax, taking Gausto with a com-
bination of ecstacy and agony and slamming out a thunderous clap of sound. She didn't duck—she stopped
herself from that—but she blinked. And when she opened
her eyes again, she found herself looking at wolf.

No. *Not wolf.*

Something akin to wolf. Something close enough to
pass, but which instantly raised her hackles, tightening
the skin all along her spine.

Nick breathed a curse.

The creature—*Gausto*—leaped for the leather
around the door, plying his teeth. Huge in the cage,
bigger than any natural wolf, he seemed at once
awkward with his body and reveling in the power of it.
Massive paws with curved talonlike nails, a dark gray
bristly coat heavy with musk, and teeth that looked
more like tusks in a broad, short muzzle with a faintly
pushed-back nose...

And the leather parted instantly beneath those teeth.

Nick swore again, more vehemently. Gausto rattled at the door latch, working at it with teeth and tongue.

"Get out of here," Nick told her sharply. "Take Eduard's route."

"He is twice your size!" Jet drew back in protest, barely glancing away to the room door as that huge paw clawed marks in the metal but made no progress. "I won't go! Together, we do this!"

He turned on her, a snarl on his face—and, she realized with shock, fear in his eyes. *Fear for me.* "Get *out!*" And then, with frantic intensity, drawing them both back toward the exam table, "He's new to this form. He doesn't know how to use it. He doesn't know how to think like a wolf or how to fight like one."

"We both run," she told him, desperate, tugging him for Eduard's escape door—but at the look on his face, slowly released him, understanding. Standing back. "No. I know. He can't be allowed to live. Not like this. Not with that amulet."

His was the smallest, most humorless of smiles, an infinitesimal shake of his head. "Heart," he said. "You showed me myself."

Fierce, wild panic seized her; it took a moment to realize why—that she saw the inevitable in his eyes. *"Not alone!"* she snarled, and she threw herself at him as he triggered his shift—swift and sure and surging through her, sensation and emotion and yearning. It swept her into her own change, the different energies mingling greedily with his—blue-white aurora and white-blue lightning licking and flickering together.

When the door to Gausto's cage clanged open, they stood together as wolf.

But when Jet would have bounded forward to meet him with death on her fangs, weakness shot through to her flank and the dead amulet there. Claws scrabbled on concrete, finding no purchase; she flung Nick a quick, frantic look—pale green eyes, hoarfrost wolf, blood scenting his shoulder, strain scenting his body. *Tortured and used and used up and back again...* For that instant, he met her gaze clearly. With Gausto leaping heavily out of the cage, he looked long enough to let her know it was more than just a passing glance. *A farewell.*

Jet flung a howl into the air. No musical thing, this, but short and full of helpless anguish—and then it was lost in the clash of fur and teeth and flesh, an impact so solid she felt the blow of it in her bones. No dancing around. No playing games. Just the intent to kill, to do it quick and fierce. Blood spattered the floor, a pattern instantly smeared by the battle—wolves rearing up against one another, grappling for hold through ruff and skin. Gausto's deep, unnatural bellow of pain marked a sensitive ear slashed and streaming blood; Nick's grunt came as massive jaws closed over his already wounded shoulder.

They broke apart, just for an instant—Gausto bleeding more profusely because ears always did, yet whole on his feet; Nick favoring a foreleg but still full of power and grace, head low and ears flat and muzzle wrinkled with a terrible snarl. He gave Gausto only that brief moment and then flung himself forward, his swift economy of movement crisp and clean against Gausto's clumsy shuffle-step, one that left him unprepared when Nick feinted at his ripped ear, waited for Gausto to jerk his head aside, and then dove for a foreleg, jaws closing down hard. When he danced away, the flesh of the leg hung shredded and dripping—and Gausto's black eyes had gained a film of red.

Gausto dove for him. Jaws that seemed more bear than wolf closed over Nick's spine behind his shoulders, and brute strength took Nick off his feet...lifted and shook.

Shook him hard and held him limp, hind legs barely trailing the floor.

The door came down.

It crashed into the shelves, torn from its hinges and slammed down into a ramp, smashing through the first set of bookshelves and resting on the second. Jet froze in shock, for there crouched upon it—for only the briefest instant—a massive beast in golden orange and black and white, stripes and pale underbelly and tremendous head with an exposed set of fangs that could have engulfed half of Jet on the spot.

Another of Gausto's creatures. The Sentinels, if they'd been out there, had already lost. And maybe Nick was already dead and maybe he wasn't—but Jet wasn't going to let this creature have him.

I'm standing next to a Siberian tiger and his name is Maks.

This was what she'd wanted, right?

Marlee squeezed her eyes tightly closed. Right. *Change,* she'd said. *Do it!* she'd said.

And only now did she realize exactly how much they'd been holding back. Every moment, every interaction...restraining themselves.

It both terrified her and reassured her.

Around the corner, the noise of conflict faded. Ryan had returned at a run moments earlier, snarling and chuffing disgruntlement and taking his claws to the wall while Maks worked on the door. Once he stopped, snarl-coughing in surprise…staggering slightly and sitting down on his haunches with a resounding thump.

Dignified, not so much.

But she knew what it meant. *Power.*

And then Maks broke through the door. Slammed it down off its hinges with one final blow, a move he probably could have made some moments earlier had he not so obviously been cautious about the unknown behind the door.

Restraining himself.

But now, with a single powerful leap, he cleared the teetering, fallen door and landed amidst the wreckage of shelving beyond.

Marlee couldn't stop herself. There hadn't been gunfire. She had a vest on.

And she was surrounded by Sentinels.

She stepped out onto the slanting door and looked.

And then she gasped, and the door tipped beneath her, and she snatched for the nearest solid object. Her hand sank into warm, clean fur and she nearly snatched it away again but self-preservation made her stick it out.

The tiger never so much as looked back at her.

The full impact of what lay before them hit. Marlee forgot to be intimidated by the tiger—she pushed up by his side, clutching that fur, gaping at the carefully excavated, carefully hidden chamber of horrors—high ceiling and block walls and concrete floor, every inch of it splashed with inhumanity. Stains and gore and stench, cages and instruments and barbaric gear. Kenneled wolves frantic at the end of the room, empty kennels agape beside them; sturdier cages along the wall filled with piles of twitching flesh—fur and skin and limbs and features all jumbled around, none of it pieced in any sensible way.

Two metal exam tables, one of them wet and bloody, sat off to one side—and the rest of the space was pure roaring ferocity. Two wolves, battling it out—one of them a familiar sheen of silver over black, the other twice its size, twice the size of *any* wolf. Wolf with an ugly stout face and tremendous tusklike fangs—and if a front leg hung shredded, it still had the smaller wolf—familiar somehow, sleek and silvered—flailing in its jaws. Right off-the-floor, gripped just behind its shoulders and surely something was about to give—

And between them, standing braced with one back leg trailing awkwardly and her head low, stood a black wolf bitch. Smaller, unsteady...terror in her eyes. But no simple wolf, not to stand her ground this way—protecting one of the other two in spite of her fear.

Joe Ryan charged through the doorway behind her, still looking a little dazed—and coming up just as short. "Oh, hell," he said, and Maks chuffed a tiger's response.

And behind him, Treviño, always blunt. "What the fuck is that?"

"Is that—" Marlee whispered, unable to quite voice it.

"Carter," Treviño said with some disgust. "And who the fuck knows what." The merest of pauses. "Damn, it's Gausto. It's got to be."

"But the bitch..."

Unaccountably, Marlee thought of a sweet husky

voice on a dozen phone messages, the accent inde-
finable but definite, the phrasing not quite right...

"She's with Nick," she said suddenly. "She's protecting him. From you."

"Poor little bitch." Ryan's voice held compassion as
he stepped away just enough so Marlee knew what was
coming. Corruscating flash of blue-white power
washed over her eyelids and then he was cougar,
ignoring Lyn's annoyed ocelot bouncing up through
the doorway as he leaped the jumbled shelves and
glass and scattered books before them and came down
before the black wolf, she who crouched even lower
with her fear and snarled even more fiercely—would
even have set herself to the attack if Ryan hadn't quite
simply thrown himself on her, pinning her—his
crushing jaws closing on her head with gentle but inexorable restraint.

Maks sprang over the shelving debris and out onto the
floor, nothing more than a few of those profound steps
and he was close enough to leap at the massive wolf.

But he didn't.

For Nick still hung from its jaws. And the wolf held
him *just so*—head cocked a little, angled for the far
wall...angled at the barely discernable, partially ajar
door in the far wall.

Marlee understood it just as quickly as the Sentinels.
They would let the wolf—*Gausto*—leave, carrying
away his new amulet, his new working...or he would
finish rending Nick Carter in half.

Beside her, Lyn's plumed tail twitched. Marlee
couldn't stop herself from voicing the question so far
unspoken. "Is he even still alive?"

From beneath Ryan's careful hold, the black wolf wailed, an eerily human cry of grief.

Tremendous pressure clamped down around Nick's ribs; one tusk pierced through skin to impale him, leaving the steady drip-drip-drip of blood to trickle to the concrete below. His vision filled with gray and red veils over greasy dark fur. A snarl still clung to his muzzle, teeth exposed…intent lingering.

He'd stopped fighting almost immediately; gone limp. He'd be dead, if Gausto had had any idea what he was doing. Dead with an instant and precise snap and flip. But Gausto hadn't known that trick, and now something had caught his attention; he gestured with his head, sending Nick swaying. Enough movement so Nick got a glimpse of round, small eyes, a glance of the creature's saliva-roped flews, an excellent view of the foreleg he'd taken apart.

Not yet. He forced himself to hang, limp and dangling. *Wait for the moment.*

In the background, doubt surfaced by way of human voice—he couldn't make out the words, couldn't recognize the voice. Jet sounded a sorrowful wail; the kenneled wolves picked up on it. Gausto looked their way without thinking—a quick gesture of his head.

Not quick enough.

Nick went for it. Twisted within that death grip, feeling that single tusk drive deeper—a sickeningly *wrong* sensation that gagged him but didn't slow him, driving in quick and neat, teeth flashing—

Gausto might have him in death grip…but Nick had Gausto by the throat. Jaws around the thin fur over his windpipe, Gausto's breath rattling between Nick's teeth, his warm blood pulsing through the jugular just beneath Nick's canine.

Gausto froze.

For a long moment, sounds and sensations enfolded Nick, muffling him from the rest of the room. Gausto's rattle, Nick's own gurgling breath around Gausto's greasy fur—a harsh sound, filling his ears…a dull roar came with it, filling his head. One flex of Nick's jaws, and Gausto was dead. No longer a bane to the Sentinels, no longer a bane to the earth or its creatures. He knew it; Gausto knew it. The moment hung on the quiver of his jaws.

It's not why you're here.

Not to kill, but to stop.

He eased the pressure of his jaws. Ever so slightly— a clear message. An opportunity to surrender. He didn't think Gausto would play it straight…he thought he'd be forced to end things. But this came first.

The moment hung…

Gausto hesitated…

You can close your jaws, Nick thought at him. *But I won't die before I tear your throat out.*

It must have come through unspoken. In his body, in his intent.

Gausto eased his grip. Lowered his head slightly.

And then Lyn Maine's voice rang clear. "Release him," she said, "and we will not kill you." A pause, and she added dryly, "By that, I mean *put him down gently.*"

Lyn. When had she gotten here?

She wouldn't be alone. Relief washed over him. Even if he failed, here and now, Gausto would still be stopped. Jet would be helped.

Her wail echoed in his ears; her fear echoed against his body. *Jet! These are my people.*

She silenced; her fear faded. Worry flooded in to replace it…a thready whine.

Not much he could say to that.

The mountain lion relaxed as Jet stopped resisting him. He released her and stepped back—albeit not without a thoughtful lick across the top of her head and again along the side of her face, spreading the saliva from their encounter into spiky black fur. Absent in nature, that gesture, with every bit of his focused attention on the giant hybrid that Gausto had made of himself.

A big part of Jet wanted to stay right where she'd been. Cowering. Anguished. Hiding in a mountain lion's jaws.

But she had other things to do.

"Look!" Marlee's voice went high. "Looklooklook! Oh my God!"

For hadn't she just been right. Hadn't that little black wolf been a shapeshifter after all.

Just not one of theirs.

Even the Gausto-creature hesitated to watch as flickering sharp lightning strobed the room—and she could have sworn those small dark eyes of his held something akin to wistfulness, even as his jaws still held Carter's wolf. Ryan made a surprised sound—undignified, that—and flung himself back from the bitch, evading those energies while Maks growled deeply…a vibration that reminded Marlee that she had her hand on a tiger.

She snatched it away.

By then, the wolf had become something else altogether—uncurling long limbs to raise her head and look directly at Gausto.

The woman behind that voice.

She wore what had to have been Carter's shirt, oversized and bloodied, and was obviously surprised to find it around her. Its coverage was incomplete enough to make it clear she wore nothing else; it fully revealed strong, lean legs and draped over an athletic form. Her one leg, like the wolf's, didn't seem to work quite right. Her hair, black and short, was spiky wet; her features reflected every bit of the wolf—wild and exotic, with sharp cheek bones and sweeping untamed eyes.

Her expression, as she found Nick, plain and simply broke Marlee's heart.

Who she was, Marlee didn't know. *What* she was, Marlee didn't know.

That she loved Nick Carter was more than obvious.

That she thought him dead…

Marlee lurched under the possibility, suddenly realizing all she'd taken for granted.

That the Sentinels could survive anything. That they risked nothing.

And yet there hung the man who had been strong enough to lead them all—and if his teeth were still buried in Gausto's throat, it seemed but a token…or a final effort. Blood pooled on the floor beneath him.

"Gausto," the woman said—that same voice, a sweet song in minor key hidden beneath her words. "If you need one of us, it should be me. You know that."

Lyn moved past Marlee. "He takes no one."

The woman cast back a look, eyes resting on Lyn with no acknowledgment of her authority. "If it will save Nick, he takes me. Do you not know he is like that? He needs to win, even to lose."

"We don't even know if Nick is still alive," Lyn said, and her voice went rough with it.

"*I* know." The woman raised her voice slightly, looking directly at Gausto. "So you can take your revenge and die, or you can take me. I will go with you. I will fight these people with you or I will die before you. Whatever you want."

"That's not the way it works." Lyn's voice grew hard-edged and even brittle. "You can't bargain with this man. You can't trust him."

"He will bargain with *me*," the woman said, making herself a little straighter, looking a little taller—even as she sat on the concrete in her oversized button-front shirt, legs curled beneath her and wounded.

And it seemed that Gausto might just do that. His piggish little eyes grew hard and calculating and full of a new kind of triumph. He used his shredded foreleg to point to the floor—imperious. Gesturing.

"You can't—" Lyn started.

The woman made a low noise, a dismay. Lyn started again, "There's no way—"

And now the woman turned on her, her expression turned to desperation, her voice low…her words touched not so much by accent as formation. "Nick has passed out," she said, striking out with those words. "Do you understand? This is now a gift."

Lyn muttered a curse. She took a step forward anyway. "You can't," she said, but her voice had no power behind it, no conviction. "To let him get away… even if we accept your sacrifice—and I'm not saying we do, whoever you are—then Gausto is still loose in the world and he's still got stealth amulets and now he has *this*..." She shook her head. "You can't."

"One of the hidden amulet blanks is there," the woman said. "By the table. Take it. And Gausto has an assistant named Eduard—he is the man you need to find. He is the one who makes the new amulet workings now."

Gausto growled, a ratchet of rough sound. She turned on him. "They would learn it from Nick," she told him, unflinching. "This is to convince them to do it my way!"

After a moment, he pawed the ground again.

"You can't," Lyn said, but it was little more than a whisper, and Maks shifted just enough to block her way.

Maks, it was clear, had made up his mind. Ryan gave Lyn a chur of reassurance and an unhappy twitch of his tail—but made no hint of attempt to stop the woman as she climbed awkwardly to her feet, bare buttock flashing below the shirt. She stood an unsteady moment, her leg dragging, and she made her careful, pained way across the room.

While the Sentinels watched.

Marlee couldn't keep it in any longer. "Aren't you going to—"

"Be quiet, Marlee," Lyn snapped at her, but the command came wreathed in misery.

"But—" It squeaked out, cut short at the glare... finished in her thoughts. *Don't you think he's already dead?*

The woman didn't. The woman stood before Gausto, unflinching. More small black bear than large wolf...a modern-day Grendel. He eyed the woman with hungry satisfaction, and Carter's jaws slid away from his throat without resistance as Gausto dropped him by the woman's feet.

Ryan shifted back to the human, so swiftly and smoothly that Marlee barely saw him do it. Lyn's voice, low and just as swift, stopped him. "No," she said, reluctance coloring her words. "Not...yet."

And Gausto tapped the ground with his paw—one last, imperious command. *Mine,* said his eyes. *You are mine.*

Impact jarred Nick back to his senses. Impact with the cold hard floor, impact with Jet's fear. His mind whispered with lingering sensation—fangs withdrawn from his flesh, pain so deep it registered as a new experience altogether. His thoughts came a muddled confusion. Jet touched his head, his neck—tender hands, careful hands...fiercely protective hands.

Just like that, he pushed through the muddle to clarity. *She gave herself to Gausto.*

And then there was Jet, giving to him again. Pushing herself at him. Blunt, unskilled...like swallowing a giant gulp of water too big for his throat—eliciting a sound of surprise from Ryan, who must have felt it all too clearly, all too strangely.

But it was enough. Enough for Nick to lift his head, to glare at Gausto. To see those teeth reaching out for the chains of Jet's collar. Fury blasted him right through the change to human; he briefly surged up, knocking Gausto's malproportioned muzzle aside. Gausto came back at him with a snarl.

"No!" Jet snapped at Gausto, her hands on Nick's

arm, touching his shoulders, his torso…lying flat against the constant bloody seepage just below his ribs as if she could heal him with that touch. "You give us this! You have everything else you want!"

Gausto snarled. He hovered far too close…but he held back.

Nick found Jet's face—found all the worry he'd felt, his fierce protective dominant bitch. He dragged her close for a hard kiss, readily ignoring the sounds of surprise in the background. She returned it, matching his intensity—drawing back only when he grew breathless. He coughed against his arm and then staring briefly, stupidly, at the blood sprayed across his skin.

Jet saw. Jet knew. He caught that whiskey gaze of hers and held on hard and tight, even as he spoke to the team. "He's stalling," Nick said, a raw voice in a pow-erless throat. "He's expecting help. Son-of-a-bitch is just enjoying himself until then. Don't play it, Jet. Don't give away your life—" And coughed again, holding his side as if he could hold himself together, while Jet held her hands over his and nudged his face with a dozen little kisses.

"If I cannot have you," she said, "then I must have the choice that lets you live."

Too late, Nick thought, and then winced and knew the mistake, for instantly Jet grew fierce, and she bit the line of his jaw.

"No!" she said. "It is not! I'm doing this thing, and then you live!"

"Heart—" And had to double up over the ripping sensation deep within.

Ryan's voice rose over the sound. "No worries," he

said, that matter-of-fact manner that only a fool took for lack of intent. Ryan, at least, had a plan.

Nick glared anyway. "Don't let this happen," he rasped. *He'll take her and leave you surrounded by Core!* He projected the thought, out of breath—Lyn was deaf to it but Joe stiffened and Maks snarled gently and Dolan Treviño came running up the hallway from behind, paws slapping the carpet, thunderous intent charging along with him and oh yes, they understood now. *Core incoming.* Black jaguar and now ocelot and cougar, splitting up to take the room—to surround them.

Gausto's nerve failed him. He snatched Jet's chains with careless teeth, directly over Nick—and Nick found strength he hadn't known he'd had left. He exploded upward, launching in under Gausto's head. Jet's shifting energy washed through him; her snarl followed. His fingers clawed through a harsh, greasy coat and Gausto flung his head, swinging Jet against Nick like a weapon but *too late*—

Nick's hand closed around hot-cold metal. He found the energy resonance; he matched it. He poured what little he had left of himself into the amulet—a sudden, piercing blast until it flared beneath his hand and crumbled away into dust.

Nick fell away; Jet landed beside him. She shifted back to long limbs and black hair and strong, exotic features—and if she had a quickly swelling bruise beside her eye, the blood now smeared alongside her nose and mouth wasn't hers at all. She took one look at Nick and one look at Gausto—looming over them, pinned in place by swelling energies—and scrabbled back, dragging at Nick—frantic and for the first time sobbing with it. Her leg failed her and she fell heavily, and suddenly Lyn's hands at Nick's arms dragged him back with swift care, and Joe Ryan at Jet's side—and a jaguar standing guard to their retreat, black-on-black rosettes gleaming subtly in the stark overhead lighting.

Lyn, gasping with effort, said, "No amulet—he'll revert," while Marlee Cerrosa, whatever the hell she was doing there, said, "How the hell did he do that?" and Ryan, grim and intent, said, "Who the hell cares— we can plow through backup but we're going to be carrying a dead man if we don't do it *now.*"

To which Jet snarled, turning on him—and then cut off cold.

For Gausto fell heavily, keening a high, thin shriek and twisting, *twisting,* black energy spiraling around him. His cry crescendoed to a scream, loud and agonized; he caught Nick's gaze, his flat, piggish eye bulging in terror. The dark energy sucked in around him, obscuring him, tightening down hard—an imperfect working, thrashing itself to death in reversal until—

Implosion.

And then there was nothing. No Gausto. No wolf.

Nick spat blood. He panted into the silence, harsh and shallow. Jet came to his side, her hands on his body—soothing, touching, owning. Desperation, there, and plea. He found her gaze again—hunted for reassurance. *Gausto is gone. Brevis is secure again. You're safe, and you're free. Your pack will be safe and free.*

Instead he found himself frowning. "Why is your hair wet?" he asked, and then his eyes rolled back in his head and that was that.

Chapter 19

Nick hadn't expected to hear Maks's voice.

To be truthful, he hadn't expected to hear any voice at all. He struggled, trying to put meaning to the rumbling undertones, and realized he'd been hearing conversations all along. Light voices, prodding him. More serious voices, hushed and concerned. Boisterous voices, luring him. And Jet's voice, Jet alone…sweet voice, singing to him. Calling him.

But never more than snatches of words, because words were still too hard.

Until now.

Maks must have been sitting beside him. The voice held lazy tiger in the sun, power coiled within, waiting and ready…restrained. "Today," he said. "Or tomorrow. He'll open his eyes and start ordering us around—as if he's still the only one who can hold brevis together."

"That's the way it's been," Ryan said—an uncommon amount of understanding for a man who had once nearly been ruined by Nick's belief that he had been suborned by Gausto's machinations. "Might take him a while to get out of the habit."

"We'll take care of it," Maks said. Simple words, for a man who habitually said little and who had said even less since his profound injuries in Flagstaff. Simple but confident. Strong again.

Ready for the field, Nick thought, and then found himself struck by sudden amusement at the assessment. Maybe he'd open his eyes and start ordering them around at that.

His eyelids, however, rested with absurd gravity over his eyes.

Ryan must have been pacing. Missing his mountains, no doubt…restless to return to home turf and his power wrangling. How long—?

Nick's amusement faded. He had no idea. *How long?*

"It's going to take the Top of the World to deal with the stench of that working," Ryan was saying. The Top of the World…his own private little power-surfing perch at the height of the San Francisco Peaks. When he spoke again, his voice came from another part of the room. Restless, all right. "Jet…she's a different taste altogether. What Gausto put her through—" anger, there, just a quick shot of it "—but as clean as they come. Just different. Where is she, anyway?"

"Hey," Lyn said, from the room's doorway. Critical care section of the brevis medical center—a place Nick knew all too well from the worrying side of the equation. "She's out on her walk therapy. Marlee's showing her around."

Doubt rumbled in Maks's chest—no real words behind it. Lyn's response came closer. "It's actually part of *her* rehab. She's made remarkable strides, considering the way the Core has interfered with her—since childhood, dammit. We should be protecting our children better than that."

"You can't find them all," Ryan murmured, although her quest to root out dark Sentinels hadn't diminished in the least since their time in Flagstaff.

"I can try," Lyn said, acerbic in response—but she added, "whether we'll ever be able to trust Marlee with brevis again remains to be seen, but she doesn't get out of here until we're satisfied she's stable. And anyway, she likes Jet."

"Nick's not going to like it," Ryan pointed out.

"Hey, until he's more than incoherent mumbles again, I'm the boss." Breezy, that. Too breezy. *Incoherent mumbles, my wolf ass!*

"—ass!" he said out loud. Not with much coherence.

He managed to open his eyes for the unfocused sight of three Sentinels taken completely by surprise, all converging at bedside and babbling at him until Lyn managed to shoot a silencing glare at the men. "Nick," she said. "Do you need anything? What did you say?"

Answers to the first question also seemed likely to involve the word *ass* or possibly *hell damned ow son-*

ofabitch, so he skipped it. "How the hell am I waking up alive?"

Ryan grinned—a satisfied expression. "We beat feet before the Core backup arrived—you were right, he'd signaled 'em. Treviño grabbed that motorcycle—turned out to be Jet's—and ran interference for us...we might have broken a few speed limits getting here."

"Damned mess," Maks said.

"He means," Lyn said dryly, "that your spleen is gone, your lung was collapsed, your diaphragm punctured...and of course your liver is bruised and there are ribs broken everywhere. You didn't have a whole lot of blood left, either. You might get out of that bed in a week or so, just because you're Sentinel. Truth is...no one's sure how you survived—except that maybe a certain someone didn't want you to die."

"Me," Jet said, there in the doorway as if she'd quite suddenly appeared. Nick saw it in the eyes of his Sentinels, then—the recognition of what she was, the core of her wolf striking a wild note that echoed amongst them. Wolf who just happened to look human at the moment; human who would always be wolf.

"Heart," he said, and they moved aside for her—and if she came into the room with a slightly uneven gait, that's all it was. The healers had done well for her.

Just the sight of her did well for him.

She came straight to the bed, usurping the spot by his side—owning it. She wore scrubs, but he already knew her body too well—the slouchy loose garments did nothing to hide it from him. Something hummed between them; she smiled at him, whiskey gold eyes wise and warm and as always just a little bit untamed,

and it startled him to realize…*this is what we have.*
This is what it would be like when they weren't desperate and hunted and wounded unto death. An undertone
of connection, pleasure responding to pleasure and
building into—

He couldn't even imagine. Didn't *want* to imagine,
with an audience. But Jet knew, and she picked up his
hand and took it to her mouth for a small wicked bite
of greeting. "Gausto is dead," she informed him.

"The amulet," he said, hunting his memory for the
sterling bright recollection of closing his hand around
it, destroying it. "That working should simply have
reversed when the amulet was destroyed."

"It was flawed," Lyn told him, her glance taking in
Marlee as she, too, appeared in the doorway—much
more hesitant than Jet, but relaxing slightly as no one
turned on her. "Joe felt it…I felt it. Deeply flawed. Far
more complex than they gave it credit for. And since
when have you been able to do that?"

Nick looked straight at her—the woman he'd taken
into his trust as his second—and he said, "Do what?"

She narrowed her eyes—definite undertones of *we'll
talk later.* But when she spoke, she told him, "The Septs
Prince has made noises, but they're token. Gausto was
way too far over the line. They can't even whine that we
have the stealth amulet blanks…we're making headway
on studying those."

"And no more of your people are dying," Jet
informed him. Nick glanced at Lyn, who closed her
eyes briefly and held up three fingers. *Three.* That's
what Gausto had cost them this time. *But no more.* Jet
caught the byplay—Jet caught *everything*—but she

touched his face and drew his attention back to her eyes, and the fierce wisdom there. "My pack is healing and then they will go home. And Marlee is showing me everything about your world, the things Gausto never let me see."

And then they will go home. Nick lost his focus for an instant, drawn away by sharp and sudden understanding. By fear. *And then they will...*

Jet. Wolf in being. Wild in soul. Beyond what he could ever know, and the one woman who set him free to fully be who and what he was meant to be.

And then they will...

Jet turned those eyes on him, more fierce than ever. "*They* go home. I am no longer what they are. I may not be what *you* are—"

"Oh, who *is*," Marlee muttered, reaching out to tug Lyn's hand and pull her away, drawing Ryan and Maks in their wake.

Out the door they went, closing it behind them— so no one was there when Jet sat on the bed, or when she bent over Nick to put those wise, wild eyes so close to his.

Without her pack, now. Caught between two worlds. She who had shown him what it was like to strip away the complications and find the heart of himself.

"Jet," he said, his voice breaking on it—searching for words when he didn't really need them. She knew. *Heart.*

She knew as she touched his face; she knew as she settled more firmly beside him and she knew as she drew his hand to her chest and splayed it flat over her heart, her sweet voice husky-lilted with the music of the wilds. "Not what I was, not anymore. Not what you are, ever. But together—"

"What *we* are," he said.

And knew it to be true.

* * * * *

INTRIGUE

Coming next month

2-IN-1 ANTHOLOGY

PEEK-A-BOO PROTECTOR
by Rita Herron

An abandoned baby in Samantha's care is the target of merciless kidnappers. Police chief John's sworn to protect the pair – even if he loses his heart in the bargain.

UNDERCOVER FATHER
by Ann Voss Peterson

Someone wants to harm the baby boy left aboard Reed's ship. Tenacious PI Josie can get answers. Could she also be the thing that's been missing in Reed's life?

2-IN-1 ANTHOLOGY

A VOICE IN THE DARK
by Jenna Ryan

A serial killer's brutal attack left criminal profiler Noah scarred and determined to hide from the world, until he met beautiful FBI agent Angel – the killer's next target!

TERMS OF SURRENDER
by Kylie Brant

Targeted by a revenge-obsessed criminal, hostage negotiators and ex-lovers Dace and Jolie are reunited. Yet can they heal their hearts for a second chance at love?

On sale 21st May 2010

Available at WHSmith, Tesco, ASDA, Eason and all good bookshops.
For full Mills & Boon range including eBooks visit
www.millsandboon.co.uk

™ INTRIGUE

Coming next month

2-IN-1 ANTHOLOGY

TWIN TARGETS
by Jessica Andersen

Sidney would do anything to save her twin sister, even break the law. Could Special Agent John set her straight – or would both she and her sister pay the price?

DESERT ICE DADDY
by Dana Marton

When Akeem, billionaire and heir to a sheikhdom, learns that his ex Taylor's little boy has disappeared, he vows to bring her son home – and reclaim his woman!

SINGLE TITLE

HIS SECRET LIFE
by Debra Webb

Her mission is to find a hero who doesn't want to be found, but Colby Agency PI Jane always gets her man. She just didn't count on her irresistible attraction to him!

On sale 4th June 2010

Fill your summer with four volumes of red-hot Australians!

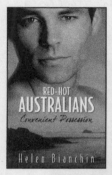

Convenient Possession
by Helen Bianchin

Available 4th June 2010

Billionaires' Marriages
by Emma Darcy

Available 2nd July 2010

Ruthless Seduction
by Miranda Lee

Available 6th August 2010

Outback Engagements
by Margaret Way

Available 3rd September 2010

"You've been warned twice. Stop prying into Anne Trulane's death."

INTERNATIONAL BESTSELLING AUTHOR

Nora Roberts

Partners

'The most successful novelist
on Planet Earth.'
Washington Post

After someone comes to journalist
Laurel Armand and claims her sister Anne was
murdered, Laurel's determined to get the truth.

When a copperhead snake is left on her
doorstep, Laurel realises that the warning
means she's close to discovering an answer that
someone doesn't want her to know...

Available 4th June 2010

www.millsandboon.co.uk

millsandboon.co.uk Community

Join Us!

The Community is the perfect place to meet and chat to kindred spirits who love books and reading as much as you do, but it's also the place to:

- **Get the inside scoop from authors about their latest books**
- **Learn how to write a romance book with advice from our editors**
- **Help us to continue publishing the best in women's fiction**
- **Share your thoughts on the books we publish**
- **Befriend other users**

Forums: Interact with each other as well as authors, editors and a whole host of other users worldwide.

Blogs: Every registered community member has their own blog to tell the world what they're up to and what's on their mind.

Book Challenge: We're aiming to read 5,000 books and have joined forces with The Reading Agency in our inaugural Book Challenge.

Profile Page: Showcase yourself and keep a record of your recent community activity.

Social Networking: We've added buttons at the end of every post to share via digg, Facebook, Google, Yahoo, technorati and de.licio.us.

www.millsandboon.co.uk

0510_IOZED   FE

2 FREE BOOKS
AND A SURPRISE GIFT

We would like to take this opportunity to thank you for reading this
Mills & Boon® book by offering you the chance to take TWO more
specially selected books from the Intrigue series absolutely FREE!
We're also making this offer to introduce you to the benefits of the
Mills & Boon® Book Club™—

- **FREE home delivery**
- **FREE gifts and competitions**
- **FREE monthly Newsletter**
- **Exclusive Mills & Boon Book Club offers**
- **Books available before they're in the shops**

Accepting these FREE books and gift places you under no obligation to buy, you may cancel at any time, even after receiving your free
books. Simply complete your details below and return the entire page
to the address below. You don't even need a stamp!

YES Please send me 2 free Intrigue books and a surprise gift. I
understand that unless you hear from me, I will receive 5 superb new
stories every month, including two 2-in-1 books priced at £4.99
each and a single book priced at £3.19, postage and packing free. I
am under no obligation to purchase any books and may cancel my
subscription at any time. The free books and gift will be mine to keep
in any case.

Ms/Mrs/Miss/Mr _____ Initials _____

_____

Surname _____
Address _____

_____

_____ Postcode _____
E-mail _____

Send this whole page to: Mills & Boon Book Club, Free Book Offer,
FREEPOST NAT 10298, Richmond, TW9 1BR